CW01096271

Eve Ainsworth is a p̶   ̶ ̶ ̶ ̶ ̶ative workshop
coordinator and award-winnı̶ ̶ ̶ who draws from
her extensive work with teenagers managing emotional
and behavioural issues to write authentic, honest and real
novels for young people and adults. Eve's adult debut,
Duckling, was published by Penguin Random House in
2022. She has had short stories published in magazines
such as *Writers' Forum* and *Prima* and articles posted online
for the *Guardian*, *Metro* and BookTrust. Eve is also a cham-
pion for working class voices, has set up the Working Class
Writers Network and is an experienced mentor.

Also by Eve Ainsworth

Somebody I Used to Love
Pieces of Us

EVE AINSWORTH

PIECES OF US

CANELO

First published in the United Kingdom in 2025 by

Canelo
Unit 9, 5th Floor
Cargo Works, 1–2 Hatfields
London SE1 9PG
United Kingdom

A CIP catalogue record for this book is available from the British Library.

Print ISBN 978 1 83598 141 2
Ebook ISBN 978 1 83598 142 9

This book is a work of fiction. Names, characters, businesses, organizations, places and events are either the product of the author's imagination or are used fictitiously. Any resemblance to actual persons, living or dead, events or locales is entirely coincidental.

Cover design by Caroline Teagle

Cover images © Getty

Look for more great books at www.canelo.co

Printed and bound in Great Britain by Clays Ltd, Elcograf S.p.A.

1

To my amazing brother Iain. Thank you for the love, support and laughter and for always believing in me. You also make the best cake x

Day One

Sara

I can't get out of bed. This is due to both emotional and physical reasons. Emotionally, I'm too hollow and empty inside to move, like a deflated balloon left on the floor after a party. Just the idea of moving causes a wave of exhaustion to roll over me. Physically, my body is pinned down by the heavy presence of Goose, who has decided to plant herself right on top of my breasts, her fat tail curled across my neck like a fluffy scarf and her paws kneading urgently at my stomach like it's a heavy lump of dough that she desperately needs to make smooth again.

I peer down at myself. In fairness, dough is a pretty good description.

I touch my stomach gently, setting off the anxious butterfly flutters that seem to be constantly bubbling under my skin. How have I put on so much weight? I can't remember the last time I've eaten properly, let alone binged on chocolate or cake. Is my body trying to wind me up, too?

Carefully, I ease myself up a little, ignoring the angry mew from Goose as she swishes off me in protest and makes herself comfortable by my feet instead. I reach across for my phone and tug it free from the charger, perhaps a little too forcefully as the cable snaps back hard against the table. I stare at the too-bright screen and the time blinks back at me in an annoyingly cheerful manner: six a.m. Really? How can I be this wide awake already? When the hell did I become such an early riser?

And then the cold hard truth slams into me.

Today is the day. It's finally here. And you have to face it.

A sob bubbles in my throat but I force it back. All I can think of is Lottie. If she was here, she would laugh in my face.

'*Early riser! You? My God, usually I'd be lucky to see you before eleven in the morning. I swear you're half-vampire. I mean, I wouldn't even expect you up early today, really. I'm flattered… honestly I am.*'

Despite myself, a tiny smile forms. 'Well, I'm awake, Lots,' I whisper. 'Although I'm not bloody ready for this.' Not one bit.

My eyes settle on the date and my head throbs, heavy and thick, like my brain had been replaced with wet cotton wool. I shake it carefully.

Twenty-two days. How can it be that long already? The heaviness inside of me seems to shift to the pit of my stomach. With a shiver, I throw the phone back down onto the bedside table. There is nothing more to see, nothing that I want to read. My notifications and messages have been left unread for days now. Everything feels so flat and pointless.

Twenty-two days have drifted by so aimlessly, and the sad fact is Lottie is still dead.

Lottie is dead.

Will I ever get used to those words?

She is never coming back. This isn't some awful dream or some daft thing I've made up in my head out of anger.

Lottie is dead.

Every bloody morning for twenty-two days that same realisation has come back to me over and over again like some sort of sick showreel being played on repeat. And every morning, the truth hits me like a knife slicing through my chest, allowing icy air to seep through.

This isn't getting any easier.

And today is the day when I have to say goodbye to her forever.

–

My flat is squashed on top of a row of local shops that sit in one of the rougher neighbourhoods at the edges of Brighton. I am unlucky enough to live above a fish and chip shop and, most days, the smell of cheap fat and cod permeates through the walls like a stale air freshener. It's particularly bad on days like today, when I feel sick, hungover and sad – and really don't need sudden fishy wafts catching me unawares.

I stand in the tiny kitchen, static for a moment, waiting for the kettle to boil and wondering grimly if my queasy stomach can manage a single slice of toast. I peer into the bread bin and discover that the half loaf that is sitting there is far more green than white. I think I'll give it a miss. My shrivelled stomach doesn't seem to be putting up much of a complaint.

Coffee – that's what I need. And lots of it.

I need to drown this hangover out of my body and trick it into behaving properly again. I can't get through the day like this, I have to force myself to function like a proper human being.

If only I could remember what one was.

I didn't want to go out last night. Jess had practically dragged me along, making out it was some kind of crime

3

not to celebrate our boss Sharon's fiftieth birthday. Besides, as Jess hissed while we'd scrubbed our hands after another long shift, we needed cheering up and apparently getting very drunk on cheap wine and listening to your work colleagues talk rubbish about their crappy lives was the perfect way to do that.

I hadn't been feeling very cheery. Sharon was a pretty obnoxious boss at the best of times, but she was even worse with four Jägermeisters inside of her. She seemed to think it was fun to tell the entire bar how 'proud' she was of her fledgling care home and how she was so thankful for her 'hard-working and compassionate staff'. Jess and I ending up glaring at each other over our drinks. This was something Sharon would never say to our faces. It certainly hadn't been an easy twelve months. I was about to tell Sharon this myself (fuelled by an additional vodka shot), but she was already too busy snogging the barman. He could have only been twenty and didn't seem particularly keen. Sharon was definitely getting worse in her old age.

To be fair, Jess was no better, having begged me to come, saying she needed my company, then spending most of the night texting her boyfriend and giggling about the amazing sex she was about to have when she got home. I'd been quite glad to slink off early, my head woozy and already throbbing, and my mind swirling with dark, intrusive thoughts about the day I knew lay ahead of me.

Drinking obviously wasn't a solution. It hadn't made me feel any better. If anything, it had made things so much worse. Drinking was the thing I did with Lottie. And long before that, with Lottie and Jay – the three of us together – merry, talking nonsense and putting the world to rights.

4

It had never been a lonely event. It had been inclusive, fun and silly, our time to relax and be daft.

I could've called Tyler of course. He might have taken my mind off things for twenty minutes. Perhaps twenty-five if I was lucky, but in all honesty, I hadn't felt that desperate. Not yet, anyway.

Peeling back the greying net curtains that Lottie used to tease me for, I stare out the window. '*What are you, some kind of nosy old lady, peering behind them, looking for trouble?*' she'd say. I never got rid of them to spite her – they're cosy and old-looking, and they make me feel safe. I don't think that was something Lottie could ever really understand – her life had always been draped in privilege and security.

Down on the street I can see early signs of life, of another morning starting. A man is jogging at pace, a couple of people are already gathered at the bus stop, and an old lady is moving tentatively towards the news-agents, dragging a battered shopping trolley behind her, the wheels zigzagging haphazardly on the path.

At my feet, Goose purrs loudly. She likes constant attention; she's always been a bit of a prima donna. Her large, slightly overweight body slips between my bare feet, her tail gently slapping my legs.

'I know...' I whisper to her. 'I know I need to sort myself out. I need to get ready. Surely it won't be as bad as I think.'

But I know the answer to that before I even say it. It's there in the heaviness of my bones and the burn in my stomach.

This is going to be the worst day of my life.

And I'm going to have to face him.

Goose yowls again and somehow manages to persuade me to move. I quickly feed her, ignoring my own raw and now growling stomach, before slinking into the bathroom for a much-needed shower. The hot water helps to clear my head a little. Then, as I step back into the bedroom, I see that my phone is glowing with a new notification and reach for it tentatively, my heart seeming to skip a beat for a second.

So silly. Even though I know it can't be Lottie, I still expect it. In the last year, we used to message each other every day without fail. How could a habit like that be easily forgotten? I swipe at the screen.

His message waits, unopened. I hover over the notification for a moment, debating whether or not to open it. Something shifts and stirs and within me. Memories rattle like old marbles in my mind.

I turn the phone off.

I'm not ready for this.

I'm not ready for any of it.

–

Outside the old bleak church, I clutch my bag to my chest like a lifeline and wonder why my legs have suddenly forgotten how to work. I'm wearing Lottie's favourite dress of mine, which clings to my body, far too tight, far too short, far too bright and, despite the heat of the day, I'm still shivering. I wish I'd worn something simple, a black suit or something shapeless. I just want to hide in the shadows and not be noticed by anyone. My face feels tight and stiff and my lips are sealed shut, desperately trying to suppress the sobs. My eyes are already sore and red, blurring the world. I can barely make out what's going on around me. It feels surreal – sick and horrible.

For a start, this funeral is in the wrong place. St Andrew's Church is a small, stuffy building that always smells faintly of cabbages. I used to go to Brownies here and I always hated it. I can almost feel Lottie's disgust as I step over the grey threshold. '*Sara – good God, why here? It's so drab – so grey! This isn't me! Get me the fuck out!*'

At the front of the church, I can make out Lottie's mum, Erica, stiff and proper as always. Her dad is slightly removed from the action, watching everyone with a grave expression. They don't acknowledge me, but I have never been their favourite person. I was too rough, too loud, too dangerous for their precious daughter. Even now, as I creep in, I wonder if they are judging my cheap haircut and market-bought handbag.

'*Ignore them.*' Lottie laughs. '*Why do you care what they think?*'

Erica never liked me. I swear she blamed me for all of Lottie's fuck-ups. She probably blamed me for the pissing cancer too. I suppose my council estate germs were always a worry. There was always a concern that I would contaminate their girl in some way.

I sit at the back, away from everyone else. I don't want to share sad stories or pretend to care how anyone else is feeling. Half these people barely knew Lottie. I recognise a few of her relatives sitting behind her parents but, in the main, the congregation is small and threadbare. Numbers have been restricted due to Erica's controlling and paranoid ways. Plus, Lottie wasn't in touch with many people at the end; she pushed people away, not wanting them to see her when she was weak and sickly and losing her hair.

A woman sits beside me and nods politely. I recognise her as the nice nurse who cared for her at the end. Sally, I think her name is. I watch as she picks up an order of service. Lottie's face is plastered on the front and it's not the most flattering photo. She is mid-giggle, and although her eyes are sparkling, her chin has doubled and her teeth are exposed. I know Lottie would've hated it.

'*Too right.*' I hear Lottie say with a laugh.

I look through the service myself. Erica has picked some awful hymns to be played on the organ and has requested that Lottie is played out to a bloody ABBA song. I slam the thing down on the bench so hard, it makes Sally jump up and I have to mutter 'Sorry'. I glare at the back of Erica's head. Did she really not know her daughter at all? Lottie *hated* ABBA.

I want to shout. This isn't right. Lottie loved to sing, she had such a beautiful voice. This wouldn't be what she wanted. She would want her favourite Beatles song played at max volume. She would want us all singing along – loudly and proudly, filling this grey space with happiness and light. She would want songs that mean something to her.

I twist and wiggle in my seat, hot and uncomfortable and just wanting to get out of here. I twist my head towards the door, longing to get a glimpse of sunlight, and then I see him.

Jay.

My stomach sinks at the sight of him. I have to turn quickly away before he notices me looking. I will him not to sit near me, and luckily he drifts past our pew and sits on the other side, a row or two up. I'm not sure if he even noticed me. I find myself breathing out heavily, my body is shaking a little and I have to clutch my hands on my lap.

I knew he'd come even though he lives in Newcastle now, but it's still a shock seeing him. He still looks the same, the short curly dark hair, those startling blue eyes. Nothing has changed and yet everything has.

The coffin sits at the front of the church, flowers heaped on top of it. It looks lost. A photo of Lottie is propped on top – not her worst, but not her best – probably picked in haste by Erica. She could've come to me. I have beautiful photos of Lottie. In this one she is squinting slightly in the sun and her hair is sun-frazzled, not straight and glossy as she loved to wear it.

I half expect Lottie to jump out from the coffin itself. To yell 'Surprise! I didn't really die! This is just a big sick joke!' But the coffin doesn't move. It seems far too small and constricting. I can't imagine how she would even fit in there. Is she comfortable? Is her hair combed as she liked it? Did anyone properly check on these things?

I glance over at Jay, noting the slump of his shoulders, the curl of his dark hair on his neckline. He seems smaller somehow, more vulnerable. I wonder if he's trapped in his own tumbling thoughts and regrets. He has enough of them.

There is part of me that longs to get up and move next to him. To take his hand in mine. If anyone knows how much I'm hurting today, it's Jay. I think of the years we've known each other, our history that has knotted us together like the roots of an old tree. He loved Lottie just as fiercely as I did. Or at least he used to. Together, the three of us used to be so strong. So happy.

My hands curl on the wooden seat in front of me.

As much as I want to, I can't talk to him today. Not after what he did to her. What he did to us.

I don't think I could ever talk to him again.

Thirteen Years Earlier

Lottie

'I just need a few more seconds, OK? Just a few more...'

This was it. My first day at this sixth form college and I was absolutely terrified. What if it was a big mistake? What if I didn't fit in – again!

Mum shifted on her seat. She hated it when I tried to delay things, just wanting me to get out and let her drive off in peace. I could see how her fingers were gripping the steering wheel, I could practically feel the tension bleed into the leather. I suppose I should've been glad she even took me at all. I knew she was missing another one of her important social meetings.

'You'll be fine,' she repeated for the second time, but her voice was stiffer now. 'We've been over this – just walk in there with the biggest smile on your face, act relaxed and everyone will want to be your friend. Why wouldn't they?'

'I'm sixteen, Mum, not five. I can't win them over with sweets.'

Mum shrugged. 'All kids are shallow when it comes down to it; teenagers are the worst. Tell them about our pool. I'm sure they'd love to know you then. You'll be batting them away with a stick.'

'You reckon?'

She seemed to consider this. 'Be careful who you tell though. I don't want our back garden to be a hook-up for the local delinquents.'

'Mum!'

She frowned but didn't say anything further. We both knew this wasn't her first choice of sixth form school for me. If she could've squeezed more money out of Dad, I would be going to a private college across town, but Dad had limits and for that matter, so did I.

I squinted out, over the playground where hordes of students were congregating in large groups, distinct in their grey and maroon uniforms. The same drab uniform that I now wore because, sadly, sixth formers here weren't allowed the freedom I'd had in my previous school. I'd already hitched the skirt high on my hips. The material itched, unlike my Meadowbank High one, which had felt softer and had fitted me better. At least I didn't have to wear a tie and blazer.

'They do look very... loud...' Mum shook her head. 'It's quite different.' My gaze moved towards the building itself. A grey, squat-looking block with thin-framed Crittall windows. The school looked tired and dated, even the wide-open door looked like it was yawning from exhaustion. 'It's so drab,' Mum continued. 'Not a bit like Meadowbank. I wish you'd waited. I could have easily got you into a better college. There was no rush, I could have worked on your Dad a bit more and easily got you a tutor in the meantime, you know that.'

She sighed and, for a moment, I almost felt sorry for her. Mum loved my old bloody school more than I did, the sweeping gravel drive, the ancient manor house that looked more like a hotel than a place for kids. Mum loved everything about it and our life before. This was all

11

too much for her. I could tell she was struggling to hold everything together. This move had hit her much harder than it had me.

Carefully, I laid my hand on hers. I felt her resist, almost stiffen. I guessed she was fighting the urge to pull away from me, but instead a tight smile appeared on her carefully made-up face.

'I'm going on again, aren't I?'

'A bit…'

She nodded. 'You'll be all right, Lottie. I know that, really. Just like your father – you fit in everywhere.' Her voice broke a little at the mention of my dad. She withdrew her hand and lifted her sunglasses from her head, rubbing them clean on her top and at the same time removing any emotion that would threaten to show behind the lenses. 'Go on, go,' she whispered. 'You'll be late. You need to make a good first impression.'

As I got up to open the door, I heard her next words, muttered with hidden spite.

'Though God knows why you'd want to…'

This was meant to be our fresh start, mine and Mum's, and it was pretty clear we both needed it. The last year had been hellish – the divorce, Dad moving in with his young PA Zoe (so bloody stereotypical and yet still shocking at the same time). Suddenly we were left rattling around in a huge house that Mum could no longer afford, wondering what the hell we were going to do with our lives.

Dad had been the money-maker, the businessman, the rock – wheeling and dealing his way to the top of his game, selling prestige cars to the rich and famous. Soon it had been flashy motors that lined our own drive and Mum had given up her hairdressing job so that she could lunch with friends, treat herself to the best beauty treatments and shop until she dropped. I grew up thinking that it was normal to own five cars, have at least two holidays abroad a year and own a second home in the country.

When Dad left, we were left rootless for a while and Mum lapsed into some kind of dazed panic. What would we do next? How would we cope without a man in the house? It was a strange, confusing time, until Mum finally got her act together and became angry instead. She made Dad sell his assets and split them fairly with her and then she told me we were moving away from the village completely. We needed a fresh start.

I wasn't bothered. I wasn't particularly close to my dad; he'd hardly been around even before he left us. I had no real friends and found Meadowbank stuffy, pretentious and competitive, so when Mum said we were moving back to her hometown near Brighton, I was relieved. Maybe this could be something exciting for me. And we could still afford a lovely, detached house, with a small pool in the garden and fields and lakes beyond. We were better off than most.

The sticking point was the nearest school. I flatly refused to go to another private school to do my A levels. I didn't want to spend another term feeling like an outsider, never quite posh enough to feel like I belonged, always trying desperately to fit in. I was the one who insisted I go to St Margaret's. There was something about the rough exterior that drew me in – it looked well-loved and homely. Even better: it looked friendly.

I wasn't particularly academic and knew in my heart that I was only staying on at school to please my parents, so suddenly being in a place that seemed relaxed and welcoming seemed ideal.

It ended up possibly being the best decision I ever made.

I first spotted Jay in my maths class. He was sat at the back with some other lads, his body spread out lazily on his chair, his long legs taking up far too much room. He glanced up as soon as I scuttled in. I saw him look me up and down, a hint of a smile appearing.

'You're new,' he said finally.

I smiled back shyly. 'Yes, yes I am.'

Obviously intrigued, he leant forward. He asked a few questions about where I'd come from, what subjects I was taking. I could smell the mint on his breath. He had an interesting face. Not handsome as such, more attractive. Dark eyes framed with long lashes, a nose that was slightly too large for his face, thin lips that curled easily into a cheeky grin. Dark curls that were slightly messy but still very cute, almost old-fashioned.

I have to admit that looking at Jay was enchanting. I wanted to know more about him.

I'd already decided that the only way I was going to make a memorable entrance in a new school was by being interesting and having a strong set of friends around me. I was an avid romance reader and it always seemed to work for those characters, so why not me? I couldn't bear the thought of disappearing into the background again. It was important I stood out this time. Maybe this time I could be the romantic lead?

The lesson started and soon I became absorbed in my work, relieved to find I had covered the topic before, so I was feeling confident. I even helped the girl beside me who was struggling. This first day wasn't turning out to be too bad after all.

As I swept through the rest of the morning, I looked out for Jay – but it was clear he wasn't in any of my other lessons. I tried to ignore the tug of disappointment. It was silly really, I had only spoken to him for a few seconds. Why did it matter so much? Instead, I tried to focus on my work – to be warm and smiley and approachable. To attempt to fit in.

It was later, at lunch, when I saw Jay again. As I was walking back from the food counter, a tray clutched against my chest and my eyes warily scanning the busy scene, I spotted him in the far corner. He looked up and, seeing me, waved me over.

'Hey, sit with us,' Jay said as I approached.

At his table was another boy with bright ginger hair and dark glasses, who barely acknowledged me, and a girl, who was sat close to Jay. The free seat was next to the boy, and he grumbled slightly as he removed his bag and made me the space to sit down. I sat opposite the girl. She was petite, with dark hair that fell like a cloud over her shoulders. Her eyes studied me from under her heavy fringe, lined with thick kohl and ever so slightly threatening. I noticed her hand was on Jay's knee. Were they a couple?

'Ah,' she said softly. 'Is this the new girl I've heard so much about?'

I nodded, and for the first time that morning felt a little intimidated. This girl's face was hard, unmovable. There was no warmth there, no welcoming smile. Instead, she reached for a chip and chewed on it thoughtfully.

'I'm Sara,' she said finally. 'Do you want to tell us a bit about you then?'

What was there to say really? I told them a little about my life. That I'd moved away because of my parents' divorce. Sara's eyebrow rose when I mentioned my last school.

'Meadowbank High? That's the really famous posh school, isn't it?' she questioned. 'Didn't a load of MPs go there or something?'

I hesitated for a second, surprised that she knew this. 'Yeah... but it's not that posh. Not really.'

'I bet it cost a bomb though.' She scowled a little. 'Where are you living now?'

'Quintin Avenue.'

Sara's eyes widened but she didn't reply, continuing to munch on her chips, her dark eyes still studying me. The ginger boy made a low whistling sound.

'Quintin Avenue? That's the nicest street in town. Don't some of their houses have pools?'

'I'm not sure...' I thought of Mum's comment earlier, how she assumed I could make friends by telling them about the stupid pool in the garden. Judging by the dark look on Sara's face, this would be the last thing to impress her. And I needed to impress Sara if I would have any chance with Jay. It was clear, just watching them together, that they were good friends.

'Do you have one?' she asked finally, wiping her lips.

'Well, yes... but it's in a bit of a state. Nothing special at all.'

'Right...' Sara stretched the word out.

I shifted in my seat, suddenly uncomfortable. It was Jay who broke the ice, his voice rich with enthusiasm.

'How cool is that! A pool! You could have pool parties. Sara, imagine that!'

I nodded meekly. 'Sure, maybe when the weather is better.'

Sara shrugged; she looked bored now. Her gaze was no longer fixed on me. 'Maybe – yeah. If there's nothing better to do.' Her fingers drummed the table lightly; I noticed that her nails were painted black. A couple were chipped in places. 'I guess it's going to be exciting having you around, Lottie,' she said softly.

She sounded anything but.

'And are you two going out?' I said, nodding towards her and Jay. They were still sat pressed close together.

Sara seemed to stiffen slightly. Jay grinned sheepishly and Dec snorted.

'Don't even ask that,' Dec told me. 'it's too complicated for us lesser mortals to understand.'

'Don't be a dick, Dec,' Sara flared. Her eyes studied me. 'We're just friends, that's all.'

'Yeah, just friends,' Jay said, shrugging, but he didn't sound so convinced.

–

Over the next few weeks, I found myself hanging around with this new group. It was just the way things worked out. I sat with them every lunch and found it easy to talk to the lads. Jay was the calm, friendly one who seemed to know everyone in school and had an opinion about everything. We got on straight away; there was an ease there, something that I'd never had with anyone before. I loved being around him.

The boy with ginger hair, Declan – Dec – was actually really nice, shy but with a sharp sense of humour. The others teased him for being a bit of a geek, but I secretly thought he was kind of cool in an understated way. We quickly bonded over our love of gothic horror films.

It was Sara, though, who intrigued me most. She wasn't as friendly as the boys and seemed to be constantly studying me with those dark eyes of hers. Jay told me not to worry. He whispered that Sara took a long time to trust people and that I shouldn't take it personally. They'd been friends since they were kids, so I guessed he was used to her cool manner. I tried not to be worried by her, but it was hard when I felt her hard gaze on me all the time like she was assessing me. I wondered if I had overstepped a mark, walked into a group that I had no permission to belong in. So, when Jay told me they were going to Sara's after school one Friday, I hesitated, unsure if I should go. Would I even be welcome?

Jay simply tugged my arm, grinning. 'It'll be fine. She won't bite.'

To be honest, I wasn't so sure. But I knew if I was going to have any chance to make friends with this group I would need to win over Sara. So I smiled sweetly and agreed.

After all, what harm would it do?

Day Two

Sara

I called in sick today. I could hear Sharon's fake sympathy down the phone, but I know she wasn't impressed. I can picture her sitting on her stupid swivel chair, staring up at the timetable and rolling her eyes.

I've managed to get out of bed at least, daytime TV playing while I feed Goose the last of the tuna that I found at the back of the cupboard. There is no bread or cereal left, so I munch on a few dry biscuits while I watch a posh politician try to convince the bright, bubbly TV presenter that he sympathises about the latest housing crisis. The biscuit crumbs lodge in the back of my throat.

When my phone rings, I consider ignoring it but then see it's Jess. She's probably picking up extra flack at work because of me not going in, so guilt makes me pick up.

'Hey.'

'Hey.' Jess's voice is gentle. 'Are you OK? Sharon told me you're poorly.'

She has the decency to leave out the word *again* and I'm grateful. I turn down the TV volume and flop back on the sofa, Goose curling up next me, my personal hot water bottle.

I like Jess; she is sweet and fun and doesn't really give a shit about anything. She's only a couple of years younger than me but seems a lot more somehow. I think it's because she's so petite and skinny, like a fragile little doll. The first mistake I made was assuming that she was delicate and needed looking after. On one of our first shifts together, Jess showed me how strong and tough she was, easily manoeuvring patients into the hoists and practically running between floors. At break times we would have a quick drink and compare lives. We both had quite tough upbringings – Jess had lived on an estate just across the way from me, and her dad had been a violent piece of work. She'd quickly learnt to be savvy and thick-skinned in a tough world.

My current problem is that Jess is looking for a friend and, while I understand that, this isn't something I could ever offer her. I already had a best mate. Once upon a time I had two. I'm not interested in replacing those people.

'Sara?' Jess asks, breaking my train of thought. 'Are you still there?'

'Yes, sorry. I was just sorting the cat out.'

Goose stretches out a paw and glares at me, like she knows I'm lying.

'I wanted to know how yesterday went? The funeral…' She pauses. 'I understand it would've been hard.'

Hard. That's one word for it. I sigh and try to ignore the burning feeling that is ripping through my skin. 'It was OK. It went as well as it could. To be honest, I didn't stay long.'

Thinking back to yesterday physically hurts; my chest constricts and my heart thumps hard. I couldn't bear to stay. As soon as the service was over, I'd rushed out into the fresh air. The sun had been too hot, and I'd felt suddenly dizzy and sweaty in the courtyard. I couldn't stand to hear the sad voices as people drifted out, I hated the way their expressions softened once they saw me.

Even Erica had been quite sweet, walking over and touching my arm briefly. 'Will you come to the wake? It's just a small thing at our house?'

'I–I don't think I can…'

She had patted me, like I was a small dog. 'I'd like you to come, Sara. There's something I need to show you.'

I was about to answer, to offer poor excuses, when a small crowd of relatives came towards Erica and took her to one side. I found myself pulling away and beginning to walk out of the grounds. I was desperate to get back to the safety of my flat and didn't want to be in Erica's house. I didn't want to be where Lottie spent her last days. Everything was too painful, just being here was too much.

'Sara?'

I turned.

Jay was on the path behind me. He looked destroyed. He'd clearly been crying. His skin had an unhealthy grey hue, his eyes and nose red, even his hair looked flat and lifeless. It was all I could do not to run into his arms and bury my face in his chest.

'Sara,' he said again. 'I wanted to talk. I'm staying at my Mum's for a bit. It feels wrong to go back straight away.'

I shook my head. I couldn't. I could barely look at him, let alone speak to him. 'I'm sorry, Jay…' I replied, my voice splintering. 'I–I can't.' His expression twisted, his mouth opening to protest but I wasn't interested. 'Leave me alone, Jay, please. I don't want to see you again.'

I walked away and he didn't stop me. It felt like my heart was breaking all over again.

'But you got through it. That's the main thing,' Jess says now, snapping me back into the present.

I run my hand over Goose's soft fur and let myself relax a little. My eyes are dry from lack of sleep and my body hurts all over, but Jess is right: the worst is over in some ways. I don't have to face Erica again, or Jay. The only problem is, what happens next? I can't simply move on. I feel like I'm stuck in limbo.

'I'm here if you need to talk,' Jess continues. 'When you come back to work, we can grab a coffee and you can lean on me if you need to, OK? And please don't worry about Sharon. She's told me to tell you not to worry. She said to do something nice. Take the opportunity to get your head together.'

'Something nice? I'm not sure what that'll be, Jess. I'm broke and feeling shit.'

'It doesn't have to be anything major. Take a long walk somewhere or watch a soppy film. I dunno – just do the stuff you like doing.'

I nod, like I'm agreeing with her, but I'm not. The things I'd liked doing involved Lottie and it wouldn't feel right to do them without her. Maybe I'll just sleep. I'll sleep this whole nightmare away and everything will feel better. I like sleeping.

'Call me whenever you need to,' she says softly. 'I'm right here waiting.'

'Thanks, I will,' I reply.

'Hopefully I'll see you tomorrow.' She pauses. 'It will be better soon. I promise.'

But it's another lie, and we both know it.

The truth is, I like work normally. I love our little care home with the range of residents and their ever-changing needs. I like chatting to them as I wash and dress them and make them feel good about themselves. It's a special job, and although it's pressured and kills my back, I couldn't imagine doing anything else.

Lottie always used to laugh at me. She never understood the appeal of being around old people all day. Lottie had an exciting job working for her dad's car firm. She was paid well and always dressed the best. I think she would've lasted about twenty minutes on one of my shifts.

'I can help get you a job,' she told me. 'With your travel experience and writing ability, you're wasted there. You could be working in journalism, or publishing. My dad has contacts. Or you should be doing something with your art – you're so talented.'

I scoffed. As much as I still harboured a dream to pick up my art again, I knew that was just what it was – a dream.

Besides, I was happy enough. Lottie didn't understand the thrill I got spending time with my favourite residents. How I loved feeding George his dinner and listening to his war stories, or how I would take Esme for a walk and let her chat about her days as a ballet dancer. My favourite though (and this was naughty of me, as I wasn't supposed to have favourites) was sitting with Derek while he talked about his life. He had such interesting and exciting tales – it was like I could escape into different worlds for a while.

'Don't you get bored listening to them going on?' Lottie had asked me.

'No, never. It's a privilege to hear their stories,' I told her.

I thought of Derek now and a stab of sadness shot through me. He was quite poorly, his cancer having spread to his bones. He wouldn't talk to anyone else, saying Jess was too 'daft' and Sharon too 'snappy'. The other staff members didn't even register on his radar. Derek liked me because he said he saw something in me.

'You understand what other people have gone through. You have empathy.'

I wasn't sure if he was right about that, but I didn't argue. I was just honoured that he felt I was worthy of listening to his stories.

And yet, here I am, sitting on my sofa, staring at a daytime TV show about house repairs that I have no interest in, when I could be with Derek and the others.

'You could go,' I hear Lottie say in her matter-of-fact way. 'Nothing will change if you stay here mouldering.'

I think of Derek's sad eyes and the fact that he is suffering the same way my friend was. There is no way I can face that now.

'Just one more day,' I whisper into the air. 'Just one more day and I'll be OK.'

Goose mews softly beside me. She always knows when I'm talking rubbish.

The rest of my morning passes without much event. My letterbox rattles and a few bills flutter onto the doormat. There is one card that I open reluctantly. It's from Dec. I'm surprised he knew my address, but then I remember we swapped details the last time we caught up – when Dec had come for a flying visit three Christmases ago. He lives in America now. The card is a sweet one, with a cat on the front, and I'm grateful for this touch; it looks a little like Goose. Inside, Declan's message is short and sweet.

> Hey Sara,
>   I've been thinking of you all. I only spoke to Lottie a few weeks ago, it's such a shock this happened so quickly. It feels so wrong and unjust.

I'm sorry I can't be there for the funeral. Jamie is due to give birth any day now and I can't leave her, I hope you understand.

I tried calling, but I appreciate you might not want to talk at the moment. When you are ready, give me a call? I'd love to catch up. There's a spare room in LA if you ever need it.

I did speak to Jay a few days ago. He was in bits. I really think you two need each other right now, more than ever.

Love you,
Dec

I read it a few times and then cast it to one side on the table. It'll sit with the others on the pile, collecting dust. Dec is lovely and I miss him with all my heart, but that guy is far too soft. He thinks things can be resolved so easily, that mistakes from the past can be erased like I'm holding a magic wand. Just the thought of contacting Jay makes my heart feel as though a hand is clutching it too tight beneath my ribs.

I go back to my mindless TV and the warmth of Goose and try to shut out my thoughts.

–

Later, I eat some soup that I've found at the back of the cupboard and stare out of the window. It's another hot day and the sun is blazing through the glass. I watch as people walk on the pavements below, girls wearing pretty summer dresses, guys dressed in shorts and loose-fitting shirts. Cars drive past with their windows rolled down, music blaring through.

Lottie loved the summer. She hated being inside on a nice day, she would call it a waste. If she was here right now, she would grab my hand and drag me out into the sunshine. 'Let's get some rays onto that pale skin. It's good for you.'

I've always been more of a winter girl. I like comfy jumpers and long, dark nights. Maybe that's why Lottie and I worked so well in the end; we were total opposites of one another. Fire and ice. Summer and winter. Sun and moon.

I draw the curtains against the heat and step away. I'm not ready to face the brightness yet.

I pick up my phone instead.

There are three text messages waiting for me. The first is from Sharon, hoping I'm OK and reiterating that I can take a couple of weeks off work if I need it. It's very tempting, but I don't reply straight away. After all, what am I going to do with my time? Sit around the flat feeling sorry for myself? Surely keeping busy would be the best thing to do, it's always helped me in the past.

The next message is from Tyler. I can't say that my heart lifts reading his words; if anything my stomach shrinks a little.

> Hey sexy, we need to hook up soon.
> Thinking of you.
> Txt me
> Xx

I immediately delete it. I don't have the headspace for Tyler right now. There's no denying that he could be a useful distraction, but I can't face him. Maybe later, but

26

not yet… The last message is much more of a surprise. As I open it, I can feel my skin cool a little. A scowl settles as I read the words. It's all I can do not to throw the phone across the room.

> Hi Sara.
> I know what you said yesterday, and I get it, I really do.
> But I need to speak to you. There's things you need to know.
> Can we meet?
> Jay

Irritation prickles throughout my body. What the hell is Jay going on about? I re-read the words again. Does he really, honestly think that talking about things will make everything better? The cheek of him makes me want to laugh.

If this had been a few years ago, yeah, I might have listened because then it was only me he ended up hurting. However, I still can't get out of my head the image of Lottie crying. Of her pulling me into a hug and whispering the words, 'He's left me. He doesn't want me any more.'

Jay left Lottie just months before her diagnosis. Sometimes I think it was a blessing because Lottie was spared from a man who clearly didn't love her. Someone who moved far away and didn't even bother to check how she was. I should have known better after what he did to me, but I guess there's no fool like an old fool.

I quickly delete his message too. This is his guilt kicking in, it has to be. He wants to meet with me and

27

be absolved for his shitty behaviour. He wants his oldest friend to hug him and tell him everything is going to be all right, just like I always used to. Well, he can think again. I am not prepared to play that game. Not again.

Now Lottie is gone, what's the point of holding onto the past? Everything has changed now. We have no need for each other. Unlike what Dec believes, I can't act like nothing happened. Nothing is ever going to be the same again. It's just something I have to come to terms with.

I've just thrown the phone back onto the table when my doorbell rings. I freeze, puzzled. No one comes here. I'm not expecting visitors and the thought of having to face another human makes me feel slightly queasy.

Pulling the dressing gown tighter around my body, I pad to the front door and open it cautiously, gasping when I see who it is. Erica. Sour-faced and clutching what looks like a beautifully wrapped present, complete with bow and curly ribbons. It's not my birthday and even if it was, Erica would be the last person to come and celebrate it with me.

'Erica…' I say, my voice catching. 'I didn't expect to see—'

'I'm not stopping.' Her reply is as curt as always. Her small eyes, sharp like cut diamonds, blaze through me. 'I can assure you this is the last place I want to be.'

Even as my body wants to curl up protectively, I pull back my shoulders, trying to channel defiance. I never want Erica to see the effect she has on me.

'I have something for you,' she says bluntly. 'It's from Lottie.'

I don't say anything. I can't. I don't really understand what she means. Lottie is dead. Is this some kind of sick joke?

'I would have given it to you yesterday, but you rushed off.' Her eyes fix on mine. 'It was a difficult day, I get it. But I thought, maybe—' She shakes her head. 'Never mind. It doesn't matter now.' She shoves the box in my hands. It feels quite light; the paper is silky smooth. I swear, and this might be my imagination, that I can smell the scent of Lottie's perfume. For a second, it's almost as if she is here beside me.

'What is it?' I ask, still confused.

Erica, as always, is totally clueless and seems almost put out that she had to make the delivery. She dusts her hands on her coat and tuts under her breath.

'It was Lottie's wish that I give it to you in person,' she says. 'She even wrote it down on her to-do list before – well, before she died. You know how she could get silly ideas in her head sometimes… It was the same, even at the end.'

'I don't understand,' I say, because I just don't. 'Why would she give me a present now? It makes no sense.'

'Well, neither do I really. I just hope it makes you happy,' Erica replies, before turning on her heel and striding off.

I am left standing there, clutching a box that my best friend had carefully and beautifully wrapped for me. It's all I can do not to crumble right there on the doorstep.

Lottie has one last gift for me. So typical of her to think of me, even right at the end. Just the thought of it makes the tears well in my eyes again.

But what on earth can she give to me that I would want or need now? All I want is her.

Thirteen Years Before

Lottie

I could tell that Sara really didn't want me at her flat. Her shoulders were all stiff and her face was turned away from mine. The few times she caught my gaze her eyes were as hard as flint. She kept muttering things to Declan and Jay under her breath and I could hear traces of the sentences.

'...*I said no*...'

'...*annoying*...'

'...*your fault*...'

I drifted behind, feeling like the outsider, a pain in Sara's neck that she clearly didn't need. I hadn't even wanted to come here. Jay had insisted; he said they always went to Sara's after school and told me that it would be 'no problem' for me to tag along. It was fine as long as Sara's mum was at work apparently – Dec and Jay exchanged a glance between them then. I wasn't sure what the problem with Sara's mum was, but I got the impression Jay didn't like her.

I guess this was the normal routine. I had a sudden desire to turn and leave, to remove myself from this awkward situation and get myself away. But where would I be going? Back to a cold, empty house where my mum would no doubt not be. She would be out with her own friends or shopping or having something on her body plucked or finessed. I would be going back to my sad, tired thoughts that rattled around in my head. Back to a lonely sort of nothingness where I didn't belong either.

I knew I had to make this work – it really was my last chance to fit in somewhere. I had to convince Sara that I was worth getting to know. If I could make that work, things might open up for me.

'It's a nice place, Sara,' I said brightly. 'Really cosy. I love it.'

Sara finally turned to face me. We were stood in her small living room – well, all of us except Jay who'd already thrown himself down on the nearby sofa and picked up an Xbox controller. I could see two spots of pink appear on Sara's cheeks, she pushed aside her dark hair and stared at me flatly.

'Are you taking the piss, or what?'

'No–no, I meant it?' I was flustered as I tried to gather my words together, my stupid voice breaking and stammering like it always did when I was nervous. 'It's lovely in here – warm and nice.'

'Leave her, Sara!' Jay said, his eyes now fixed on the screen. 'She's only trying to be friendly.'

Sara's mouth turned into a sort of snarl, her eyes still on mine. 'Yeah? Well I don't need her to be nice, OK?'

I shrugged, trying to look relaxed and cool and desperately ignoring the gnawing in my stomach. I didn't see her problem. It *was* cosy in here. OK, it was a bit small. The sofa and large chair took up most of the space. A coffee table in the corner was piled up with newspapers, books and a few used cups. There wasn't a carpet on the floor, but a red rug brightened the space and photos lined every wall. Most were school photos – a girl who I instantly recognised as Sara, with her heavy fringe and dark eyes, seated next to an older boy with the same serious look on his face.

'I didn't know you had a brother,' I said. 'Is he at our school?'

Sara's gaze fell on the picture I was looking at. She didn't answer for a moment, and then she spoke in a flat tone. 'No – he was excluded. And he doesn't live here any more.'

I got the sense I shouldn't ask any more questions. 'Oh, I'm sorry,' I muttered.

'You don't need to be. He isn't.'

'Kyle was one of the hardest lads on the estate,' Dec told me, throwing himself down next to Jay. 'You wouldn't want to mess with him.'

I flinched – I wasn't planning to.

Sara trailed off to the kitchen and I followed her, not really keen on staying with the boys who were now playing a shoot-'em-up on the TV. I watched awkwardly while Sara filled the kettle. It was another small room; packets and jars lined the small counter and the sink was full of unwashed plates and cups. The walls were painted yellow but stained darker in some places. It smelt thicker and greasier in here, like the windows hadn't been opened in some time.

'I'm sorry if I said something wrong out there,' I said.

She shrugged. 'It's OK, don't worry about it.'

I was struggling to find things to talk about. I wanted to keep the conversation moving. 'How many bedrooms do you have?'

Sara flicked on the kettle and chuckled softly. 'You really are a little estate agent, aren't you? Full of questions. Would you like me to take you on a tour of the place so that you can take proper notes?'

'No… I was just interested.'

'No, come on – you must see!'

Before I could say anything more, she grabbed my arm and swept me down the thin dark hallway. The first doorway was open, revealing a small toilet, sink and bath – all in pastel pink.

'That's where we shit and wash. No fancy showers for us I'm afraid and certainly no swimming pool.'

'I–I didn't—'

'Come on! There's more!' She pulled me down towards another door, this one firmly shut but she forced it open, pressing my body towards the opening. I could see a large unmade bed. A mess of clothes. 'That's my mum's room. She's not in, though. In fact, she's never really in. She's either working or up in London caring for Nan. Or doing other stuff. But you wouldn't know about that, I expect.'

Prickles of frustration began bubbling up inside me. 'Lottie, I—'

But she was pulling me again. This time towards the final room. She opened the door with a flourish. It was tiny. A small bed pressed against the wall. A wardrobe. And books – so many books – they littered the floor and were piled up high beside her bed.

'And my room. Small and poky – no space to swing a cat. Not that we'd ever have a cat. Books everywhere, I'm hopeless at looking after them, always losing my place. I bet you don't, do you? You probably own loads of the things. And one of those posh beds I bet and—'

I pulled my hand out of her grip. 'Enough!' I could feel the anger suddenly explode out of me. Sara actually recoiled a bit, her eyes widened, and a tiny smile formed on her face.

'Wow. I wasn't expecting that,' she said. 'You do have some fire in you.'

'I've had enough of you going on like you know me – talking about your flat, your things like they're shit compared to mine. I'm sick of you making judgements about me when you don't even know me.' My entire body went rigid, and I made myself look her straight in the eye when all I wanted to do was flinch. 'You know nothing about me. You haven't got a clue. So just shut the fuck up.'

I could've blown it then. That could've been it. I suppose Sara could've slapped me, or told me to leave. In that split second, I could have lost it all.

But instead of screaming at me or reacting in anger, Sara just threw her head back and laughed.

We stepped into her bedroom, and she gestured towards her neatly made-up bed and I sat myself down. My head was spinning a bit, I could taste something hot and bitter at the back of my throat and tried to swallow it down. What was going on here? Why wasn't Sara mad at me?

'I've been a bit of a bitch, haven't I?' she said frankly. For the first time, her expression was softer. There was a hint of a smile on her lips. I could feel myself begin to slowly relax.

'Well… yeah, just a bit…'

She laughed again. I liked it. I liked seeing her eyes light up, her face filling up with warmth. She was like a different girl standing there in front of me. I watched as her fingers clawed into her palms, how her teeth worked at her bottom lip.

Was she nervous? Surely not?

'Sara,' I said softly. 'I don't get what the problem is. I never meant to muscle in on you guys or try to change anything. I just wanted...' I let the word hang. It sounded so pathetic, so hopeless. I just wanted a friend. That's all I ever wanted. Why was it always so bloody hard? Even in my last school it had been a struggle. There, the other girls had money too, but it didn't make it any easier for me to fit in; I was always on the periphery, looking in, wondering how everyone else made friendships seem so easy.

Sara studied me for a second and then sighed softly. She sat herself down next to me; the bed was small and overcrowded with cushions and a pile of clothes, so we were pressed up close together. I could smell her perfume – it smelt like the musky ones I had tried on at the Body Shop when I was bored in town. I could also smell cigarettes and the sickly-sweet scent of hairspray. Together it was quite a heady mix.

'I guess I hate people making judgements,' she said finally. 'They do it all the time with us, with my family. They make assumptions because mum is on her own, because Kyle is in a young offender's unit...' She breathed out as she picked on the loose threads of her jeans. 'It winds me up that other people must be thinking all these things about us – that we're rough, or poor or not worth knowing. It puts my back up, you know, because they don't know the truth. They don't know what we're really like.'

'You shouldn't care what other people think.'

I thought of my mum – how impressions meant everything to her. How she wouldn't answer the door without her make-up on or leave the house unless she was wearing her best clothes. I always hated how those things mattered so much to her and yet other things, the things that I needed so much, barely featured in her mind.

'I know… and I try not to, and yet…' She paused, shook her head. 'And yet, I ended up doing the same thing to you, just because you have a posh voice and live in a nice house.'

I flinched. 'I don't have a posh voice.'

Sara snorted. 'You do! You just don't notice! I suppose you're used to it.'

'It's normal. It's just my voice.' I couldn't help feeling a bit offended.

'I know… I know, I'm just saying.' Sara was still smiling.

'And I'm not posh… not really. You should have seen the kids at my last school, some of them even had connections to royalty. I'd always felt left out there too,' I said. 'Maybe that's the problem. Maybe I don't belong anywhere.'

Sara reached out and took my hand. It was warm and soft. She squeezed gently. 'You do. You belong with us. And I'm sorry if I made you feel any different.'

I managed a weak smile. 'Are you sure?'

'I'm sure. I need a friend, too. The boys drive me nuts. I've been hanging around with them too long on my own. I need a girlfriend for once.' She squeezed my hand again. 'Can we start over?'

I nodded. 'I'd really like that.'

All at once, in that small room, I felt safe. We sat for a few more minutes together, listening to the sounds of the boys shouting at the Xbox in the other room. It was perfect in a simple way.

'And you're not getting in between me and Jay,' she said quietly. 'There isn't anything to get in between, not really…'

'You seem so close though?'

'I've known him since I was tiny, but Dec is right, it's so complicated.' Sara sighed, her face looked pained. 'One day I'll explain but it's a long, boring story – for now, can we just chill, Lottie? Have fun just us two?'

I couldn't stop my grin from spreading. 'I'd love that.'

And in that moment, I guess, our friendship began to take bloom. Like two vines in the same garden, we were drawn to each other, but while Sara was fresh and blooming, I was struggling to thrive. I was twisting towards her, in the hope that I could benefit from her section of sunlight.

I needed her.

Day Three

Sara

Sunday. Urgh. Could it just disappear please?

It used to be my very favourite day, but now it feels like my very worst, hanging over me like a heavy, endless cloud threatening to break into rain at any moment. I am quite possibly the only person on earth right now who is praying for Sunday to end, so that I can move onto the structure and banality of Monday.

In the last few months, Sunday had become mine and Lottie's day. A day we always shared together if possible, whether it be lunch down the pub or walking around the lake. It was our day just to ourselves.

Lottie's illness had affected that, of course; we had started with short trips out before Lottie had become too tired. Then I started visiting Lottie at home – painting her nails or doing her hair or watching films. Anything that made her feel better and more human. It may have been different, but it was still special. I even ignored the fact that Erica had been there, hanging around in the shadows, listening to our conversations.

However, Lottie's cancer soon made her too weak for even that. I used to go and see her as often as I could, but it was clear that Lottie struggled with too many visitors. Erica became stricter, like a brittle gatekeeper at the door, scared that I might bring more risk to Lottie because I worked in a care home. She wrapped Lottie up in cotton wool, restricting her to short meetings in their huge living room or tiny walks in the garden. It was hard. I hated those times. I didn't know what to say to my friend who was angry one minute and scared the next. I was consumed with rage too, a rage that was so strong it frightened me. I just wanted to whip Lottie out of her mum's grip and do fun things with her again like we used to – a trip to Brighton beach, shopping in London, drinking milkshakes at Roxy's cafe in town.

Anything was better than seeing her curled up in a chair, bored out of her mind, slowly wasting away.

We called each other, but that soon tired Lottie out, and it wasn't the same. I couldn't hug her. I couldn't rub cream into her dry skin. I couldn't wipe away her tears when she cried, but Lottie cried so rarely even then…

Lottie had needed me more than ever in those last few months and I was kept away from her. I was a danger. A threat. And in no time at all, our Sundays had been broken forever.

I haven't opened her present yet. I can't bring myself to do so. It's just sitting there, looking at me in its pretty paper, almost like it is taunting me.

I don't know what I'm waiting for. I think maybe knowing this is Lottie's last gift to me is making it too hard. I don't want to rush opening it, it's too special. But also, I'm scared. What could she possibly give me that I would want? What if this present makes me feel a whole lot worse? Sometimes it easier to just leave things alone and remember things as they were. Sometimes things are best left unopened – I've learnt that to my cost.

Goose buzzes around my legs as I busy myself having a shower and tidying the flat. I am trying to get a grip of my life. I hate sitting around in my own misery, I feel like it's starting to seep deep into my bones, making my feel heavy and listless. Out of boredom, I even ring Tyler.

'Hey babe.' His voice is sexy and soothing. 'How are you doing?'

I picture him in his chaotic flat, probably walking up and down with his top off. To be fair, Tyler does have a lovely body and I can understand why he likes to show it off.

I met Tyler when I was at university waiting tables. We dated on and off for a laugh and then hooked up again when I came back from travelling three years ago. We are *not* dating. I don't think either of us wants that. Tyler is happy being free and single and I am happy meeting up with a fun guy occasionally for uncomplicated sex and a few laughs. It's always been like that between us. From the night I met him, dancing crazily whilst trying to protect his pint of beer, I felt a kind of affection towards him. Tyler is daft, kind and undemanding – which is just what I need right now. It's all I've needed for quite a while…

'I didn't want to call you,' he continues, 'in case, well – you know. I didn't want to barge in where I might not be wanted. How did it go? I was thinking of you.'

I smile. I doubt this is true, Tyler's life is too busy and crazy, I can't believe he even had time to send me that text. 'It was tough, but I'm glad it's done now.' I stare at Lottie's present and tug a little at my hair. 'It's just going to be hard, I guess. Moving on.'

'Yeah, I guess it will.' He pauses. 'I've made a curry, you're welcome to pop over?'

'That's nice, but I don't think so. Maybe tomorrow? We could meet up?'

I don't want to sound needy because I'm not. I'm really not. I just like the idea of slipping into Tyler's arms, having him whisper some dirty words into my ear before he pushes me up against the wall. I can't be thinking about sad things when I'm turned on, can I?

'Well, the offer is there if you change your mind,' he says. 'What are you planning on doing instead?'

I stare again at the present. 'I dunno. I guess I still have a few things to sort out.'

'I'll book us a table for tomorrow, somewhere nice. You need spoiling. Shall I text you the details?'

'Sure.' My smile feels forced. 'Sounds perfect.'

When he ends the call, I feel sad and a bit jealous. Tyler's life is so simple and unproblematic. He loves his job as a chef and he's good at it. He's close to his family and has a huge gang of friends that he regularly hangs out with.

I think of what we used to have together – me, Dec, Lottie and Jay and I suddenly feel hollow inside. We once were that happy, sociable group but then, bit by bit, it all came apart until only Lottie and I remained.

I glance at the photo that I still display on the mantlepiece. It's my favourite one. In it we are all huddled together after a party at Lottie's house. Lottie is in the centre; her cheeks are rosy and her beautiful thick golden hair is loose around her face. Dec is crouched beside her, his face turning to look at her, laughing. Even looking at the photo from here I can remember the rich, hearty sound of Dec's laugh – it always sounded a bit too big for his body somehow. Jay and I are standing behind. Jay has his arm slung around my shoulder; his cheeks are glowing from too much drink, his eyes are sleepy. I'm the only one not smiling, but I never did in those days, I was always so paranoid about my teeth. My fringe is heavy against my eyes and my skin is deathly pale against Jay's tan.

I may have looked miserable, but I remember the joy of that night. How we had laughed for hours because Dec had drunk too much cider and started talking nonsense about his career aspirations. I remember how Lottie had tried to get us all to dance, putting on her favourite Madonna songs and begging us to copy her moves – poor Jay hadn't had a clue.

We'd been eighteen there. Just after our A levels. We'd been so happy.

I walk over to the photo, and I turn it against the wall. I can't stand to see the open smiles and the hopeful faces. So much has changed – too much – and I'm not sure that I can deal with much more.

–

Later that evening, after a small dinner of beans on toast, I sit in my living room with music playing softly in the background – something nondescript on a local radio station that forms a nice backdrop. Beside me, Goose is sleeping soundly, gentle purrs escaping her body every few minutes and making her whiskers flutter against my leg. On my lap is the box that Erica had given me. I still haven't opened it. Once it's opened, it's opened forever.

Lottie had always been a fervent present buyer. She loved lavishing gifts on others. When we were younger, I had resented this a bit – I saw it as Lottie flashing her privilege in my face, trying to win people over with her money. However, it hadn't taken me long to realise that

Lottie's gifts were not about the expense at all. They were thoughtful and kind and had taken her a lot of time to choose. Lottie gained pure joy from simply giving them out, and soon it became hard not to be won over by her charm and excitement.

I remember the first gift that Lottie had given me just after we met. A simple bookmark. So silly now, looking back, but at the time it had meant the world to me. I still have it, tucked away in my drawer. Lottie told me it was to help me keep my precious words safe and I liked that. I realised that in very little time Lottie had worked out that books meant a lot to me. The bookmark was a reminder that not all first impressions are right ones.

And now, here I am with another gift on my lap. My mind is whirling. When did Lottie have time to shop? She must have purchased it online, surely? She was so tired, so drained at the end. And what on earth could she have thought I needed?

'You shouldn't have bothered, babe,' I whisper. 'This will be a waste. There's nothing I need. Not now anyway…'

I imagine Lottie sitting next to me frowning. '*Just open the bloody thing and stop wasting time. You're such a drama queen!*'

My fingers touch the fancy paper, always the most expensive kind. Lottie said that half the fun came in the wrapping, and stuck beside the ribbon is a small handmade label, cut out in the shape of a heart. Lottie's curly writing sweeps over the glossy card. I take a breath before reading the words, imagining Lottie's soft voice reading them to me.

> *I think this might be the greatest gift I could ever give to you. I hope you agree.*

You deserve this. You really do, but you need to believe it too.

Forever your friend,
Lottie
x

It feels like I'm being watched by her. I remember how impatient she used to get when I took ages opening presents, especially in the early days. She hadn't realised then how much they meant to me – how I wasn't used to getting them, always overwhelmed by a heady mix of awkwardness and excitement.

I picture her beside me, her face pulled into a scowl. Her hands slapping the sides of the sofa. *'C'mon Sara – get a move on. I'm dying to know if you like it.'*

'All right. All right,' I mutter to myself. 'I'll do it now.'

I peel the paper back carefully. I don't want to tear the beautiful wrapping. It's so shiny and expensive looking, glossy black with tiny white diamonds. I want to treasure it forever. It reminds me of the tiled floors in Lottie's mum's house. Clean and glistening and slightly slippery underfoot. Her house was always elegant, modern and tidy. So unlike mine. We were so different in many, many ways.

I remember the first time Lottie had come back to my house, and a lump forms in my throat, making it difficult to breathe. How sweet she had been, so kind and unjudgmental. It was like she couldn't see the dust and clutter, the worn carpet and the tatty curtains. I just wish now that I could rush back in time and be with her again. I would do things differently. I would thank her for making me feel OK.

'I wouldn't have been so defensive back then,' I whisper, my fingers stroking the paper. 'I never thought you'd understand. How could you, really?'

Imaginary Lottie is still sat beside me, nodding her head gently. Telling me it's OK. We never talked about this stuff, not really. I guess there was never the need. We just began to understand each other in that comfortable and quiet way that makes friendships so perfect.

I pick gently at the Sellotape, feeling a smile tug on my face. Lottie always knew how to use the right amount, how to wrap a present properly. I was the complete opposite, I would always rush and cut corners and end up twisting yards of tape over the package just to hold it together into one huge sticky mess. It used to drive Lottie mad. She would break a fingernail simply trying to open one of my specialities and would be a be a hot sweary mess by the time she got it open.

'Here we go,' I say, as I break through the seal.

I pull away the paper, hardly able to believe how fast my heart was beating. Inside is a box. A plain white box. Pushing the wrapping to one side, I gently turn the box upright on my lap. I can feel the thud of something moving inside. It isn't that heavy, but it feels substantial. Carefully, I tug at the lid of the box, keen to see what is contained inside. I tip the box slightly and peer in.

It takes a few seconds for my mind to compute what I am actually seeing.

'Oh, Lottie,' I breathe, my voice breaking. I almost don't want to go on.

Because I now know what Lottie has given me. Immediately, I feel my heart crack open once again.

It's a jar.

One of Lottie's Jars of Joys.

Eleven Years Before

Lottie

It wasn't meant to be a big thing. I was just having some people round, that was all, to celebrate the end of sixth form. It was a small party while Mum was away. I don't know why it was becoming such a big deal in my head.

The boys were late, so I showed Sara up to my room. I wasn't planning to, but she insisted she wanted to see. In all honesty, I was a bit embarrassed to show her.

I stood back as Sara opened the door and walked into the large, mainly pink space. It was a huge room, and I was achingly aware of how much bigger it was than hers. However, unlike Sara's room, this space had no warmth and said nothing about me. I cringed as Sara padded across the fluffy pink carpet and scanned the floral wallpaper. The scatter cushions covered my bed and everything – my make-up, clothes and books – were stored neatly away in shiny white units (not by me; Mum insisted that Fay, the cleaner, came in every day to keep everything spotless).

'My mum decorated it,' I said quietly. 'She insists she has a better eye for these things than me, but I wanted something far more neutral.'

'It's nice,' Sara said, but the stiff smile on her face told me she thought differently. 'It's so bloody clean though.'

'My mum is a bit OCD, if anything is out of place she kicks off.' Including me, I wanted to add, but I didn't. The words remained stale on my tongue instead.

Sara seemed quite caught up in looking at my things, admiring the amount of stuff I had decorating my shelves and units. Most of it was silly little knick-knacks, things that Dad might have bought me on his travels away or gifts from Mum when she was having a moment of guilt about something. You could tell the difference between them: Dad's objects were interesting curios, rocks or crystals that he thought I might find 'pretty', while Mum focused on ornate dolls, jewellery boxes and scarves and bangles that she longed to decorate me with.

It just went to show that neither parent knew me very well at all.

'It's so interesting in here,' Sara said. 'You have such a mix of stuff.' She walked past my bed, pulling a face at my overdressed bed and picking up an old teddy that sat amongst the cushions. 'You still sleep with this?'

'Fay – I mean, I – just put it there to keep it out of the way.'

Sara grinned but luckily didn't ask any more about Fay. I didn't want her to know I had a cleaner. For some reason I thought she might find that bad.

She was looking at my books now. My collection was far smaller than hers. In truth, I'd never been much of a reader. I didn't really see the point of it. These were books my mum bought for me because she expected me to have the same taste in things that she did. Most of them were ancient.

'Interesting selection here,' she said, squinting at the titles. 'So you like romance mainly?'

'I guess.'

'That's cool. I like romances too. I can recommend some to you if you like? There's some great recent releases.'

'I'm not sure... I don't really read that much any more.'

'Hey, what's that?' Sara had spied a glass jar sitting on the bookcase, stuffed full of folded paper. She carefully lifted it up, peering into the jar itself. It was decorated with tiny silver stars and in gold pen the letter 'J' was written. I immediately stiffened. I had hoped she wouldn't spot that.

'Lottie? What is this?' She asked again, shaking the jar.

I knew my cheeks were turning a deeper shade of red. I was already used to my mum teasing me for my 'little craft projects and funny ideas', I didn't want Sara to think the same thing or to take the piss out of me for having such a daft object in my room. At the same time though, this was important to me. It was something I always did and if Sara was going to scorn me for it, it was probably better to get it out of the way.

'It's my Jar of Joy,' I said as casually as I could. 'I've been making one for myself every year now since I was little. You should try it. It's fun.'

Sara eyed it suspiciously, like it was some kind of trap. 'What, this jar is going to make me happy? I doubt it somehow.' She shook it again. 'What's inside? Self-help messages? Words of wisdom? Answers to problems of the universe?'

'Don't be so quick to scoff.' I gestured for Sara to sit down on the bed. 'It's just a thing I've done for ages. It helps me a bit. It's nothing special.'

'I want to know what's written on these things though?' Sara was still peering in the jar, almost as though she expected one of the messages to jump out and unravel themselves in front of her. 'I've never seen anything like this before. How does it help you?'

I carefully took the jar from her. It was funny how a simple jam jar felt so valuable in my grip. I still remember the first time I washed one out and carefully wrote out my first messages. I'd only been eight but at that time in my life I needed something to help me through the bleak days. The days when Mum and Dad's arguments were dark and destructive, the days when I realised that I was beginning to disappear from their attention. I needed reminders of the good things in my life.

'I write myself messages every day of things that make me grateful or events that have happened that have made me happy. Then I put them in a jar.' I paused, smiling shyly. 'Then, every time I feel a bit sad, or maybe I'm having a bad day, I take one of these messages out and read it. It helps me remember. It reminds me to appreciate the small things. It helps keep me going.'

Sara frowned. 'It sounds a bit simplistic to me.'

'Well, perhaps you shouldn't knock it 'til you try it?' I gazed at her steadily. 'I think you would find it helpful.'

'I doubt that. I'd struggle to fill the bloody thing up.' Sara grinned to show that she was joking, but I didn't return the smile. Instead, I placed the jar back on the shelf.

'One day you might find you need something like this,' I told her gently. 'And when that day comes you will be grateful for it, believe me.'

This jar, this bashed-up, crusty old jar, had got me through some really bad times and I truly believed, deep down in my heart, that it could help anyone who was struggling.

–

We started drinking while we waited for the boys to arrive.

'Do you like Jay?' I asked suddenly, needing to get to the point. 'I mean – more than a friend? You two always seem so close, and I don't know—'

'We've known each other forever, that's all,' Sara said dismissively. 'So yeah, we're close, we've been through a lot of shit together.'

'Yeah, what's that all about? You mentioned it before but I didn't want to pry.'

Sara chuckled to herself. 'God, it's so dull. Like something from a bad film.' She waved her glass at me. 'Basically, my mum had an affair with his dad. It got messy between our families. Everyone hates each other. Jay's parents especially hate my brother.'

'Why?'

'Because he beat the crap out of Jay's dad when he hurt my mum.' Sara sniffed. 'That's why he's inside. He nearly killed him.'

'Oh…' I let the words drift. That was a lot to take in.

'So, me and Jay are screwed. Even being friends is hard. Our mums hate each other.'

'But would you want it to be more than that?'

Sara's cheeks glowed red. Maybe it was the drink, but she seemed suddenly awkward. She shifted on the bed beside me. 'Oh, Lottie, I don't know. I shouldn't talk about this.'

'But we're friends, aren't we?' I pushed. 'We should confide in each other.'

She shrugged. 'I guess. But it doesn't matter anyway. It doesn't matter how I feel about Jay because everything is so difficult…' She hesitated. 'Anything more than friendship would risk everything we have. Besides…'

'Besides what?'

She sniffed. 'I don't know. He's so nice, isn't he? I think he just puts up with my crazy ways. That I'll always just be like a sister to him.'

'I could ask him,' I said with a confidence that I didn't feel. 'I could ask him what he really feels about you?'

Sara hesitated. I saw hope flash behind her eyes, and it actually hurt me, how much she wanted Jay. He was all she wanted – nothing else. There was nothing I could give her that she would ever desire more.

'Lottie, I—' The doorbell rang. Sara shot up, as if stung. Her eyes were already at the window.

'That's them,' she said. 'We have to go down. Come on.'

As I followed her downstairs, I realised she hadn't answered my question, but it didn't matter any more.

I knew what I was going to do.

–

I got Jay to myself later on that evening. We were all pretty drunk by then. Dec and Sara were flopped out on the chairs by the pool. Jay and I were in the kitchen, leaning up against the worktops. He looked sleepy and dreamy and quite cute. I could understand why Sara was attracted to him. Together they would make a pretty perfect couple.

Except perfect couples weren't good for people like me – couples excluded, they ignored others – they would change the dynamics of a friendship group.

I swallowed down my bitterness.

'This summer is going to be really important,' Jay told me softly, his words slightly slurring. 'Things will be different after.'

'How come?'

'University – me and Sara at the same place, away from here.' He paused. 'I don't know how much you know about me and Sara?'

I tried to look indifferent. 'A bit – I know some of the issues and that you're close.'

'Yeah…' His smile widened. 'We are and it's great, but I'm thinking – or maybe hoping – that we could be more…'

'Oh…' I tried to hide my disappointment. 'Is that what Sara wants too?'

Jay frowned. 'I'm not sure. It's hard to tell with Sara sometimes, she jokes and puts on a front, you know. But, I have this feeling.' He paused, his eyes suddenly fixed on mine. 'Has she said anything to you?'

I felt myself redden. 'No, nothing. Just that you're good friends.'

I could see the pain flicker in his expression before he glanced away, and I tried to fight back the doubt that gnawed at my stomach. Was I doing the right thing? But I knew in my heart Jay and Sara would be destructive together and, worse still, they would push me out. I was only being protective of my own friendship. The alcohol fuelling my body only made me feel more confident.

'If I'm honest, I wonder if we could ever make it work,' he said softly. 'There are plenty of people who want to mess it up for us. But I do want more, Lottie, I do – I think of her every day. I can't get her out of my head. But if I mention it, she thinks I'm just messing around, or she gets scared and defensive. She's so bloody scared of being hurt.'

I dipped my head. 'Because of what happened with your family, right?' I asked. 'Why do family have to make everything so difficult?'

'Exactly!' He slammed his hand on his thigh. 'And I'm sick of it. I need to try to change things. Maybe university will be the opportunity? I can get some time alone with Sara. I can show her how I really feel about her. We will be away from here finally.'

I nodded. The words seemed lost in my throat. University – I had been dreading it, trying not to even think about the day Sara and Jay would go off together and I would be left behind.

'And you, maybe you can help,' Jay said gently. 'You're her friend too. You can make her see how much she means to me. I know she's scared about university, about going away and leaving her mum – but I think it's for the best. I really do.'

'Yeah,' I muttered. 'I can try.'

My throat felt dry, and I coughed awkwardly to try and relieve it. Jay rubbed my arm affectionately and I had to fight back a shiver.

'Thanks, Lottie. You really are the best.'

–

Later, Sara slipped into the seat next to me – she smelt of heat and smoke. Her hair was a tangled mess and her eyes shone. I took another slug of vodka; the room tipped slightly. Nothing was helping the curdled feeling in my stomach.

'I saw you speaking to Jay?' she whispered hopefully. 'What did he say? Did you tell him anything?'

Sometimes, decisions are made in a heartbeat. My heart was broken and tired and beaten black and blue. I barely recognised my voice as I croaked out my answer.

'He doesn't want to hurt you,' I said. 'He only ever sees you as friends. There's too much history – with your family.'

I saw the pain flare briefly, before she took a shaky breath and stiffened. 'OK – OK, fine.'

'He doesn't want to upset you, Sara, that's why...' I hesitated; I hated seeing her like this. 'He cares about you too much.'

'But like a sister,' she muttered.

I nodded stiffly. Yeah, that. Wasn't it better she believed that? Wasn't it better that I kept her away from a potentially toxic and troubled relationship? How could it ever work if the families hated each other so much? Weren't we all safer as friends?

I convinced myself this was true as I took another slug of vodka, as I watched the walls of the room begin to narrow, and as I realised that my best friend was beginning to cry.

I convinced myself I was doing the right thing.

Day Four

Sara

The jar is still sat on the table where I'd left it the night before. The box is beside it, open and discarded. It's now seven a.m. and I have another thumping headache, probably not helped by the half bottle of wine I downed last night.

I stare at the jar bleakly. My mouth is dry and bitter tasting, and my body is cold despite the heat of the flat. I pick up Goose and hold her tight against my body. Luckily she doesn't protest and simply purrs gently against my chest.

'Why has she given me this?' I whisper into her fur. 'She knew I wasn't into that stuff. How the hell is this going to help? It's just going to make me feel even sadder, thinking about the silly things she did that I never understood.'

My thoughts drifted back to last night. Despite my earlier reservations I had made the somewhat hasty decision to invite Tyler over – I needed distraction and for someone to help me relax a little. I was so stressed out I couldn't even bring myself to open the bloody jar and read the messages. What if they upset me all over again? What if each one was like opening up a fresh wound? I wasn't sure I could face that.

Tyler's answer to everything was wine and sex in that order and, although I went along with the instructions quite happily yesterday, I was regretting it now. Sex with Tyler is like eating one of those poncey desserts in a posh restaurant. It looks nice at the time, but always leaves me feeling empty and a little bit queasy from overindulgence. That was the problem with Tyler – he was all style and no substance. He'd always been there for me when I needed fun and flattery, not when I needed to digest complex emotional shit.

'It's just a jar,' he'd said, looking at it as if it was some kind of boring specimen. 'I don't see why you're getting stressed over it.'

We'd just had sex on the sofa. Quick, untidy sex. Tyler's hair was a floppy mess, and his eyes had that sleepy, faraway look. I knew he just wanted to drag me into bed to talk about football or something funny he'd heard down the pub. He didn't have the emotional bandwidth to dissect the reasons why Lottie had decided to leave me her jar.

'I don't understand why she's given it to me,' I tried to explain. 'It makes no sense. I took the piss out of her for keeping one. I never saw the point in it.'

Tyler's frown blighted his good looks briefly. 'I can see what you mean…' He shook the jar. 'No offence, babe, but I don't think a jar full of paper is that exciting… She could have left you a watch. A necklace. Something more exciting and valuable.'

Snatching the jar away from him, I smarted – I didn't like him talking badly about Lottie. 'Lottie always does the best gifts. This isn't about value or anything like that. They're usually so special; she puts thought into them.'

But the Jar of Joy was all about Lottie: it was related to things that mattered to her, that made *her* feel good. I couldn't see how this would be relevant to me.

Tyler went to open the jar. 'Well, let's read the messages then. It's the only way you'll know.'

'No!' I clutched the jar tighter to me. 'We can't. I remember Lottie telling me before that you have to do this properly. You can't just read them all at once. Besides, they are not mine, they are for her. She always wrote these things to help herself. It feels too personal.'

Tyler looked totally confused. 'So what are you going to do? Leave them in there?'

'She probably just gave it to me to look after,' I said. Thinking about it, this made the most sense. She wouldn't want it in the house under her mum's prying eyes, it was too personal to her, and there was no way she would've destroyed it herself. Lottie was never much good at throwing stuff away, she clung onto things in case they became worthy again. If she had lived to an old age, she would've probably been one of those mad old hoarders. The thought caused my heart to ache.

'I still think it's a bit weird,' Tyler muttered. 'Leaving you a jar of a personal wishes and stuff. Where are you going to put it?'

I shrugged. 'I don't know. I haven't figured that out yet.'

Even looking at it made me feel sad. It looked just like the ones I had seen Lottie make when she was little. There was glitter and some stickers around the top, tiny hearts and stars. It was like a glimpse back into her childhood. I wondered if this was one of her original ones.

'It's so sweet how she kept it for so long,' I said.

'Did she ever show you any of the stuff inside?'

I shook my head. 'No, and I never asked.'

It was private and I'd respected that, but also, I knew – with a touch of shame – that I hadn't been interested. How could tiny scraps of paper make you feel better about your life? What if you didn't have many things that brought you joy? Did it mean your jar would be half empty? I think looking at that would have made me feel more depressed. Lottie was lucky in that she saw the best in most things and, unlike many, she had a lot to be thankful for. Well, until the end…

Tyler shook his head. 'I still can't work out why it's such a big deal. Keep it or bin it. It's a child's thing. Something she thought you might like, but obviously didn't want to upset you with. It's no big deal.'

I stare at him blankly, wondering again why I always ended up back with him when he understood so little about me. Lottie used to call him my 'shag blanket' – a kind of comfort that I sought when I was feeling upset or lonely.

'*There's better things you could do, Sara. You could get another cat. You could have a bath. Fuck it, you could just call me…*' Except I didn't want another cat, Goose was more than enough. And I couldn't call Lottie. I couldn't call her ever again.

I told Tyler to leave after that. I was quite cold about it, and he looked at me in that familiar, baffled way – like he was a dog that I had just kicked for no reason. I couldn't really explain to him why I wanted him gone; I just knew I couldn't stand to have him around me any longer. He didn't understand. He never knew Lottie that well. I'd always tried to keep those parts of my life separate. He hadn't known the stuff we'd been through together.

And the only other person who did know, who might understand, was the last person I wanted to see right now.

'I don't want any men around me right now,' I tell Goose firmly. 'Tyler, Jay...' His name catches on my breath. 'I don't need any of them.'

—

Every year, Lottie had made herself a new Jar of Joy and it would stand freshly decorated on her bookcase. She would fill it with messages, starting on New Year's Eve and continuing as the year went on, then, by December, her jar would be full. Rammed full of folded-up pieces of paper. Lottie's scraps of Joy.

'What do you do with them?' I asked her one time. I was still confused by the whole process, not understanding how she could commit to this same process every year.

'I transfer most of them into my new jar. Some I discard if they are no longer relevant, or no longer fill me with joy, but many I've kept for years and years now.'

'Am I in there?' I asked, intrigued.

She nudged me gently with her arm. 'You might be,' she said teasingly. 'There are some things you've said that I want to keep forever.'

'Like what?'

She shrugged. 'It's in the jar. When I pull it out, I'll remember and it'll bring me the same joy that it did back when it happened.'

'That's what you do then? Take them out occasionally?' I frowned. 'I'd be tempted to tip them all out at once.'

'No, no, it doesn't work like that. This is like a separate memory bank, except that this memory bank is for good things. You wouldn't want to waste them all at once, would you?' She stared at me intently and I felt compelled to shake my head. 'You take out a message when you need to, like if you feel sad, or a bit low. It's really uplifting. You immediately remember a better time. Something that made you feel grateful and then you can move on with your day.'

I shrugged. 'Sounds nice I suppose… A bit too much of an effort for me, though.' I wasn't even sure I'd have enough happy messages to fill my jar. 'What if you run out of room?' I asked.

'You never run out. Sometimes I throw away a message once I've read it and it's served its purpose, but like I said, some have been there for ever.'

'And what if you use them up?' I ask.

She smiled. 'Sara, I swear you look for problems that don't exist. I never run out. If I see I'm getting low, I'll write some more to add, but I don't use the jar every day. Only when I need it. You can make special jars for people who are having a bad time, they might need to read a message every day to get them through a dark period.' She shrugged. 'I've not had to do that yet.'

'Which ones do you keep forever?' I asked. 'I'm guessing they must be really important.'

She took a moment before answering, I could see she was giving it a lot of thought. The tiny frown lines appeared between her eyes – the same ones that were there when she was studying or worrying about something. 'You'll think I'm silly,' she said quietly. 'In fact, I know you think that anyway.'

'No, I don't,' I lied, because I did think she was a bit, but I was trying to understand. 'Tell me what makes the ones special that you keep them forever.'

'They're the ones that make me happy to be alive,' she said finally. 'They remind me to keep on going. They remind me why I'm here.'

–

I don't want this present. It's hers. Something that is so personal to Lottie. It feels wrong, invasive. I glare at the jar as if it's its fault. As if it had asked to come here and sit itself on my table. As if it's mocking me.

Then another realisation hits me. Maybe this is a mistake. Maybe the wrong gift went in the wrong box. It's an easy thing to happen, Lottie had got so muddled in the end – her medication was so strong. She was bound to have got confused. Maybe she picked up the jar without thinking, meaning to give me one of her special crystals or ornaments instead. She knew I always loved those. The jar should've stayed safely in her room. OK, there was a risk her mum might look – but would Lottie have cared about that so close to the end?

I'll go back to Lottie's mum and give it back. I'll tell her I don't think it is for me and that she should look after it.

With a glance at my phone, I realise the time and jump up with a jolt. Its already eleven thirty. I hate how I am wasting the days away. I have some time off work and I know I need to make the best of it and try to get my head straight again, so I hurry into the shower, hoping that the cold water will invigorate me. It doesn't. It just makes me grumpier, and I trudge into the bedroom to change into some clothes.

'What were you thinking, Lottie?' I mutter. 'You know I hate any attempts at forced happiness. It's not me, none of this. Was this your last joke? A little wind-up?'

'*Nothing wrong with some fun,*' I swear I hear Lottie whisper in the shadows. '*You know I love you, Sara, but you always take life so seriously. It worries me.*'

I shudder. I have to stop doing this. Imagining Lottie's voice will be enough to finally push me over the edge. I walk over to my chest of drawers and rummage through my make-up trying to decide if I can face attempting to apply some on my pale features. In front of me, a photo of Lottie shines back at me. It's of both of us, taken when we were sixteen on Brighton beach. Jay had been behind the camera telling us to strike a pose and smile. It came easy to Lottie of course. You can see it in her bright sweeping grin, her long blonde hair whipping up in the wind, catching across her cheeks like streaks of sunlight. My arm was pulled tightly around her, my expression more serious as I squinted without the protection of sunglasses.

She was the light, and I was the dark. Rose Red and Snow White. We had all been so happy then.

'What were you thinking there?' I ask her smiling face. 'Did you even suspect how things might turn out for us all?'

Lottie beams back at me. The answers are there of course. Trapped in a mind that I no longer have access to. Lottie is as far away from me now as this girl in the photograph.

I sit down heavily on the bed, my body naked and dripping from the shower, and burst into tears.

-

It isn't a long walk to Erica's but I always feel a bit self-conscious walking in this side of the city. The roads are much wider and tree lined, the driveways are sweeping and the homes themselves are detached and grand – each one as individual and intimidating as the next.

As a teenager, I used to skulk up here in tatty ripped jeans and busted-up trainers. I used to imagine what it would be like to live in a place that was four times the size of our flat. What could you do in that space! I knew Lottie was embarrassed by it. She never bragged or liked to show off what she had. Sometimes I think she was just as uncomfortable living there as I was visiting.

'It's just a house,' she would say. 'It's where I sleep. It's not home.'

I asked her what home was, but she couldn't answer. There was a sad expression in her eyes, and I knew not to push her further.

But her house – well, that was always something special. Number thirty-two sits at the end of Quintin Avenue on the corner plot; larger and prouder than the others, the house seems to overpower the rest of the street. I can see Erica's red Audi parked up and my stomach dips a little, as it always did at the thought of facing her. There is something about Erica's stern expression and her perfect, polished appearance that always makes me feel ill at ease.

Lottie never understood that. She never really seemed to take her mum seriously – said she was 'fake' and 'full of shit', but I only ever saw a rich and austere woman who looked down on scraggy-arse characters like me.

With a sharp intake of breath, I make myself walk towards the front door, press the doorbell and wait. My rucksack contains Lottie's supposed last gift to me and I am keen to give it back.

After a moment or two I hear an internal door open and see the shadow of Erica approaching behind the glass. Even now, after all these years, I feel like the same scruffy teenager. I am slouched and awkward on her doorstep, painfully aware of my scuffed trainers and messy hair.

She opens the door carefully and I immediately notice that she's wearing an old grey tracksuit – not like Erica at all, in fact more suited to what my mum would wear. Her hair is pulled away from her face, which is unmade-up and plain.

She looks exhausted. I've never, ever seen her like this.

'Sara?' She frowns. 'I wasn't expecting you, was I?'

'No. No, sorry.' I'm still thrown by her appearance. Even in the days after Lottie's death Erica had maintained a perfectly turned-out look. It's unnerving. 'Maybe I should have called ahead…' I say quickly.

She purses her lips. 'Yes, maybe you should have. I didn't think anyone would come today.'

She doesn't invite me in. Instead, she stands blocking the small gap in the door, like I'm some door-to-door salesman that she is desperate to get rid of. I think of all the times I've been here before. How I'd slept over, spent weekends here. Have I ever really been welcome?

'Sara, I'm sorry but I'm a bit busy at the moment. Is there something I can help you with?'

'Yeah… I'm sorry.' I pull my bag from my shoulder, reach into it and drew out the jar. I had carefully packed it back into the box to protect it. 'I wanted to bring this back. I think it's some kind of mistake.'

Erica takes the box and peers inside. 'I'm not sure I understand. Isn't this what I gave you yesterday?'

'Yes. But I don't think it's meant for me. Lottie knew my thoughts on these things and I would never ever want to take her Jar of Joy. It was hers.'

Erica shakes her head. 'But it's not hers. Hers is still in her room. This is one she made for you. It took her ages.'

'But I recognise the jar, the glue...' My words are jumbled.

Erica shrugs. 'Well, maybe she made it like her own for sentimental reasons, I don't know, but this was definitely for you. She worked hard on it. I watched her do it.'

I can't speak for a moment. I step forward, peering again at the jar. Had I been so caught up in my emotions that I'd failed to notice the difference? Now I look again, I can see this one has tiny butterflies painted on the glass, my favourite insect. And – oh my God, is that a robin?

My hand flies to my chest. 'She painted a robin for me. My favourite bird. How did I not see that?'

'Perhaps you weren't looking properly.' Erica's tone is sharp. 'Did you miss this, too?'

I blink, tears building in my eyes. Erica has reached deep inside the box and pulls out a large folded square of paper.

'What is it?'

Erica hands it to me. 'Perhaps you should look for yourself.'

Through the cloud of my tears, I do. I open and read Lottie's last letter to me on Erica's doorstep. And suddenly, everything makes a lot more sense.

Dear Sara,

My God, I think this is the hardest letter I've ever had to write. I did think about giving this to you face-to-face, explaining to you properly, but I knew what you'd be like. You would think that something like this is daft and unnecessary – a silly little Lottie Project that you never quite understood. Maybe you'd push it away and that would really upset me.

I'm begging you not to do that though. You need to give it a chance, even if it's begrudgingly. I know you're pulling that face right now (the one I hate) so stop that! Just chill and go along with this process, OK? I promise it's not as bad as you think.

The truth is, I think this gift will really help you. I think this might be the greatest present I've given you and I really need you to believe in me. You once told me that you thought I was good at working people out, well, let's just say this is my opportunity to prove it. I think I worked you out a long time ago. I love you more than anyone I know, and I want you to have something that is special and meaningful.

I want you to experience something that will matter. This might not make a lot of sense at first, but I think by the end it will – you simply have to trust me.

This Jar of Joy is yours – I've made it just for you. It's a little bit different to the one I used to have. I had to put a twist on it that makes it yours and yours only, I hope you don't mind. Inside, I have written happy memories and good things that we have done together – either the two of us, or with Jay and maybe others too. I want you to remember those moments. They're special. They have meaning.

My last wish – and as a dying woman it's important that you follow this through unless you want to be haunted by a neurotic, ghostly me – is that you take out a message from the jar every day. I want you to read the memory and then I want you to follow the instructions on the back as requested. There is one memory at the bottom of the jar. I've stuck it on. Please leave that one until last. The rest can be read in any old order, but I want that one to be seen last.

There aren't that many messages. I could've gone mad, but I didn't want to exhaust you. Maybe at the end of it you'll realise why I loved remembering joy so much.

I'm hoping you'll be able to enjoy the good things we did all over again. That's not so bad, is it? I know I'm not there to experience them with you again, but I need you to remember the amazing thing we had. All of us. I think it's rare to find people you get on so well with. Some people go a lifetime and never find a true friend. I count myself lucky that I found you when I did. I was so desperately lonely at times. Despite my best efforts, I struggled to see the brightness in the world – but it was you – and Jay – that helped me to find my way. You may feel like you're alone now, or that I've left you, but that's not the case. I'll always be with you really, just listen and you'll hear my voice. In time, I reckon you'll soon be sick of me and that's when I'll know you are healed.

Also, you are not alone. You know that, really. I hope you're not pushing everyone away, Sara. Now is the time to start letting others in. Your heart needs to be prepared to be open. You can't still be scared of being hurt.

I want you to be happy, Sara – that's all I've ever wanted. You will always be my closest friend, my sister and the best thing that ever happened to me.

Please don't be too sad. I would hate that.

I want to give you happiness and by the end of this, I hope you understand what that truly is.

Yours forever,

L

Xxx

Day Five

A message a day. That is all I have to do. Read a message a day and follow its instructions. I frown at the jar, which is now sitting pride of place on my coffee table. Goose sniffed it a few times as if she was hopeful it contained treats; she soon gave it a flick of her tail when she realised it didn't.

I should have started yesterday, but I was such a snotty, teary mess after leaving Erica's that I couldn't face anything. Even Erica had been shocked, her stern demeanour slipping briefly as she stepped forward to take the jar from my shaking hands.

'Are you OK?' she'd asked, her gaze drifting briefly to the letter, which I hurriedly folded away and stuffed in my pocket. I didn't want her to read Lottie's last words to me; they were private.

'It's just a bit of a shock,' I told her. 'I wasn't expecting this.' I took the jar back from Erica, feeling suddenly foolish and ungrateful for even trying to bring it back. 'I'm sorry, I shouldn't have come,' I'd said, before staggering back down the driveway, my eyes still misty with tears. I heard Erica calling behind me, offering me a lift, but there was no way I wanted to be cooped up in a car, I needed fresh air. Instead, I pretended to ignore her and continued to walk.

I'd barely slept last night, tossing and turning and thinking of Lottie. Imagining her decorating this glass, taking time to fill out each message. I wondered how long it had taken her, how she had decided what instructions to give me. A huge hole had opened inside of me, and it felt like ice was setting in. I had to pull myself into a tight foetal position and gradually rock myself to sleep. But still my dreams were full of her.

'Sara? Are you coming in today?' Jess's voice is gentle and soothing. The same one that she uses with the residents when they are particularly upset. I picture her at the other end of the phone, her soft round face, her bright purple hair, her gleaming dark eyes.

'Yeah, I'm due in at nine.' I rub my face. I'm so tired it's crazy, but work will be a distraction. I stare at the jar again and sigh. 'There's something I need to do first though.'

'OK, babe,' Jess says warmly. 'I'll see you in a bit.'

I rush around getting ready, barely bothering with my make-up and simply scraping my hair back into a rough ponytail. There are dark rings under my eyes and my lips are chapped and rough. I rub cream on my face and try not to focus on my reflection too much. Does it really matter what I look like?

Goose meows at my feet, like she is ordering me to get a grip.

'Yes, yes, I know.'

I walk back over to the jar and open it. Reaching inside, I pick the first message my fingers find. Lottie has carefully folded each one over several times, so they are just tiny squares of paper. Slowly, I unravel the note. Lottie's beautiful cursive writing hits me immediately.

Listen to our song. Loud. Sing along. Loudly.
Remember what the words mean.

The message drops from my suddenly numb fingers, drifting back to the table. My throat feels tight, and my eyes burn as if I have just rubbed dust and grit into them. I haven't listened to our song in years.

To be honest, I don't think I ever want to again.

–

Walking through the doors of Oakbridge Care Home, my legs feel a little bit wobbly, like I've just stepped off a rollercoaster ride. I have to pause in the reception area for a few minutes to regain a sense of normality. A familiar smell curls around me like a soothing blanket. It's a mix of the lavender floor cleaner they use and the flowers that Sharon likes to have dotted around the place. Sharon says it's good to have plants and pretty things, it keeps the residents in a positive frame of mind.

With a bracing breath, I walk through to the staff area and take off my jacket and bag and stuff them into a locker. Ade is sitting in one of the chairs, swiping at his phone – he's one of the new care workers, only been here for a few months. He looks up at me and smiles warmly.

'Sara, you're back!'

'Yeah, I am.' My own smile is strained. 'I've only been off a few days.'

'Well, you've been missed. The residents have been grumbling. Esme keeps asking where you are and Derek has been in a right old bad mood.'

'Really?' Guilt stabs at my gut. 'I'll check in on both today.'

Just as I'm about to leave, Sharon sweeps into the room. She's a tall, imposing woman who I always think belongs more in an army barracks than an old people's home. Her face is stern and looks like it's been carved out of granite and her long mousey hair is always pulled back into a severe bun. Me and Jess used to giggle about how much we'd like to give her a makeover.

'Sara! I'm so glad you're back. All better now?'

I blink at her; there is a lump in my throat that feels like I've just swallowed a brick. How am I even supposed to answer that? Does she think that grief is like a broken leg? After a short time, it heals up and I'd be all better again? I have to fight back the sharp words that are forming.

'Yes…' I manage to choke out. 'I'm fine now.'

'Good, good. We can do your return-to-work forms later, you know what HR are like, but in the meantime can you do your usual rounds? I'm sure everyone will be pleased to see you back.'

I nod quickly. Ade offers me another encouraging smile. I know I can do this. I'm good at my job and I love the people here and God knows I need the distraction. I just wish my brain could convince my body of this, as I move stiffly out towards the main lounge. Jess is stood in the corridor on the way through and I'm so relieved to see her friendly face.

She pulls me into a tight hug. 'It'll be OK,' she whispers in my ear. 'And I'm here if you need me. Just remember that.'

'I'll be fine,' I tell her, trying to sound convincing, but in reality, I feel sick to my stomach.

Can I really act normal again?

–

72

'You look pale. Are you eating?'

Derek stares up at me with his wise old eyes. He always reminds me a bit of an owl, not that I would ever tell him that, he'd kill me! But I mean it in the nicest possible way. He is small and hunched now with age and his face is heavily lined, overshadowed by the huge glasses that dominate his face. There's a picture in his room – a beautiful one of him and his wife from decades ago – where he stands proudly, his arm wrapped around Alice's waist and an easy, infectious smile creasing his handsome face. Although he's in a lot of pain now, I still see that handsome man, especially when he smiles and his blue eyes twinkle like jewels at the bottom of a pool.

'Of course I'm eating,' I tell him. 'You need to stop worrying about me and focus on your own food.'

I push his dinner towards him. To be fair, it doesn't look that appetising, some kind of beef stew that is far too fatty. Derek lifts the spoon with a shaky hand and moves it around a little.

'I had better stuff when I was in the army,' he grumbles. 'I miss Alice's cooking. Her Sunday roasts were to die for, I've told you that before, haven't I?'

I grin. 'Yeah, you told me, but it doesn't matter. You know I love hearing about Alice.' I move the bowl closer to him. 'Just have a few spoons to keep your strength up, Derek. They have agency staff working in the kitchen today because Gav is off. The food will be better tomorrow.'

'Do you promise?' His eyes sparkle at mine.

'Would I lie to you?'

He takes a few reluctant mouthfuls and then pushes the bowl away. 'I'm not hungry anyway. I don't work up

73

much of an appetite sitting around here.' He sighs. 'I've missed our chats.'

'I know and I'm sorry.' I glance at the time. 'I can sit with you a little longer, but then I need to check on the others. I can come after my shift?'

He shakes his head. 'No. You need to go home and rest. You look exhausted.'

I smile wanly. I don't tell him that all I've been doing is sleeping. Derek doesn't need to know my troubles.

'You don't need to worry about me,' I say, patting his hand gently. 'Although it's lovely that you do.'

Around us, the dining room is buzzing with activity. Many of the residents are talking loudly among themselves as dinner plates clash and rattle, and Ade's hearty laugh rings out as he jokes with one of our eldest ladies, Daisy. Derek's gaze moves around the room for a moment or two, as if he's taking it all in, then a small frown settles on his face, and he sighs gently.

'Is it too noisy in here for you?' I ask. I know his headaches are getting worse lately, although he likes to pretend that there is nothing wrong.

He is rubbing his temples now and manages a small nod. 'I think I might like to go back to my room, Sara. If that's OK with you?'

'Of course it is.'

I take him in his wheelchair across the corridor to his bedroom. He has a large, bright room with views out to the grounds. Often, when Derek needs to be quiet, he will sit in his chair by the window and stare out, daydreaming of times gone past. When he's feeling a little better, I will take him for a walk; the fresh air is good for his lungs and well-being.

Today though, I help him back into his bed. Although it's lunchtime and a warm day, Derek is shivering slightly, so I pull the covers tight across his body. Worries drift across my mind, although I try and force them back. I've only been away for a short time, but I can see that he has lost weight, his skin also looks greyer and dull. A spike of fear makes me catch my breath and I have to turn away from him and pretend to busy myself, tidying his bedside cabinet. Tears are building in my eyes and I don't want him to see.

Death is part and parcel of this job and although it's always difficult and sad, our job is to make sure people feel as comfortable and settled as they can, with as little fear as possible. Usually I could manage this, but after losing Lottie so recently it's more difficult.

Derek reaches across and pats my arm. 'I heard, you know. About your friend.'

I can't reply. I take a gulp of air instead and move to the end of his bed, straightening the bedding that is already straight and patting the sheets down unnecessarily.

'Jess told me,' he continues gently. 'Don't be cross with her. I kept asking where you were and, in the end, she told me. You used to talk a lot about her…' He screws up his face. 'What's her name again?'

'Charlotte,' I say quietly, my voice catching. 'But we all called her Lottie.'

'That's a pretty name. You told me she was poorly, of course, but I didn't know she had passed. I'm so sorry.'

'It was quick, in the end. Much faster than we'd expected,' I reply.

'I lost Alice young, as you know. She was only fifty which is no age at all…' He closes his eyes. 'Those first weeks – months even – were like trying to dig myself out of a hole. It was so hard and, even now, I feel an ache deep inside of me. It's like a scar that never properly heals.'

'Derek. You need sleep. Let's not talk about this now.'

The truth is, *I* don't want to talk about it. I feel a trickle of irritation towards Jess for discussing my business with Derek, she always does let her tongue run away with her, but then I remember how much I used to tell Derek about Lottie. All the time she was poorly, my worries would slip out. I had been so scared of losing her.

'Sara,' Derek says softly, 'can you put my record on? I want to drown out the noise around me. It helps me to sleep.'

The vintage record player sits in the corner of the room – still in excellent condition – and I walk over to it and the stack of vinyls piled up beside it.

'Which one do you want me to play?'

'Buddy Holly.' His voice is barely above a whisper now. '"True Love Ways".'

I carefully select the right record and slip it onto the turntable. There's a pause as the needle finds its place on the groove, followed by a beautiful crackle and spit before the rich music floods the room.

'There,' I say. 'I'll leave you to enjoy it.'

'I will,' he replies. His face has softened, and a sweet smile has appeared. I can't see his eyes, but I know they are sparkling beneath the closed lids. 'This was our song. Mine and Alice's, and every time I hear it, it's like she's with me all over again.'

–

Our song.

Waking home, I can't help thinking of Derek's words and how relaxed and calm he had become once the music filled the room. Music had always formed such an important part of mine and Lottie's relationship. We had a shared love of old bands, listening for hours, sharing secrets, fears and dreams among the melody and beats that throbbed around us. When we were most upset or stressed, we used music to relax and unwind, to heal some of the pain we were feeling.

But there was one song that linked us the most. A shared favourite that brought us closer together.

Without thinking too much more about it, I reach for my phone and open my music library. I stuff my earphones in and select the chosen track. One I have ignored for far too long.

Immediately the opening guitar chords welcome me, familiarity drifts around me like a gentle hug. The soothing words of 'In My Life' by The Beatles fill in missing parts of me, it's like I've needed them for so long and didn't realise.

Before I know quite what I'm doing, I find I'm singing quietly along. I imagine Lottie is beside me. God, it really feels like she might be.

'*I am. I'm here. And I'm singing just as badly as you.*'

I giggle despite myself and continue walking, the words flooding my soul. For the first time in ages, I feel like my friend is back and it is wonderful.

Eleven Years Before

Lottie

The summer between school and university hung over us like a weighted cloud. We were different – restless, uneasy and anxious – but no one was more different than Sara and Jay. We all noticed the change in them. It was like something had shifted. Before the party there had been a clear bond between them – it was like static electricity that was always buzzing. Sara would often needle and pester Jay, going on about him being a nice boy, a good kid, someone who would never do anything wrong, but there would also be a twinkle in her eyes, so that we could see she didn't mean it. Sometimes, she would show her softer side too, leaning into him when we were sitting together, or wrapping her arm around him when she was cold.

Now, there was a gap between them when they sat together. Sara no longer leant against his arm or pressed her back against his stomach. There were inches between them. The conversations were stilted and weird. Sara often chose to sit with me, teasing me instead – not that I minded. I liked having her attention, but it was difficult to ignore the weirdness between her and Jay.

That summer we often hung around the park, especially if the weather was good. I don't think any of us wanted to be at home. Sara always said that she found her flat too small and depressing, Dec didn't get on with his dad so he tended to stay out as much as he could, and Jay just liked being with us lot.

'Have you noticed a difference between Jay and Sara?' I asked Dec as we walked home one day.

'Those two are always up and down,' Dec replied. 'But if they've had an argument, they will get through it. They've been mates since they were kids, they're really tight, despite everything.'

'But right now, they're acting so weird – it's like they can't stand to be around each other.'

Dec shrugged. 'Maybe they need a break. Maybe it's been too intense, you know? I often wondered if those two are amazingly well suited to each other, or just completely toxic.'

Something stirred inside of me that I hadn't felt for a long time.

Hope.

I hated the feeling, I really did. It was mean and cold and not something I wanted to accept, but all the time Jay and Sara were distant, it meant there was more room for me. I wouldn't be pushed out.

–

We had been shopping. It had been a pretty fruitless trip. Sara was meant to be buying stuff for university, but she was restless and distracted and clearly not in the mood. I wasn't either, to be honest. After all, this whole experience didn't involve me. I already had a job lined up, working in one of my dad's car showrooms in Brighton. I was done with education. But knowing that Sara and Jay would soon be going to Manchester together hurt my head.

With Dec going away to Durham, I would be the only one left behind.

'It's going to be a nightmare,' Sara complained, as we walked through a bookshop. She was looking forlornly at the stationery, picking up notebooks that were too expensive for her to buy. I had offered to help her out, but that had quickly been dismissed. 'I don't have half the things I need yet, and they sent through the accommodation. Even the cheapest option is too expensive. I'm going to need another loan.'

'I'm sure it'll be OK. You'll just have to budget.'

Sara glared at me, an eyebrow slightly raised. She and I both knew that I'd never had to budget in my life. But that was hardly my fault.

'And Jay going there too…' Sara let the words hang. 'We always thought it would be a good idea to stay together, but maybe now – after everything – it's not?'

I shrugged. 'You have to do what's right for you.'

We left the shop empty-handed, and as we walked down the narrow street towards the main centre a crystal of an idea began to form. OK, maybe that's a lie. I think the idea had been there for some time, burning away in the back of my consciousness and now was the time to release it.

'You don't have to go to Manchester, do you? You could still swap to your second option?' I said casually.

Sara looked startled. 'Brighton? You mean stay here?'

'Yeah, why not? It's a great university and you told me already what a good course it is.' I paused. 'You could live with me. I'll be getting a little place of my own. I wouldn't expect much rent – none at all really.' After all, Daddy was helping me out, as Sara loved to remind me.

'Lottie. I couldn't do that!'

'I'd love the company, seriously! And you could help me learn to be a grown-up.' I forced a laugh. 'And maybe, you know, this is what you and Jay both need? Some space.'

Sara didn't answer for a moment, but her brow was furrowed in concentration.

'You still love him, don't you?' I asked quietly.

She snorted. 'Don't be daft, we've been friends for years. I think I was just overthinking things before. He is more like an annoying brother.'

The tips of her ears were bright pink, and she was chewing a little on her bottom lip – a clear sign she was lying.

'You know you can tell me, right? I wouldn't tell anyone else.'

There was a pause, just a beat. 'There's nothing to tell. Stop making a big deal of it,' she said. 'Now come on, we have to run for the bus. The next one isn't for ages!'

–

I liked it at Sara's place. She was always apologetic every time we came here, but I never understood why. There was a warmth in Sara's flat that you would never find in mine even if you searched in the deepest darkest corners. I liked nothing better than sitting huddled together on Sara's bed, flicking through the latest magazine we'd bought, or searching on her phone for the latest gossip. It was probably my favourite place to be.

Today, Sara had made us buttered toast and tea and had turned her attention to her record collection. Another thing I loved about Sara was that she had a record player; I didn't know anyone else who did.

'It's one of the few things I have of my dad's,' she explained, touching the plastic top carefully. 'It's not much, but this and his records make me feel like I'm closer to him somehow.'

Sara didn't talk about her dad much. There was a photo of him on her bedside table, tatty and old. In it, he was holding Sara as a baby. It must have been taken at Christmastime because there was tinsel draped around his neck and a paper party hat sitting at an angle on his thick dark hair. His eyes were large and intense like Sara's – in fact, she looked the spit of him. I knew that he died when she was little, but I wasn't sure of the details. Sara just said that everything went 'to shit' after that. They struggled for money, her brother went off the rails and her mum was never the same.

'Sometimes I'm angry at him for being dead,' she said to me once. 'How unfair is that? He can't help it and yet I'm so bloody angry that he decided to leave us. That he gave up. That he didn't try harder to stay.'

I didn't say anything because in truth I didn't know what I could say. My dad had buggered off without looking back. He thought he could stay in my good books by sending me cheques in the post and occasional postcards from the latest exotic island he'd travelled to and more recently offering me a job. I understood the anger all right, but I didn't understand the grief.

At least Sara had this connection to her dad though – a love of music that seemed to light her up from inside out. The music was mainly Seventies and Eighties stuff and when she played it to me, I didn't really have a clue.

'I don't really like music,' I admitted. 'Except Sixties stuff. I know it sounds mad, but it's what I used to listen to growing up. I love it.'

I expected Sara to laugh, after all my music taste would probably not be seen as cool. However, instead of laughing, Sara stared at me intently, her large eyes glinting.

'Really? Who are your favourite bands?'

'The Kinks, Small Faces…' I paused. 'But mainly The Beatles. When I was younger my mum used to play this stuff all of the time. I think my nan used to be a bit of hippy, so it made her feel happy. It used to be so fun to see my mum relaxed and singing along.' I stopped, suddenly uncomfortable. Mum never played her music any more. I couldn't remember the last time I heard her sing.

'Do you still see her, your nan?' Sara was now rummaging through her records, her back turned away from me.

'No, not any more. Her and Mum used to clash quite a lot and in the end she moved to Dorset. I kept wanting to go and visit but Mum put me off.' I shrugged. 'She died when I was thirteen. I barely knew her. I was angry with my mum for a bit, but you know what she's like.'

I don't really know why I said that. Sara had only met my mum briefly when she was leaving my house and my mum was perfectly polite, putting on her best hosting act and pretending to be interested in my new friend. It was only after Sara had left that her true colours had bled through, as she had sneered at Sara's scruffy trainers and 'rough accent'. I was only too glad that Sara hadn't seen that side of her.

'She doesn't seem that bad,' Sara said, confirming my thoughts. 'I wish I had some Beatles records you know; I really like them, too. There's one song that is just perfect. It's slow and haunting and really sad, but I can't remember its name.'

She sat next to me on the bed and picked up her phone. We went online, clicking on different tracks – listening carefully as the beautiful voices of the Fab Four flooded our ears.

'Hang on,' I said, pointing to a track name. 'Is it this one you like? I always loved it. My nan told me Lennon wrote it about his friend dying, but I'm not sure if that's true.'

Sara clicked on 'In My Life' and as soon as it started, we both beamed.

'This is it,' she said in a breathy tone. 'I've not heard it for ages, but it always makes me feel tingly.'

'Me too.' I whispered.

We sat back and just listened, the words and melody were perfect. When the track finished, Sara played it again. I closed my eyes, allowing myself to drift away, the only thing I was aware of was the music and Sara's soft breathing next to me.

'Sometimes I think I do love him, you know?' she said softly when the music stopped.

'Who? Jay?' My eyes opened to see her reaction.

There was a pause and then she nodded. 'Yeah, Jay. I think I always have; he drives me nuts, but I also can't imagine being without him.'

'Really?' I paused. 'So why do you always tease him and wind him up?'

Sara shrugged. 'I dunno. It's complex, isn't it.'

'I guess…'

'It's no big deal.' She sat forward. 'But he can never know, Lottie, OK? He's my mate. If he thought I felt differently about him it would mess everything up completely. He clearly doesn't feel the same way about me. I don't want to ruin things.'

There — in that moment, as we sat side by side, our bodies pressed tightly together, I was ready to tell her the truth. The words were already forming on my lips.

I'm sorry, Sara — I lied before. I don't know why. I think I was scared or something stupid. Maybe I was worried about you being hurt, but I lied. Jay does like you — he really does. You two could be something more than friends...

But Sara burst into my thoughts, her voice firm and sure.

'I'm glad he said what he did, it's helped me see sense. We can never be together. It would just never work out. It would be horrible and messy and make everything so much worse between us. I think you're right, Lottie. I think I need a break from him. It's been too intense for too long. Maybe I should stay in Brighton.'

I wanted to ask more but I could see from her expression that Sara had closed down again. Instead, I reached for her hand.

'I'm your friend. I'll always be here for you.'

She smiled at me. 'Just keep me away from Jay, Lottie. It's a bad idea, OK. I need you to remind me of that.'

To be honest it wasn't something I was likely to forget.

Day Six

Sara

I nudge Tyler awake. It's an obscene hour, and he lets out a groan of frustration. After a few minutes, he's reluctantly pulling on his jeans and gathering his clothes off the floor. This is a pretty usual routine for us.

'I could stay,' he says softly. 'I could make you breakfast. Bring it to you in bed?'

'I have to go to work soon and I need a shower.' I pull the covers tight over my body, suddenly self-conscious. In truth I just want an hour or so to be by myself.

He leans forward and plants a kiss on my cheek. 'Last night was good, Sara. It always is.'

I watch as he exits the room, his arse looking great in those bloody jeans. I groan again and pull the duvet over my head. The bed stinks of stale sweat, sex and Tyler's potent aftershave.

He's right. Last night *was* good. Tyler had called me up earlier and I realised that I needed company. When he came over, I'd actually been pleased to see him. I was still buzzing a bit from playing Lottie's and my song and remembering the times we used to listen to it together, whispering our secrets and becoming even closer. It reminded me too of Jay, feelings that I had tried so hard to hide. Thinking about Jay again was hard. I had worked so hard to push him to the back of my mind, I thought he was safe there. I was obviously wrong.

Tyler had cooked me a lovely chicken dish telling me that I needed filling up. I didn't think I was hungry but as soon as I started eating it was like I couldn't stop.

'It's because you've been existing on a diet of baked beans and tinned soup,' he told me, his eyebrows raised. 'You need proper nutrients to recover.'

'I'm not sick,' I argued.

'A broken heart is a kind of sickness,' he said, leaving the table to check on the dessert (hot chocolate torte cooked to perfection). 'My mum is half Italian. She always tells me food is healing. I guess I kind of agree with her.'

'Only kind of?'

He opened the oven, and the waft of hot, rich chocolate overtook my senses. 'Yeah, only kind of. I think there are other things that can help too. Far more fun things.'

I think of the sex now and my body tingles. Tyler might not be the best for in-depth conversations, or being able to commit to anything more long-term (not that I would want that either), but he is an incredibly good shag. I relive the moment he came up behind me while I ate my dessert and began to slowly and delicately kiss me on the back of the neck. It wasn't long before he was leading me into the bedroom and peeling off my clothes, taking his time to touch and stroke every single part of me. It was no surprise that I was aching for him, that I actually had to beg him to fuck me. I know I was more insistent, more frantic last night as I clawed into the back of his skin, pulling him in closer, clamping my legs against his body so that I could really feel him. I know that I needed him to be fast and hard.

When I finally came, it had been like a small explosion, taking my breath away. I dug my teeth into his shoulder and moaned softly. He didn't see the tears; they surprised me even. I'd never cried during sex before and I swiped them away quickly, angry at their presence.

I didn't want sex to become tangled up in my other emotions. I'd always been so good at separating them, since Jay at least. He was the last man, the only man, where I'd let my guard down. Where sex had become something more than just a satisfying act.

Jay had been the only one where I'd let my defences down, and look what a mess that got me into.

After the sex, Tyler had picked up one of my old sketchbooks that I'd left lying around on the floor. Lazily, he'd skimmed through it.

'Your art is so good, why don't you do this any more?'

I pulled the book away from him, groaning softly. 'Not now, Tyler. You're ruining the mood.'

He nibbled my neck gently. 'But I don't get it. I never see you draw now, or paint. Surely you miss it.'

I tugged his hand, leading him back towards my body. 'I'm too busy, Tyler. Too busy focusing on other things…'

I tried to focus on where his hand was going, and not on the book lying splayed on my carpet. Art was such a complex thing for me. All my hopes and dreams had been coiled around it. I had had dreams of doing something linked with my drawing, living a life that was creative and fulfilling.

But like so many of my dreams, this was another one that had been discarded and forgotten.

-

The jar is waiting for me again. Goose sits next to it like she knows, her tail curled around the base like she's protecting it. I glare at her.

'Since when did you get so bossy?' I demand. Goose mews lightly and her green eyes flash, like she is telling me to get a move on. I don't even know why I'm hesitating. Yesterday's message had worked out OK – in fact, in some ways it had helped. A little.

'But it's not just that,' I whisper. 'Every message I read, means that another one has gone. Soon there will be nothing left of you.'

The curtain stirs in the breeze. I picture Lottie leaning up against the sill, her blonde hair catching in the light.

'But I'm not gone – not really. Now stop being an arse and choose your next one.'

Quickly, I open the jar and select the next folded piece of paper.

'I hope this is something achievable, Lottie.' I mutter. 'I'm working until six. I can't do something crazy like a hot air balloon ride today.'

I read the words, a smile soon settling on my lips.

> *Go to Greta's. Order the same crazy milkshakes we used to and try to sit in our seat by the window (if someone is already there, kick them out).*
>
> *Remember the stuff we used to talk about. Remember when I told you about my fear.*
>
> *You did something magical after that day. You need to connect with that.*

—

'So what's the plan? You're going to go there after work?' Jess sips her coffee and looks at me in interest.

'Yeah, I guess so. We often used to go late afternoon so the timing works. I might even order the messy burgers we used to eat.'

'I thought you hated fast food.'

I shrug. 'Not all of it. Actually, Greta's always used to be pretty decent, though to be fair I haven't eaten there for a while.'

She and I were chilling in the staffroom, taking a much-needed fifteen-minute break. The morning had already been full on. We were short-staffed due to staff illness, which had stressed Sharon out to start with, and then we had to call the doctor out for Jenny who had taken ill in her room. Likely, it looked like it was a virus and nothing too serious – but these kinds of things unsettled everyone, the residents included, and as a result there was a heavy feeling in the air. Jess had made us both mugs of steaming hot tea and ordered me to rest for five minutes because I hadn't stopped since I'd arrived. Jess is a great advocate for taking breaks where you can.

I'd explained to Jess about the Jar of Joy and how I was having to follow an instruction every day. Jess seemed to get it straight away.

'It's like that movie I watched once, where the guy dies and sends his girlfriend messages and stuff.' She screwed up her face. 'I don't remember much about it, but I know it was sweet.'

Jess also seems to be excited about me going to Greta's tonight, although God knows why. It's just a cafe after all, and an old and scruffy one at that. I'm surprised the place is still going; there are so many chains that have opened up all over the place now.

'It sounds like it's important to you both,' Jess says. 'Hopefully by going there it might bring you some, I dunno, peace?'

I hadn't told Jess all of the message; I had kept back the bit about Lottie revealing her fear to me. That was too private, too important, to just share recklessly.

'It might,' I reply. 'But it might also be painful. We went there all the time, either as a group or just me and Lottie. I don't know why we loved it so much, but we did.' With a sigh, I push my tea away, suddenly not wanting to drink it any more. 'It's going to be full of memories, they will be everywhere I look.'

'Memories aren't bad, Sara,' Jess says gently. 'You don't have to fear them, in fact sometimes it is better to embrace them completely.'

–

Greta's stands at the back of town, down a side alleyway that would be easy to miss if you didn't know it was there. It is a tiny, narrow building with a scattering of seating outside and a beat-up noticeboard that seems to be displaying the same specials that it had years ago. I'm not sure who Greta actually is; for as long as I've known the place it's always been run by a slightly overweight and red-faced man by the name of Frank, occasionally helped out by a range of young and flustered minions. Lottie and I used to joke that Frank had a secret life and lived as Greta by night, dressing in the finest gowns and wining and dining in high-end eateries. This memory immediately makes me smile.

As I walk in, the door rings and a familiarity floods through me. The smells hit me at once, roasted coffee and fried bacon, mixed with something a little sweeter, like cinnamon. We hadn't been here for so long, I'm not even sure why. I guess we kind of grew out of the place. This was our teenage haunt, looking for cheap drinks and a place to hide from the rain and the cold, a place that didn't mind if we took up a table for far too long. As adults, Lottie and I were far more likely to go to the usual nationwide cafes that filled the high street. The thought of that made me sad, like we had given up on a traditional and much-needed independent business in favour of something more commercial. It's pretty empty in here, only a couple of tables are taken, and I wonder how they've managed to survive.

Frank is still serving at the counter, helped today by a young boy with short greasy hair and a hint of acne on his cheeks. I scan the menu even though I know exactly what I'm going to order. To my relief, it's still there.

'I'll have the Super Strawberry milkshake please,' I instruct the young boy. Then I pause, remembering Lottie's instructions. 'With extra cream and sprinkles.'

Frank had been cleaning the surfaces, but he looks up when I speak. His eyes sparkle and he points a stubby finger in my direction. 'I remember you. Double trouble!'

I grin. Surely, he can't recognise me after all these years. Double Trouble was the nickname he'd given us when we used to sit giggling in here all of the time. He used to joke that we were cooking up some dangerous scheme or other.

'It's been a few years,' I say. 'But I'm pleased this place looks the same.'

'Some things never change,' he says lightly, his eyes still on mine. 'It's good to see you here. Greg, make sure you put extra cream on this one. She's a special customer.'

I feel myself blush. I don't deserve this attention, especially as I haven't been here for years. With a quick scan of the room again, I'm glad to see that our seat by the window is free.

'She said you'd come,' Frank says softly as he hands me the milkshake, and I blink in surprise.

It is just as I remember: a huge jug of bright pink milk topped with thick squirty whipped cream and hundreds and thousands. A massive, sickly delight – but we always loved it.

'She came here?' I whisper.

Frank nods and then gestures for me to follow him to our seats. Instinctively, I move towards the chair facing up towards the church. It was where I always sat; Lottie would be opposite me, her legs stretched out so that they touched mine.

'She told me about her illness,' Frank says gently. 'Cancer is such a shitty, shitty thing. She was so young.'

I bow my head. 'I know. It wasn't fair.'

He touches my arm lightly. 'She came by to tell me that you would be coming here one day soon and that you might be sad.' He pauses. 'But she told me to tell you to remember how it felt when you spent time in here with her. She wants you to remember those good times. How silly and daft you both used to be. How you drove me mad.'

'Oh my God, we were so loud, weren't we!'

Frank nods. 'You were, but you lit up the place. Two pretty girls full of hopes and dreams. It was always a pleasure to have you here.'

I smile sadly. 'Thank you.'

'She also wanted me to give you this.' Frank reaches into his pocket and delicately pulls something out. It takes a while for my eyes to register what it is, but when I do, I nearly start to cry again.

'Oh, Lottie,' I whisper under my breath. 'How could I ever forget?'

Nine Years Before

Lottie

I loved our flat. It was small but perfect. Yes, it was damp, but that kept the price low. The two bedrooms were a decent size, and the tiny kitchen didn't bother us as we barely cooked. Sara was only a few minutes' walk from university, and I could easily drive to work. It didn't bother me that most months Sara couldn't afford her rent – after all, I was only there thanks to Dad's bulging wallet. All I cared about was her company, and in those years together, we got so much closer.

We fell into an easy routine. Sara didn't mind cleaning up after me – I was always a bit of a chaotic mess – and I didn't mind giving her lifts to places or ordering in the takeouts. We'd spend evenings curled on the sofa, gossiping about all sorts of inane things and talking about our dreams.

Sara had one goal. She wanted to work in the creative industry – maybe in graphic design or illustration. One day she dreamt of displaying her art in a gallery.

'It's daft.' She giggled. 'But I truly believe I could make it happen.'

'Of course you can,' I told her. 'You can do anything.'

I didn't tell her that my dreams were small. I just wanted to stay safe and secure. I wanted to keep this feeling of having someone close to me for as long as I could.

The boys visited every summer. That second summer of university, Jay brought a guest with him. His new girlfriend, Rae.

We had invited Jay and Dec over to our flat, keen to show it off. Sara was attempting to cook some kind of curry on our dodgy stove and was already hot, bothered and frustrated by the time Dec and Jay arrived. I saw her gaze fall on the girl holding Jay's hand and her expression stiffened.

'I hope you don't mind,' Jay said. 'But I wanted Rae to meet my friends.'

Sara flashed her brightest smile. 'No, of course not. It's lovely to meet you, Rae.'

I greeted her, too. She was a pretty girl, with long dark hair and dark eyes. In many ways she looked like Sara. I wondered if Jay realised quite how much.

Dinner was strained. The boys talked about their courses. Jay was loving his Art History course and Dec bored us for some time talking about Economics and Mathematics. I ate my food thoughtfully. There was a shift between us, but I wasn't sure why. Everyone was acting very polite and formal – almost as if we barely knew each other.

Maybe we didn't any more. I suppose university changes people. Dec was certainly more laid-back and confident. Jay seemed more aloof and distant. He spent a lot of his time fussing over Rae, who in turn didn't seem interested in us at all.

Sara barely spoke at first. She drank quite a bit though. Then she told the boys about her boyfriend 'Ben'.

'I didn't know you had a boyfriend?' Jay said, suddenly looking interested.

That was funny – because neither did I. I knew she'd shagged a guy a few times when she was bored. I wondered if it was the same one.

'Yeah...' Sara was playing with her hair, staring Jay down. 'We're pretty close actually. I'd have brought him tonight but he's busy. He's a fireman, you see, on shift.'

'Oh, I'd love to date a fireman,' Rae gushed. 'That's a fantasy, isn't it?'

'It really is,' Sara said, her eyes still fixed on Jay.

There was a pause. Jay was smiling, but it looked forced. His eyes were blazing. He sniggered and nodded.

'Yeah, well, I'm glad you're happy, Sara.' His arm snaked around Rae. 'I'm glad we are both happy. It's about time, isn't it?'

The evening ended soon after that. Sara left me to clean up. She slammed into her bedroom and refused to talk about it.

–

A few days later, Sara and I ended up at Greta's cafe. It was one of Sara's favourite places to go. At first, I hadn't been keen on going there. I didn't tell Sara, but I had found it a bit shabby and cold-looking, and the smell of grease was hardly appetising but, after time, I had grown quite fond of sitting at our little booth by the window. It was never crowded there so we always seemed to get the same seats. It became a routine to go after school on a Wednesday when the boys had football. Sara would order us both the ridiculously sickly strawberry milkshakes and although I privately worried about the calories, I would gulp it back because I knew it made her happy.

Sara was noisily slurping out the last of the cream from her glass, a troubled look on her face, and her gaze fixed at something far off in the distance.

'Are you OK?' I asked, pushing my own glass to one side. I felt a little sick and knew I wouldn't be eating much later.

'Yeah…' She turned back to me and smiled weakly. She began to stab at the last of the cream with her straw. 'I'm sorry about the other night – just seeing Jay like that was a surprise. I mean I knew he was going to be dating other people, I guess I just find it hard to see it in my face.'

'He's obviously happy. You're pleased for him, aren't you?'

Sara gave me a funny look. 'Yeah, of course. We've practically grown up together. I'll always care about him.'

'It's nice.' I paused. 'I guess I never had anything like that.'

I realised how pathetic that sounded and felt my skin burn. Sara slid her hand across to mine.

'Seriously, though,' Sara continued, her voice more intense now. 'You're lucky, too. You seem to have the perfect life. Money, a decent house, freedom. What is there for you to stress about?'

I looked away from Sara, unable to bear the way her eyes were blazing into mine like she was trying to see right into me. An itchy feeling had taken over my skin, it was all I could do not to claw at myself right there and then.

'There's loads for me to stress about,' I said quietly. 'It's not always been easy.'

'You never talk about this stuff.' Sara gently stroked my hand. 'I'm your friend, Lottie. I want to know these things.'

'There's not that much to say.' I managed a weak smile. 'Yeah, I have money and stuff and grew up in a decent house, but I'd give that all up for stability, for security, for...' The word sticks in my throat. It sounds so pathetic, so childish to admit that the one thing I craved more than anything was love. 'One time,' I said quietly, 'when I was about four or five, my parents went away for the weekend. They thought it was fine to leave me there, in the big old country house with some plates of sandwiches left out and jugs of water. They didn't care about how scared I was. How I wet myself because I heard noises in the dark. How I was terrified that they wouldn't come home. They just treated me like a pet that they had grown tired of, someone that got in the way of their partying and drinking.'

Sara sat back. Her face was white, her mouth drawn into a frown. 'That's awful, Lottie. If someone did that on our estate, they would have been reported to the social immediately.'

'People forget that rich people can neglect their kids, too,' I said. 'They did it a few times after that, they never saw the point of a babysitter. I could tell you other stuff too, but I really wouldn't want to depress the pair of us. I just wanted to show you that my life hasn't been this amazing experience you think it has.'

Sara nodded. 'I understand now. I'm sorry.'

'And I guess now, I'm so scared of being left alone again...' I turned my face to the window again so that Sara couldn't see my tears start to form. I hoped she didn't think I was some weak and pitiful creature, but I wouldn't have blamed her if she had. It was often how I saw myself. She wriggled around on the seat opposite and then she gently nudged me to look at her again.

'Lottie, I want you to have this.'

Sara was holding out a necklace – the pretty gold one she always wore.

I shook my head. 'Sara. Don't be silly, I can't—'

Sara pressed it into my hand. 'I won't take no for an answer. It's yours now. I want you to wear it all the time. It's a silly old thing my mum got me, but I never filled it with a picture, I never knew who to put in it, but now I do. I want you to put a photo of us in there.'

'But it's your locket,' I insisted.

'And I'm giving it to you.' She smiled. 'That way you'll never be alone, even when I'm not there. Every time you open it you will remember me. You'll remember that I am with you.'

'This is beautiful,' I whispered. 'And you have me, too. You don't need Jay now. He's moved on. But I'll always be there for you.'

Sara nodded. 'I know. And it means everything.'

Day Seven

Sara

'*…you'll never be alone. Every time you open it you will remember me. You'll remember that I am with you.*'

The locket sits in my hand now, and I remember those words I had said to Lottie, how she had cried a bit but finally accepted my gift, placing it around her own neck. And there it had stayed until…

I'd always loved this silly old locket, going back to the day when Mum first gave it to me after spotting it in a charity shop. The necklace wasn't valuable or particularly old, but I loved the pretty leaf detailing on the front. I open it now and see the tiny photos that Lottie had managed to squeeze in. On one side, she is smiling shyly at the camera, her blonde hair in a bun and her cheeks pink and healthy, as if she'd just been for a run. On the other side, I look dark and haunted. My dark hair is gathered loosely around my face, my eyes painted with heavy liner and I'm almost scowling at whoever is taking the picture.

The sun and the moon – complete opposites and yet we worked.

I couldn't stay at Greta's yesterday after Frank gave me this. Suddenly overwhelmed, I made hasty apologies and rushed out. It was too hard being there, in the same spot we always sat, remembering that difficult conversation – the first time I had seen Lottie's true vulnerability.

With my head lowered so that no one could see my tears, I nearly barged straight into him.

Jay.

'What the hell?' I looked up startled, hastily blinking my tears away. The last thing I needed was Jay's sympathy.

'Hey.' He smiled at me, and it was difficult to resist the urge to fall into his arms. Jay always had such a warm, cheeky smile that reminded me of everything that had once been good – teenage years, cuddles, laughter, love…

I frowned instead, memories clawing inside of me like birds with sharp talons trying desperately to escape.

'Are you OK?' he asked. 'I tried messaging you after the funeral, but you didn't reply.'

My mind was whirling with everything that had just happened and I sucked in a breath, trying to get my head straight. 'I didn't think there was much to say.'

He visibly shrank back, his shoulders slumped. 'I'm not so sure, Sara, I think we have a lot to talk about.'

I glared at him. Yeah, sure he did. He had loads to go through. The only problem was, where would he start! Would he go back as far as when were eighteen and he first broke my heart, yet I forgave him and somehow we still remained friends? Or would he skip a few years and focus on the part when he misled me again, forcing me to go away travelling for two years to escape the humiliation, only to find that he and Lottie were together when I returned? I flinched at the memory. No, maybe not that – maybe he'd talk instead of his regret at dumping Lottie not long before she was diagnosed with cancer and then not coming back to see her while she battled it.

'I know I should have seen Lottie sooner,' he said as if he was reading my mind. 'I just—'

'I don't want to hear your excuses, Jay.' I sighed. 'It's not going to change anything. Lottie told me everything that happened. She was broken when you left.' Just as I had been all those years ago – knowing that the man that I thought was the one for me had no interest in me whatsoever and never had.

At least Jay had had the decency to avoid my gaze. His feet scuffed the ground.

'I have lots of regrets, Sara. I shouldn't have left like I did. I should have stuck around, but it was hard being here. This place was getting to me, there were too many memories. I didn't even find out about Lottie's cancer until right at the end. By then Erica said she didn't want visitors, least of all me.'

'I guess she didn't want to see you.'

'So I gathered.' He lifted his head slowly. His blue eyes sparkled in the cool evening light. I hated how they still made me feel a bit wobbly. 'I wanted to call you, so many times, but I didn't think you'd want to hear from me, either.'

'Well, you'd be right,' I said stiffly.

'I'm sorry.' He shook his head. 'You're right, I should let you get on. I don't want to stress you out. That was never my intention.'

'Why are you here anyway?' I demanded.

This cafe had been mainly mine and Lottie's place, although the boys had come on occasion – in the school holidays or if their football practice had been cancelled.

Jay shrugged; he looked a bit shifty. 'I dunno. I'm staying here for a bit and I just had this idea to come here. It's a memory, isn't it? I never thought you'd be here.'

'What about your work?' I asked coolly.

The last I heard, Jay was a partner at some fancy architecture practice in Newcastle. I couldn't imagine he'd want to be away from there for too long.

'They understand. I'm due some leave anyway.'

'OK.' I nodded and made to move away. 'Maybe I'll see you around some time…'

Jay reached out, touching my arm, and a flicker of electricity buzzed deep into my skin. I pulled my arm quickly away, as if I'd been burnt.

'Please…' he whispered. 'Call me, or something. We do have to talk soon, Sara. There are still things I need to talk to you about.'

I frowned at him again and then I strode off. There was nothing that Jay could say that I needed to hear. I wasn't in the mood for pitiful excuses or prolonged apologies; the guy had caused too much pain already. As I walked away, I could feel his eyes burning into my back and an uneasy feeling overtook me. What if he hadn't bumped into me by coincidence? What if he was following me?

–

I think over these worries again now, the locket still in my hand. I'm not working today and have managed to waste most of the morning sitting on the sofa, staring at the Jar of Joy and tipping Lottie's necklace from one hand to the other.

I hate remembering about Jay. Really, he should be with me now. We should be together, helping each other through this grief – but instead, he stuck up a great big, nasty divide between us. He caused this.

Jess had called me last night. I'd had a few glasses of wine, so I was a bit of a snotty, soppy mess by the time we spoke. She was keen to know about Lottie's last message and what had happened, so I told her about the locket and seeing Jay outside.

'Who is this guy?' Jess asked. 'Another mate of yours?'

'He was…' I took another slug of drink and then coughed as the acrid taste hit the back of my throat with too much force. That would teach me to buy suspiciously cheap wine again. 'It's a long story, Jess. Me and Jay were friends for years but then I ruined it all by fancying him.'

'Ah!' Jess drew a breath. 'The age-old problem.'

'It would have been fine if I'd let things just stay as they were, we had a good thing, you know? The four of us – Dec too – but then in the last year of sixth form there was a party and me and Jay got drunk and—' I'd shut my eyes, cringing. How was it possible to both love and hate a memory at the same time? Even now, the thought of it made my chest burn.

'Oh God, so you slept together!' Jess gushed. 'Was it everything you hoped it to be? Or was it a total disaster?'

'No, not then. We just snogged. Silly teenage stuff, but I thought he liked me.' My eyes smarted at the memory. 'It was just a drunk mistake. We shook it off, went to uni, stayed friends, until…'

'Until what?' Jess's voice had gone up a pitch. It irritated me how excited she was.

'Until I made another stupid mistake a few years later. We were drunk again, stuff happened.'

'And you slept together.'

I took a slug of my wine. 'Yeah. We slept together. It was nothing.'

Such a simple lie to say, because I've spent so long trying to convince myself the same thing.

I couldn't tell Jess how I still remembered those hot, stolen minutes at the beach. How Jay had ripped off his own clothes and then tenderly unpeeled mine. How his mouth had been on every part of my body, and it had felt so right. How he had said things that had made me groan in need and cry in disbelief. How I had been the happiest I'd ever been.

I couldn't tell her any of that, because it was pointless.

'It was a one-off six years ago,' I had told her coolly. 'I wanted more but he didn't. I found out he regretted it, so that was that.'

'Shit. And then what?'

'I couldn't stick around, so I left. I went travelling. When I came back him and Lottie were a nice little couple and I was very much on the outside.' I hiccough-sobbed. 'I kept away for a bit – well, until Jay showed his real colours and dumped Lottie. He buggered up north to live with his dad and I was left to pick up the pieces. Just months later, Lottie got her diagnosis and needed me even more.'

'He sounds like a total wanker. You're both shot of him.'

Numbly, I'd nodded. 'I know, I know – but I thought I knew him, really knew him, you know?' I sniffed. 'I just feel like I'm too full of pain, Jess. There's too much inside of me. I don't know where it can all go. I didn't even realise how hurt I still was about all of this. It was so long ago, and yet it feels like yesterday. I always stupidly thought that me and Jay were meant to be together. I was such an idiot.'

'He clearly meant a lot to you.'

'He was part of my life for so long, it took a lot to walk away,' I said. 'I was always angrier with Jay for getting with my best friend. Lottie, I could excuse. She was so desperate for love and affection, but Jay – he should've respected me better.'

'I get that,' Jess replied. 'I would be the same. It will get easier though.'

'Maybe…'

But what does she know? What does anyone know really? The reality was the man I loved had smashed my dreams into bits twice over. Then he'd moved on and broken my best friend's heart too.

And now they were both gone. And I am left totally alone.

Goose purrs at my feet. I take this as motivation to get moving. I can't sit around here moping and feeling sorry for myself.

In the shower, the radio plays – in the old days, I used to sing along loudly, and sometimes Lottie would be sat in the living room shouting abuse at me through the door.

'How the hell can you be so tone deaf?' Or, 'Don't you make your own ears bleed?'

I know I'm not a great singer, but I used to find it soothing to belt out a song at the top of my voice. Now, it's almost impossible to open my mouth. The words get choked up in my throat, as if they are stuck there, unwilling to come out. It's easier to swallow them back down.

Although it looks quite warm outside, it's bloody cold in the flat and I'm shivering as I dry myself. After throwing on an old pair of jeans and a loose long-sleeved T-shirt, I stare in the mirror, barely recognising myself. I was never one for long beauty regimes, that was always Lottie. I was always happier slapping on some moisturiser and a slick of mascara, some eyeliner, and that was me done. Jay used to say he liked the way I looked natural, that I had a 'glowy, healthy look about me'.

There is nothing 'glowy' about me now though. My skin is dry and dull. I have shadows the size of tents under my eyes and my lips are chapped and sore. I rub cream into my skin and attempt to comb my messy hair into a half-decent ponytail.

'*You need a haircut,*' I hear Lottie whisper in my ear. '*Those split ends are shocking. You can't blame my death on not looking after yourself.*'

I twitch and actually check behind my shoulder. Am I going mad? How do I keep hearing her voice so clearly?

'You have to stop doing this, Lottie.' I whisper. 'It's driving me nuts.'

Goose is standing by the door, staring at me with knowing eyes. She knows I'm losing the plot, either that or Lottie has a more powerful hold on me than I realised.

–

I tip a message from the jar into my hands. I figured there is no point messing around, it's almost like I can feel Lottie breathing down my neck and to be honest I don't need that kind of stress. Besides, there is a part of me that wants to see what she has lined up for me next. These messages are little parts of Lottie that are bringing me closer to her again and with each one, I feel less alone.

This one is fairly straight forward and an uneasy smile settles on my lips.

> *Go for walk in the woods and find your tree.*
> *Remember the time I found you there.*
> *Remember why that was important.*
> *Remember the mark you left.*

'You picked a good day for it, Lots,' I say, gazing out of the window. The sun is properly beaming now, and the street below is lit up in its golden rays. 'But really? You want me to go back there? Why?'

'*Just do it*,' I swear I hear her reply.

–

The woods – Gasson Woods, to be precise – are about a thirty-minute walk from my flat. They lie perfectly between my old estate, where I lived with Mum, and Lottie's house and because of that we often used it as a cut-through if it wasn't too dark.

The woods themselves aren't that extensive, having been cut back for the numerous new housing projects around, but they are dense and pretty. A well-worn path snakes through the middle, running alongside a small clean stream. There is a small glade in the centre where many late-night drinking sessions take place, but in the day it's mainly frequented by dog walkers and joggers.

The tree is just off the beaten track, to the left of the glade and away from the stream. I still remember us coming here. Hot clammy hands leading us away from public sight and towards a more private area. I remember how excited, but scared I'd been. How my head was dizzy with self-doubt. Together we had found what we thought was a perfect spot, away from everyone else.

I have to check to make sure I'm walking through the right bit; the area is even more overgrown now. Prickles swipe at my skin and my feet struggle on the uneven ground but finally I see it: the huge oak tree that I'd loved so much.

'There's something about trees,' Mum once told me. 'I swear they are spiritual or something, the older ones especially are so calming.'

This tree is huge so there is no doubt it is of a good age. A fuzzy familiarity fills me up as I walk towards it, like my blood is being warmed. My hands touch the rough bark, as memories drift and settle in my mind. Where is it? Where is it?

And then, as clear as day, I see the tiny marking made with my compass.

I feel like I'm falling again.

Eight Years Before

Lottie

I always put off visiting my mother. It was easier living away, as though the constraints around me had been loosened. I was even beginning to restore some of my relationship with my dad now that I no longer had her breathing down my neck. Don't get me wrong, I didn't forgive him for what he did to us, but I could start to understand some of the strain Dad had been under. I of all people understood how difficult my mum was to live with.

On the way to another obligatory visit, I tried to straighten my thoughts. There was a lot going on at that time. Sara, Jay and Dec had recently graduated from university and, after a burst of local parties, were now back together in the same town. Jay had sent us a simple message, asking us to meet him in the woods by the lake. He wanted a get-together, he wanted it to be 'just like old times'. Just those words made me feel an immediate resistance. I knew I wasn't being fair; Jay and Sara had history, he knew all of the issues she had been through before, while I'd barely scratched the surface. How could I expect them to forget and move on? They would always be close, wouldn't they?

It was meant to be different for girls, though. We were meant to be the ones to support each other, to whisper our secrets to one another. I desperately wanted Sara to trust me enough to talk to me properly. Despite living together for three years, I still didn't feel like this had happened for us. I was just her surface friend – the one she talked to about TV shows and fashion trends. Sara kept so much of herself locked away and I knew, deep inside, that the only one that had got even close to penetrating that had been Jay.

And now he was back. For how long, I wasn't sure.

As I reached the house, a familiar feeling of loneliness tugged at me. I stared up at the building that Sara once pointed out was the largest one on the road and could probably fit her flat in it three times over – but to me was a great yawning space.

Inside, all I could smell was floor polish and bleach and a slight scent of the fresh flowers that our cleaner had placed in the hall. At Sara's mum's flat, you had to step into a crowded, narrow hall where coats were overflowing on hooks on the wall and shoes littered the carpet. It always smelt warmer somehow, more human – like people actually existed in the space and hadn't been tidied away.

I kicked off my shoes on the mat and moved through to the kitchen, planning to get myself a drink or something, nearly leaping in shock when I saw Mum sitting at the breakfast bar, staring at her phone.

'Hi Mum. How are you?'

She looked up. Mum always had a slightly frozen look on her face, probably not helped by the years of Botox. Her eyebrows were always slightly too raised, her skin too stretched.

'I'm surprised you even care.'

I inwardly sighed. Great, she was in a bad mood too. This was all I needed. I walked over to the sink and got myself some water, feeling her eyes burn into my back the entire time I stood there.

'I spoke to your dad today.'

Her voice was a little too high. I turned off the tap and took a sip of water; it did nothing to take away the bitter taste in my mouth.

'Oh, did you?'

'Yes, I did, though God help me I wish I hadn't. That smug bastard always has to get one over on me. You know he's marrying that tart? That woman he was sleeping with behind my back?'

I almost asked 'which one' but held my tongue. I didn't want to wind Mum up any more. As it happens I did know that Dad was marrying Emily. They had a lovely place in Essex. I hoped Mum didn't know that it was twice the size of this house.

'You knew though, didn't you? Of course, you did' – her tone was colder now – 'because you've been having lots of lovely chats with him.'

'Well... he is my dad. And my employer now, too.'

Mum sucked in a breath. Her face had that pained look, like I'd just stabbed her with one of her hideously expensive chef-branded knives.

'Yes, of course, I know all of this... but after everything he did to us. I thought you understood—'

She was looking distraught now, and I felt a tug of guilt. I was angry with him too. I hated him for leaving us, for finding someone he'd rather live with, but that didn't mean I wanted him out of my life forever.

'He's still my dad,' I said quietly.

'Oh, I know he's your dad,' Mum sneered. 'It's funny how he seemed to forget that when he walked out on us.'

Dad had told me that Mum had blocked his calls and wouldn't let him visit after he left. He told me that their break-up had been more complicated than Mum had led me to believe, however, looking at Mum's rigid expression, I knew that there was little point in raising this now, it would only make her angrier.

'He took great pleasure in telling me about you on the call, seemed to think he knew more about you than I did. He was telling me how well you're doing at work…' She pulled a face. 'I never see you, so I wouldn't know.'

I shrugged. 'I've been busy, Mum.'

'But you have time to go bleating away to dear Daddy instead.' Mum pulled herself away from the breakfast bar and started pacing the room. 'He told me that he's offered you a promotion at his place. Oh, yeah – he was all smug about it, like he'd fixed all of our problems.'

'Mum – the promotion would be a great opportunity. I might not even get it.'

It had only been a passing comment by him, although I had to admit I was hoping Dad might be able to use his influence. I was currently working as a receptionist for his dealership in Hove, but the sales role in the Brighton office was far more lucrative. Dad would just need to convince the manager there.

'Yeah, well, he can stick his options where the sun don't shine.' Mum pointed a well-manicured finger at me. 'I'm telling you now, if you stay working for that cheating arsehole, well – you stop visiting here altogether. It'll be clear whose side you've picked.'

'Mum – it's not about sides!'

'Of course it's about sides! And that shit always wins!' She was shouting now. 'I can't believe you can't understand that. All this time I've been doing all I can to look after you, to keep my own sanity, and the minute Daddy turns on the charm you go running back to him trying to manipulate him to get what you want.'

'It's not like that,' I whispered.

'It is. That's the problem with you Lottie, you're always so desperate for love and approval.' Mum was properly sneering now. 'And you go the wrong way trying to get it.'

-

I left soon after, unable to stand being in a house with a woman so twisted with bitterness that she could no longer see straight. As I walked, I tried to process some of the things she had said to me about Dad and how I was manipulating him. That comment stung, but was she right? It was true that I had hoped Dad would sort things out for me, come to my rescue like he'd always done when I was a kid. The truth was, I lacked motivation and commitment to make any important decisions for myself – I just wanted to take the easiest route possible.

That was why I was so jealous of Jay and Sara – they both had ambition and desire. Jay had often talked about his plans to train as an architect and Sara was keen to move into graphic design, or something where she could use her art. They were both hugely talented and had fire in their bellies to drive them on. Even Dec knew that he wanted to work in the tech industry. It was different for me. The only thing I had was Dad's money and even that was of limited use; it wasn't like I had the brains or ambition to set up my own business or use it to fund studies. At this rate, I would end up like my mum, marrying a man I could barely stand in order to sustain the life I had got used to. My heart felt heavy just thinking about it.

I didn't even realise where I was walking to until I got there. The woods were soon surrounding me, the trees swamping me, a familiar hug as I followed the curvy path that ran alongside the bubbly stream. I wasn't due to meet the others for another hour, but it seemed my feet had automatically brought me to Jay's spot. It didn't matter though, I could wait here. It was a warm afternoon. I'd have time to clear my mind before the others arrived.

I walked briskly until I reached the small clearing. This was usually where we would meet up. A couple of tree stumps made useful seats and the view to the stream here was particularly pretty. There was no sign of any of them. I had time to relax. I settled myself down on a nearby tree stump and started to get my headphones out ready to play some music.

I heard them before I saw them.

'I don't know why you do it, Sara.'

I froze. The voice was Jay's. Pushing through brambles, I edged closer to peer through the branches and spotted him and Sara together, Jay looking angry while Sara sat defiant with her arms drawn tightly across her body.

'Do what?'

'Blow hot and cold all the time. One minute I'm your best mate, you call me up and we chat like it's old times, and the next you're cold towards me. I don't know where I stand.'

'Stop making a big deal of everything, Jay. I'm not in the mood.'

'No – you never are. That's the problem.'

'For God's sake…'

'You know I loved those calls. Every time we spoke it felt like the old days. It felt like us.'

'I know…' I heard the crack in her voice. 'You know I like talking to you. It's always been so easy.'

A chill passed through me. I didn't realise they had both been talking so much. That explained what Sara had been doing when she was shut away in her room.

'And now I'm back, I just thought…' He let out a breath. 'I miss our time together.'

'I know, me too – but I'm confused too. It's hard, Jay. Kyle is coming out of prison soon. Mum is stressed out about it. She still won't have your family mentioned. And there's the other stuff… I'm not sure I even want to go into that now.'

'What is it? Why do you push me away all the time?' He sighed. 'I thought we came here to talk about everything before the others got here. You know, finally work out what we wanted.'

'I know, but—'

'But what? I try and get close to you, and you freeze. I don't understand what you want.'

Sara sniffed. 'I don't know – it just freaks me out when you get too close.'

'Freaks you out?' Jay sounded hurt. 'Sara, do you even like me?'

Sara laughed. It sounded cruel, but I knew it was because she felt awkward. 'Jay – I don't know why you're asking that. It's you that doesn't see me that way. I'll always be the little sister to you, won't I?'

'Eh? What makes you say that?'

'You've made it pretty clear,' Sara muttered. 'And what about Rae? I thought you were all loved up?'

'Rae was never that serious. You know that. You must know that?'

'You're crazy.'

'So I'm crazy now? I came here to try and clear things up, to talk to you, and you just treat me like shit.'

'It's not like that—'

'So what is it like?'

'I dunno. I just…' She sighed. 'I can't be bothered with this, Jay.'

'Yeah, and that's the problem isn't it! You can never be bothered.'

'Jay, don't be like that!' Her voice was wobbling. 'We don't need to destroy what we have. We're good friends, aren't we? Or at least we were. I want that back. I really do.'

'You want friendship?'

'Of course.' She paused. 'I'm seeing someone now – I met him at uni. Carl. I think you'd like him.'

Carl? I frowned. Sara told me she didn't even like him that much. He was just another lad she was hanging around with sometimes.

Jay coughed. 'Yeah. Dec mentioned something. Is it serious then?'

'Well, it might be. I like him.'

There was a brief silence and some movement in the trees. I flinched, scared that I would be discovered.

'I'm glad you're happy, Sara. That's all I wanted. I just want to find a way where we can be around each other without hurting each other, that's all. Maybe I want different things from you, I'm not sure.'

'Jay – I don't know what you're saying?'

'I don't know, it's too hard being around you. Maybe our mums were right. Maybe we are too toxic for each other. Maybe even friendship is too much for us.' His voice was so quiet, barely a whisper. 'I'm going to go, Sara. Say hi to the others – I don't think I'm in the mood for this now.'

'But they'll want to see you. Stay, don't be daft.'

'No, I can't. I'm sorry.'

He stormed off, luckily in a different direction to where I was standing, and Sara was left on her own. She slumped to the ground, sniffling. She looked broken. Her eyes stared out and, at first, I thought she could see me but then I realised she was looking into nothingness, her fingers gently tracing a marking on the tree.

I stayed and watched until Sara slowly got up and left a few minutes later. She left in the same direction as Jay, her body still slumped, her eyes downcast. I thought of running after her, but then she would've known I'd followed her here. She would've known I'd been watching.

Instead, I walked over to the tree. The words were carved deep into the bark.

Sara & Jay
4Eva

Day Eight

Sara

This isn't like me. Usually when Tyler is top of me, thrusting and groaning, I'm totally swept up in the moment. I claw at his back, I bring my legs up so that he can enter me more fully, I groan and shout and sometimes I bite. Usually, I love sex.

Today, I'm staring at a dark mark on the ceiling and wondering if it might be mould. How do you even fix that?

Tyler sighs and rolls off me.

'Did you come?' I ask him.

'What do you think?' He gets off the bed and starts gathering his clothes up from the floor. 'It's not right, us doing this. You're not the same at the moment. Do you even want this?'

I turn on my side, pulling the covers over my body, suddenly self-conscious of my exposed skin. 'I'm sorry, I thought I did want it, but...'

He shakes his head sadly. 'It's OK. You've been through a lot. Maybe you just need to talk or something?'

I laugh. I can't help myself. I'm not supposed to talk to Tyler. He's not exactly the kind of guy that you sit around with and have a cup of tea and a heavy chat.

'Why is that so funny?' Tyler looks hurt, standing there clutching his T-shirt against his perfectly ripped chest. 'Do you think I'm too thick to have proper conversations with or something?'

'No, I—'

'I'm sorry I'm not one of your university-educated mates like Declan or Jay,' he continues, his cheeks flushed. 'Maybe that's why you're so embarrassed to be seen with me.'

'No, Tyler, it's not like that.' A giggle erupts from me again. I can't help myself. He looks so daft standing there, glaring at me with an angry expression whilst only wearing one sock and a pair of pants.

'You call me up. You expect me to drop everything to come and see you and every time it's just for sex. It's not even fun sex lately, it's angry, cold…' He shakes his head. 'I don't feel comfortable with it, Sara.' He tugs on his jeans. 'It's like you're using me.'

I'm a little shocked. He's clearly being serious. 'Tyler. I thought you liked it how it was between us,' I say instead. 'It's easy, uncomplicated.'

He pulls the T-shirt over his head and then stares down at me. His eyes are so pretty, he has long lashes that most girls would pay for. This morning his eyes look larger, if that's even possible, and so sad. He reminds me of Bambi.

'Well, maybe I don't want that any more, Sara,' he says. 'Maybe I need more. I keep trying to hint that I want to change things but you never want to do anything with me apart from this.' He points to the bed and pulls a face.

'I thought you liked sex with me,' I say. I know I sound sulky, but I can't help myself.

'I do. You know I do, but it can't always just be about that, can it.' He grabs his coat. 'It's all just feeling a bit – I dunno – pointless.'

He walks out of the room without saying goodbye and I feel a spike of anger. How dare he make me feel bad for wanting sex, for wanting something easy and normal.

When the front door slams shut, my anger drains away. A wash of desperation rushes over me and I curl up on the bed in a tight foetal position, trying to fight back the tears. I called Tyler thinking I wanted sex, but was that true? What I probably needed most was a cuddle.

The last message from Lottie had floored me. I didn't understand why she had taken me back to the tree. It still hurt to think of that day, to that time when Jay had said those things to me. And how did she even know about it? Did Jay tell her about it? The thought of those two laughing about the whole thing makes me want to sob.

Yes, I had been cold with Jay then. I had flinched when he'd tried to pull me into a hug. I'd tried to make light of things by being casual and then by telling him that I was happy dating the idiot I had picked up at university. The truth was, I'd been scared. I was scared of my feelings for him. Those chats on the phone we'd had while at university had been long in-depth calls late into the night – usually when we were both drunk. We never talked about feelings or anything like that, but we shared other stuff – parts of me that no one else knew: my hopes, my fears, my desires. Jay had seen me at my most exposed, he knew the true depths of me. Having him back in town was both terrifying and exciting. I wanted to have him close to me, of course I did, but I also knew he was like a drug that I should stay away from.

I thought of the initials Jay had carved into the tree with my compass all those years ago. We had been much younger then, fifteen I think, and walking back from school. He had done it suddenly in an act of spontaneity.

'There – now we'll always be linked together,' he'd said, grinning, 'no matter what anyone says. It'll be you and me against the world.'

And I'd believed him. I really had. Deep inside, I think I always thought that we would end up together. It felt like destiny, like a perfect fit, like home.

But that afternoon – I couldn't tell Jay those things. I couldn't risk him throwing it in my face again. I was afraid he might have laughed, or got scared by the intensity of my feelings. It had been easier to build a wall around myself – to convince myself that he wasn't what I wanted or needed.

So we did what we always did when our feelings got too deep – we hurt each other, we pushed the other one away. God knows what we'd ever be like if we'd ever dated.

Despite it being time for me to get up and get ready for work, I close my eyes and try and make the bad feelings go away, but nothing is helping.

I hate Lottie's stupid Jar of Joy. I hate remembering everything. I just want to forget.

–

I turn up to work twenty minutes late. Sharon makes a big deal of looking at her watch and grumbling under her breath, but other than that she leaves me alone. The truth is, Sharon knows I'm a good worker. I never had any time off before Lottie got really sick. I know there is part of her that wants to have a go at me, but there is another that wouldn't dare rock the boat. I do a hard job for crap pay and barely moan – she would be lucky to replace me.

I help clean and dress the residents, working at speed to make up for lost time. Jess isn't working today, which is a shame as I could have done with talking to her. Ade is in, though, singing tunelessly at the top of his voice and making everyone smile. Another older lady is working too: Diane, from the agency. She has brought homemade muffins in and left them in the staffroom for us to enjoy. I eat mine quickly at first break, realising how hungry I am; I missed breakfast in my rush to get here and the sudden sugar rush almost makes me feel giddy. By the time I go and see Derek, I'm still a little high.

Derek has been in his bed for the last day. Ade told me he wasn't feeling that good and barely touched his breakfast earlier and, as I walk into his room, my heart stills for a second. He is lying so stiff in the bed I'm almost scared to approach. The sweet, sickly muffin starts to rise in my throat.

'Derek,' I whisper.

It's dark in the room, so I go to his window and draw the curtains back. It's a beautiful day and immediately bright sunlight floods the space. I walk closer to Derek and gently touch his hand. It's warm.

I draw a breath. 'Derek,' I say again.

He mutters something in his sleep. His mouth is open slightly, his head tipped back. I stand for a moment or so just watching him. He looks so peaceful. Just like Lottie had…

My mind drifts to the last time Lottie's mum had let me see her. She had guarded Lottie like a dog, not really allowing any guests at the end. I had begged at the door, almost in tears.

'Please, Erica, just a few minutes. I need to do this.'
Something inside of me told me that Lottie didn't have
long left and when Erica had reluctantly stepped back and
let me pass, I'd felt a mixture of fear and relief. Lying on
her back in her bed, covers pulled tightly around her,
Lottie didn't look sick, not really. She had lost lots of
weight, but her face still had that pretty, innocent look
to it — especially the way she was laying there with her
blonde hair spread out on the pillow.

'You look like Sleeping Beauty,' I'd told her. Except
there was no kiss on earth that was going to wake her
up. I took her hand and I squeezed it gently. I told her
I loved her. I said I was sorry about being angry about
her and Jay. 'It was silly,' I said. 'Silly, childish emotions. I
shouldn't have let it come between us.'

I swear I felt her move her hand in mine, saw the
slightest twitch behind her eyes. It was enough for me.
She had heard. She understood.

Erica came in soon after and ushered me out. I was
'tiring her out', so I needed to go. I slipped away without
argument, only allowing myself to glance back once. She
really did look quite peaceful, but all I wanted was for her
to sit up and start shouting at me.

That was the last time I saw her. She died the next day.

'Sara?'

I am startled back into reality. Derek's eyes are now
wide open and staring into mine. He looks worried.

'Is everything OK? Are you crying?' He rubs his face
and groans. 'For a minute there I thought I'd died and
woken up as a ghost.'

'N—no, everything is fine.' I swipe at my eyes, trying
to press away the tears. 'I'm sorry, Derek, I was lost in
thought. Are you OK, is there anything I can fetch you?'

He grins at me. 'As it happens, I'm feeling a little peckish now.'

'Well, in that case, I have just the thing.'

I watch as Derek devours the muffin. Far more interesting than the food they serve up here and he hardly has to care about the calories. I have fifteen-minutes for my break and I don't mind spending it perched on the end of Derek's bed. It makes me smile watching him wipe the crumbs away from his face and try to hide his excitement at eating such a sweet treat.

'I don't often enjoy things like this now, my sense of taste has gone right out of the window, but today this was just what the doctor ordered,' he tells me, carefully placing the empty wrapper on the side.

'You can thank Diane later when you see her. She made them.'

'Is she the one with the rather loud voice?' Derek pulls a face. 'She always wants to open my windows. It drives me mad.'

'Well, fresh air is good for you, and it is quite stuffy in here.' I look around me, considering the options. 'Derek, I still have some time. Why don't we go for a walk around the grounds, it might do you good?'

Derek shifts in his bed. 'I've been feeling a little light-headed, but I suppose sleeping all day isn't going to do me much good.'

I help Derek as he takes some wobbly steps towards his wheelchair. Despite the warm day, I place a blanket over his frail legs and then move him out towards the back door.

'I'm a big believer that sunshine makes most people feel better,' I tell him as I ease the chair out of the patio doors and down the main path into the gardens. 'Maybe you can tell me a little more about you and Alice. I love hearing about your life together.'

Derek shakes his head. 'I'm getting tired of talking about me all the time. It was nice at first, but now not so much...' he says, smiling weakly. 'I don't feel so sad about my past now. Maybe because I know I'm getting closer to seeing my darling Alice again.'

'Oh, Derek, don't talk like that, you could have years left yet.'

We've reached the small pond that sits in the centre of the garden. An unusual water fountain that is meant to look like a swan (but looks more like a lopsided chicken) trickles peacefully. It's probably my favourite place to come here and I know Derek likes it too. I wish I could sit here and draw, it's such a pretty scene.

'I'm not scared of death,' he says gently. 'It's just part of our journey, isn't it? I'm hoping that I will see loved ones again. It will be peaceful, I'd imagine, and kind. I don't think that's anything to be scared of.'

I touch his hand. 'You don't need to be thinking about those things now though. Enjoy the day. It's so pretty here.'

'Yes, yes, it is...' He breathes out a big puff of air. 'You almost feel all of your worries disappear.'

'Yes – I suppose you do.'

He chuckles. 'Sara. You can pretend all you like, but I know you're upset about something. Is this to do with your friend? The one who died?'

I nod and find myself telling him about the last note and how it made me feel going back to the place where I first let myself be true to Jay. It's surprisingly easy talking to Derek; he doesn't interrupt, and his calm eyes pass no judgement.

'I can't help wondering why Lottie wrote that message? That day wasn't a good one for me. At the time, I thought maybe me and Jay could rebuild – it was the start of something hopeful, you know? But then everything went wrong.'

'That sounds hard,' Derek says. 'You obviously cared about this boy a great deal.'

I half laugh. 'He was pretty important to me, and that afternoon was the start of the change. We were talking about deep stuff at first, before our argument. I thought maybe it was the start of things shifting between us. We had so much history, our families hating each other, the fact we'd been friends for so long. I couldn't imagine being without him and yet, being with him made me scared too, especially when he'd hurt me before.' I stop talking, feeling suddenly silly and quite shy.

Derek sighs next to me. 'It sounds a bit like my story, doomed love. My parents didn't want me to marry Alice because she was German – even though the war was long over, the prejudice stayed. When we ran away together, we were scared. We didn't even know if it would work, all we had was each other and hope. We had plenty of that.'

'That sounds so sweet.' My voice wobbles. 'That's what I once thought would happen with Jay and me, too. I thought we were strong enough together, that we could oppose the stupid beliefs our parents had. After all, it was their war not ours.'

'What was it over, if you don't mind me asking?'

The pain hits me straight in the gut just thinking about it. 'It's complicated, Derek, I won't bore you, but it was stuff to do with my mum and Jay's dad that didn't even involve us.'

'And you and Jay?' His voice is softer now. 'I take it it didn't work out in the end?'

I glance back at the home. I can just about make out the figure of Sharon pacing just inside the patio doors. She's probably looking at her watch again and cursing me for taking a longer break than I should. She won't notice that Derek has colour in his cheeks now, that he's sitting up straight and engaging in conversation.

'I need to take you back, Derek,' I say, lifting his brake and moving him gently round. 'I'll get in trouble if I don't.'

'And leave me hanging about you and Jay? What happened, Sara? Did your parents stop it? Did you both get too scared?'

I dip my head, so he can't see the tears. 'No. We weren't scared and no, my parents didn't even get a chance to ruin it. It was Jay. It was always Jay. I ended up putting my trust in him and once again he decided I wasn't what he wanted. Then he went off with someone else and totally broke my heart in the process.'

Even now, after all these years I'm surprised how much those words hurt me. I wheel Derek with wobbly legs.

'I'm sorry, Sara,' he says as we reach the doors. 'I shouldn't have asked. It wasn't my business.'

'No, it's OK, I'm sorry.' I manage a smile. 'I will never let that man get under my skin again.'

Derek reaches out and gently pats my arm. 'I'm a great believer that everything happens for a reason, Sara. There was a reason Lottie wanted you to remember that memory. Maybe you just need to understand why?'

–

Back at home, I'm exhausted. I manage to make myself a jacket potato, feed Goose and then flop out in front of the TV ready to numb my brain with an easy-to-watch thriller. I can't concentrate though. I push my half-eaten dinner away and stare at the Jar of Joy.

'Hardly joyful,' I mutter. 'It's made me feel crap all day.'

I think about what Derek had said to me about Lottie's reasonings. He was right, Lottie was always so bloody sensible and such a planner, I couldn't believe she would ever be deliberately cruel.

I picture her sitting next to me now, her gentle, kind face wearing that worried expression she often adopted when she was scared I might fly off the handle or take something the wrong way.

'*You're my best friend,*' I hear her say. '*You just have to trust me.*'

My sigh disturbs Goose next to me, who stretches out a paw and chirrups softly. I stroke her belly and allow myself to relax. It was true, the memory hadn't been all bad – in that moment with Jay, there had been hope and anticipation too. That day I'd really thought my life was going in the direction that I finally wanted it to. Perhaps that was what Lottie wanted me to tap into – the feeling of excitement and rush of early love.

'OK,' I mutter. 'I'll trust you for now, but no more big surprises, okay?'

I swear I see her grin back at me. '*Good, but now you have to open your next message. It's getting late. You should be doing one a day.*'

I shake my head at Goose. I'm clearly losing my mind, but despite this, I find myself picking up the jar and drawing out another message.

'This better not be another one involving Jay, because I swear…'

The message is a blue one today.

Do you remember all the times we spent at your flat? I loved it there. It was always filled with love and warmth.

Go and visit your mum. You know you don't do it often enough. Give her a hug from me.

XX

Guilt is trickling through me like hot water through ice. It's true, I haven't seen Mum much. In fact, I rarely visit her at all. Since I got back from travelling, things had shifted between us. I hated seeing the disappointment in her face, the regret she had that I didn't do so well after university and get myself a decent job. We'd had too many rows about the decisions I had made, and it had become easier to stay away rather than face her.

At least once a week I phone her, though, and this message has reminded me it's time to call again. I doubt very much she would want me to come and see her anyway. Mum keeps herself pretty busy – if she's not working, then she's round my brother Kyle's place helping him out, which provokes the usual twinge of annoyance just thinking of that.

Mum answers within a few rings. 'Sara? You OK? It's a bit late for you to be calling.'

I glance at the clock. It's just after nine. 'I'm sorry. I've just eaten and I thought I'd check in. I realised I hadn't rung for a bit.'

'I tried calling you a few days ago, but I knew you'd be distracted with the funeral and everything.' Mum coughs, her breathing rattling a little. 'I did think about going but I have this cold, I wouldn't want to give it to everyone.'

'Oh, Mum, you should have said…' I feel even worse now. I had no idea she was even thinking of coming. She never seemed to have that much time for Lottie.

'She was a sweet girl, a little clingy perhaps, but I expect that was her upbringing.' Mum coughs again. 'She certainly idolised you.'

'I'm not sure why,' I say with a wry smile. 'Hey Mum, I'm off tomorrow. I'll pop over in the morning. Bring you some grapes or something?'

'I've just got a cold, that's all.' She pauses. 'But if you could pick up some chocolate on the way that would be nice.'

'Yes, of course. I'll come over at ten.'

'I'll make sure the kettle is on.'

The call ends and I stare at Lottie's message again. It surprises me that she always found my flat so welcoming, it certainly explains why she was always so keen to go there.

'You have so much,' I remember her telling me once. 'But sometimes it's hard to see that for yourself.'

At the time I had rejected that notion. How on earth did I have so much? We were always broke, my Dad was dead and my brother was banged up in prison. How on earth did me and my workaholic mum have more than Lottie?

It makes me realise now how little Lottie actually had.

Day Nine

Sara

The bus is crowded, but I manage to find a seat by myself towards the back. Pressed up against the window, I stare out as we climb away from the main roads of the city itself, the signs of summer everywhere. Shops have brightly coloured displays, people are walking in short or loose-fitting clothes showing off tanned legs and arms, the trees are in full bloom.

Tyler said it was going to be a long, hot summer this year – the kind that Lottie always loved, and I always tended to complain about. If Lottie was here now, she would be insisting we go down to the beach, wearing the skimpiest dresses and giggling up at the sun as if it was a gift from the gods.

Guilt prickles in my chest, not only thinking about Lottie, but of Tyler too. I'd tried to call him last night, but he hadn't answered. This morning he sent me a text suggesting that we meet up and 'talk things through'. The thought of doing anything heavy like talking about our relationship filled me with dread, but I knew I owed it to Tyler to try and work something out. After all, Tyler was fun, he did make me laugh and for the last year or so he'd taken my mind off the mess of life. Was I avoiding anything too serious because I was terrified of being hurt again? Or maybe, like Jay once told me, I wasn't the sort of person who would ever be ready to settle down.

I haven't answered him yet. I'm not even sure what I want from Tyler, but I know I miss his company and could really use someone to cuddle up with right now. Is that enough of a reason to stay with someone? Am I just using him for sex and bed-warming opportunities like he said?

I continue to stare out of the window, blinking back the tears, when my phone buzzes, but I ignore it. It's likely to be Sharon asking if I can come in on my day off, or maybe Tyler checking the details for tomorrow. I'm too numb to speak to anyone at the moment. Instead I watch as people pass, caught up in their own lives and dreams. I wonder if any of them feel as stuck as me. A twenty-something fuck-up. An emotional wreck. Someone who pushed everyone away, except Lottie, and look how that ended up.

The bus is nearing my mum's stop so I gather up my bag and phone, glancing down at the screen. There's a voicemail notification and I click on it, suddenly worried it might be Mum or something.

It's not.

His voice still has the same effect on me, making my stomach bottom out and icy air swoop in. I have to play it twice to take in the details.

'Hey, Sara. I'm not sure whether you are getting my messages? I don't know, maybe you still don't want to hear from me. I can't say I blame you, but Sara… I really need to talk to you. I hope you don't mind me trying again. I'm using my mum's phone because I figured you might have blocked me or something. Anyway – uh – listen, I'm only going to be down here for a few weeks, I can't stay with Mum much longer, we'll drive each other mad, and then I'm going back. I think we have stuff to sort out and talk through. Losing Lottie has made me realise so much. It's made me see' – his voice breaks – 'it's made me see that life is short and we need to check in on the people we care about. I just hope maybe you feel the same. Call me, please.'

The bus comes to a shuddering stop as my phone falls silent. My head is throbbing slightly.

I don't know what to do any more. I don't even know how to think straight.

–

The estate has declined in the past few years, but I guess that's no surprise. No one wants to invest in a tatty sprawling housing estate on the rough side of town. I stare up at the dark grey flats, peppered with graffiti and surrounded by unkempt lawns and pathways, and feel a mixture of nostalgia and annoyance. This was my home for so long and I'd always had a fierce sense of pride about it. The people who lived here were kind, hardworking and looked out for one another.

Mum lived on the ground floor of the nearest block and two blocks over Jay's flat had been on the top floor overlooking the entire grounds.

It's always weird coming back, like the teenage part of me has returned and suddenly all those feelings of insecurity and freedom come flooding back. I never actually hated being a teen, there was a lot to love about it, but it was fair to say that I'd struggled with finding my place and actually knowing what were the best decisions to make.

Walking past the low brick walk that runs alongside the steps, I remember how me, Jay and Dec, and later

Lottie, would meet here, often sat on the rough top, our legs swinging in the wind. If I squint my eyes I can still picture us, like ghosts caught in a photo.

Isn't it funny how time moves so fast and yet in many ways it barely feels like it's moved at all?

I push through the heavy doors and stride across the foyer towards my mum's flat. We were always glad to live at the bottom. The lifts here were forever going on the blink and it also meant we had direct access to the small, scrappy, shared communal garden. Mum had taken over a patch, lining the area outside her back door with plant pots and sticking chairs on the couple of tiles of patio. To most of the residents that lived here, the outdoor bit was owned by her.

I knock on Mum's door and wait patiently, expecting that she's out the back and will take her time getting to me, so I'm surprised when she opens the door in a matter of seconds, and I'm even more shocked by the state of her – she looks pretty awful.

My mum never gets sick, she always told us she could never afford to. She's wearing a scruffy tracksuit and her usually well-groomed hair has been pulled back into a messy ponytail. Her face is pale and lined, make-up free, and she greets me with a loud and rather throaty cough.

'Bloody hell, you *are* ill,' I say, pushing past her to get into the flat. 'You should have told me before.'

Mum follows me down the hall. As usual it's spotless in here. Mum hates anything being dirty, but she still has loads of 'stuff'. I muscle past the bookcase that is overflowing and in the living room I notice she's added more knick-knacks to the shelves.

'I figured you had enough on your plate what with Lottie and everything,' Mum says. 'Now do you want tea or coffee?'

'Tea, please, but I can make it.'

Mum immediately pulls a face. 'I might have a cold but I'm perfectly capable of making us both a cuppa.' She smiles. 'Besides, yours are always weak as shit.'

–

I sit nursing my cup on my knee. Whenever I come back here, I'm reminded of the years I spent laid out on the sofa watching TV or sat in the kitchen wolfing down a hearty dinner. Many times, the others would be with me, although Jay would rarely come when Mum was there. She was never rude to him, but I hated the way her face would go all stiff and closed when she saw him – like he had a bad smell about him. She was always cool about me having people over though, even if she was out. That's probably why Lottie liked it so much. There were no airs or graces here. You just took us as you found us.

'I'm sorry I haven't visited for so long,' I say. 'I've just been so busy, you know.'

Mum observes me with her clever, grey eyes. 'We both have.'

I returned from travelling four years ago, and in that time I've only come to see Mum a handful of times, which is crazy when you think I only live a matter of minutes away. The last time I came was a few weeks ago when I first heard Lottie had died, but before that it had been Christmas and I hadn't stayed long. I knew Kyle was due that afternoon and to be honest I didn't have the energy to face him and his dramas. Visits to Mum's had been awkward and sometimes ill-tempered. Mum hadn't been happy with my choices after university. She had longed for me to settle down into a 'proper job' and maybe even meet a decent young man. My numerous temping jobs and long-term waitressing role before I went travelling were viewed as 'wasteful'. I tried to argue that I was just passing time until I found the right art-based job but Mum could see right through me and I knew it. I *was* too scared to commit to anything.

'I'm glad you came,' Mum continues gently. 'When you told me before about Lottie, you were in and out of here. I barely had a chance to speak to you.'

'It was hard. I thought I wanted to talk at the time, but—' I shook my head. 'You know, it was Lottie who made me come today.' I tell mum about Lottie's Jar of Joy and watch as a smile slowly spreads across her face.

'I always thought that girl had her head in the clouds, but that's actually a really sweet thing to do.' She pauses. 'She must have known that you and me hadn't been spending much time together.'

'Well, she knew that since I got back I didn't really see anyone. I just threw myself into work.' I think of Derek and the long conversations we'd had, and realise that he's been my substitution since I'd blocked my family out.

'I know I was angry about you travelling at first, but that was only because I didn't want you throwing your life away like I did. You're so bright, so talented…' She trailed off, probably because she saw the look on my face. 'I'm sorry,' she says finally, sipping her tea. 'This isn't the time. I can see that.'

'I'm happy, Mum, honestly. You don't have to keep nagging me.'

'But are you?' Those dark eyes seem to be burning into mine. 'I'm not silly, Sara. I know what you do when you're upset about things. You shut yourself away. You did the same when Kyle was arrested and then later with that upset with Jay. Now that Lottie has gone, you are even more isolated. I just want you to have someone, and something to focus on.'

'I have my work.' But even as I say this, Jess's face comes to mind – how often she's told me to call her, and how I've resisted. I wiggle in my seat, irritated. I hate it when Mum is right.

'I look back now, and I think the travelling was good for you, it made you strong and independent – but you still need your family and friends,' Mum says carefully. 'Kyle has been asking after you. You know he's in a better place now, he—'

'I'm not here to talk about Kyle, Mum,' I snap. Of course she has to bring her golden boy up again. Kyle has only ever been a cause of drama in this family – I was pretty sure he was the last thing I needed.

Kyle was the other source of disagreement between me and Mum. Every time I did visit, she would bring him into conversation, try and paint him as a new, reformed guy. I didn't buy it. Kyle was the angry, destructive force that destroyed my childhood and drove a wedge between me and Jay. No good could come from having him back in my life.

Mum is staring at me intently.

'Well – I can't believe I'm saying this – but I wonder if you should reach out to Jay.'

A half-laugh splutters from my lips. 'Really? God you must be worried about me.'

'Jay knows you better than anyone,' she says quietly. 'And maybe, looking back, I can accept I was wrong to try and stop the pair of you being friends. It was never fair. You two had no reason to fall out – the argument wasn't yours to cling onto.'

'No...' I lower my eyes. 'But Jay ended up showing his true colours anyway. You were right all the time, Mum. The Walkers were never any good. I should have listened to you then.'

'The past is in the past. Maybe you should listen to me again.' Her voice is more earnest now. 'Sometimes it's better to forgive than to spend years holding onto bitterness.'

–

I leave the estate feeling a little lighter than when I arrived. Mum had hugged me at the door as I was leaving, and I had greedily drunk in the scent of her. For too long I'd thought that I was fine as I was – that being independent was the best way to be – but standing with my Mum's arms pulled tight around me made me realise that I needed her more than ever.

'Come again soon,' she demanded. 'I want to know all the other crazy places Lottie has sent you.'

'I will,' I promised. 'Maybe one of the messages will take me somewhere hot like Spain or France. Here's hoping, eh?'

Mum was already fanning herself. 'It's plenty hot enough here. Anyway, those messages mean something, remember that. Lottie took her time to send you somewhere that was important to both you and her.'

Shading my eyes from the sun, I grin at the ugly grey building that I've always had such mixed thoughts about before. I guess Dorothy was right all those years ago. There really is no place like home.

'Hey, Sara!'

I spin around. I recognise the voice of course, but I hardly believe who I'm seeing. Surely, he can't be here too?

'Jay?'

He jogs over towards me, his dark curls floppy against his face, his blue eyes even lighter in the bright sun. He grins and my legs still wobble slightly. I hate that. It's like my body is betraying me.

'What are you doing here?' I say sharply. 'It's almost like you're following me.'

The thought does cross my mind. After all, he was outside the cafe too, and he left the message on my phone. I know he wants to talk, but this reeks of desperation.

'I've been staying with my mum. Didn't you get my message?'

My gaze automatically switches to his flat, so high up with views to die for. I've known Jay since we were little kids, but I've only visited that flat once. His mother would never let me in. I was bad blood in her eyes.

'I'm surprised you're not in some posh hotel some-where,' I mutter.

'Nah, I wanted to be with Mum while I was here. Work have given me some time off but I can still catch up on stuff remotely anyway. I saw you out of the window. You're visiting home too, eh?'

I nod. I almost tell him about Lottie's jar and then think better of it. It's better that it's just 'our' thing. I don't want it to be something else he might spoil. 'How long are you here? I thought you were just staying for Lottie's funeral.'

Jay hitches himself up on the low wall and gestures for me to sit next to him. I shift on the spot, feeling uncomfortable; we were different people when we used to sit here. I find myself leaning against it instead. A kind of compromise.

'I was going to go back straight after, but Mum was a bit low...' Jay shrugs. 'I figured it would be nice to stick around for a few more days. Visit some old haunts.'

'Like the cafe.'

'Yeah...' Jay is staring at me intently. It makes my entire skin buzz, like he's sending an electric current into my veins. 'Sara, I wanted to catch up with you, too. I know time has passed and all of that, but I still feel like there is unfinished business between us.'

'There really isn't.' I try to keep my voice light. 'We got together a few times, so what? We were young. We both knew it was a mistake.'

'We never got a chance to sort things out properly.'

'You made your choice, Jay.' I hear the wobble in my voice and quickly turn away. 'Look, I don't want to go into all this again. It's not fair now that Lottie has gone. You wanted to be with her not me, and I get that, I really do. I'm sorry it didn't work out between you.' There is so much ice in my tone, I can barely recognise myself. Jay has the decency to look away.

'I didn't mean to hurt her, or you,' he says quietly. 'It was a horrible, messy situation. I got so much wrong.'

'Yeah – well, that's not my problem.'

I go to walk away but he jumps off the wall and comes up to me. He gently touches my arm. I have to pull away quickly, remembering a time when I longed for him to grab me like that.

'Sara, please – can we just talk properly? Just one night? It doesn't even have to be about anything serious. I could just use a friend at the moment, an old friend. Don't you remember how we used to talk about everything?' I can't speak. I simply nod my head instead. 'I hate how complicated things got for us. Why did it matter that my dad was once shagging your mum? It wasn't to do with us, we were just kids. It wasn't our fault that Kyle decided to hurt him. The whole thing got into both our heads.'

'Kyle had his reasons,' I remind him a bit agitated now. 'Your dad was a controlling idiot, he made my mum's life hell and she changed when she was with him. For ages he kept telling her he was going to leave your mum for her and then he would leave her for weeks without any contact. He made her feel worthless and small.'

Jay's features stiffen. 'I know he's got his faults, Sara. You don't have to remind me. He destroyed my mum, too – but he's still my dad, whatever happened, and he didn't deserve that beating Kyle gave him.'

'He thought he was protecting our family,' I say. 'He didn't like how your dad was treating everyone. He was sick of the lies and pretence.' I sigh. 'Besides, Kyle has his own problems. He's never been able to manage his emotions. But he paid the price for what he did, Jay. Youth detention nearly finished him and he's not been the same since.'

'I know that. I don't blame Kyle, not really. I don't really blame anyone.' Jay sounds so sad. 'But it messed us all up. We always felt guilty for being close, for having a bond that no one else understood.'

'My mum used to say your family were dangerous.' I giggle despite myself. 'You were the least dangerous person I knew.'

Although he could still cause harm. I'd learnt that to my regret.

'My mum said your family were all cheats and liars, and you were the most honest and decent person I've ever met.' Jay shrugs. 'Families get it wrong sometimes.'

I think of what Mum said to me earlier, about letting go of bitterness. 'Perhaps not all the time,' I say hesitantly. 'Look, maybe we can go for that drink. But just one, OK? Tomorrow.'

'Really?' Jay looks stunned.

'It's just a drink, it's no big deal,' I say, walking away. 'It's not like it will ever be like it used to be between us.'

Because that's not what I want.

Is it?

Five Years Before

Lottie

Sara was dancing around the living room, the half-empty vodka bottle lying on the floor. I was feeling woozy, clutching a cushion to anchor myself to the sofa and laughing at Sara's cheesy moves. She looked so carefree and pretty. Her black dress fit her perfectly. I looked at my top in comparison; it seemed to just emphasise that I had no curves at all. I stared down at my flat chest that couldn't fill my clothes properly and sighed dramatically.

'I'd give anything for your tits.'

Sara cupped hers and giggled. 'What, these old things? Seriously? They do my head in.'

'How? They're gorgeous…' My words sounded a bit mumbled. I knew I was talking too much but strangely I didn't really care. 'I'd love your body, your face – everything.'

Sara snorted. She stopped dancing and wagged her finger at me. 'Stop being so daft. Look at you with your blonde hair and blue eyes. Most girls would die for that.'

'You have it all.'

Sara was still staring at me, a mockery of a smile settling on her face. 'Really? Do I? And this is coming from the girl who really *does* have it all. Look at your birthday presents.'

A sour taste filled my mouth. I knew I should be happy that Dad bought me another car, that Mum transferred another stack of cash into my account – but what did it mean really? I hadn't seen either of them for weeks. I shook my head, trying to remove the thought. I didn't want them to ruin my birthday celebrations.

'That's not what I mean.' I swiped at my mouth trying to remove the bad taste. 'It's not all about money. You have other things. Everyone loves you.'

Sara stepped forward and snatched the vodka bottle away from me. 'I think you need a break from this before the others get here.'

'You still like Jay, don't you, even after all this time?' I probed. 'And he'll be here soon. All you've done is talk about him all week.'

'I'm proud of him. That's all. His new job is a big deal.'

'It's more than that, I can tell. It's like we're back at school.' I snatched the bottle back and slugged the drink again. 'You don't go all misty-eyed about anyone else. All the men you've dated...'

'There's not that many. I'm not a slag.'

'But they've never been up to standard, have they?'

Her eyes narrowed. 'I don't want to go into this now, Lottie.'

'Why not?' I threw my arms out in protest. I knew I was talking too loudly, but I didn't care. 'You're meant to tell me stuff!'

Yet – she didn't. She thought I didn't know that her phone calls to Jay had started up again. After years of not really talking, I heard her late at night giggling to him like a schoolgirl. She met him before work in cafes and after work at bars – apparently just to 'catch up', but she was always glowing every time she spoke about him.

Sara sighed and then came and sat next to me on the bed. She took a swig from the bottle and shuddered slightly. 'I dunno. I guess I do – yeah. I mean he's always been there, Jay, hasn't he? He's always been part of my life, but I can't help thinking…' She shrugged.

'What, that you want it to be more?'

'Sometimes I get the feeling that's what he wants, but I don't want to wreck our friendship. It's hard enough being as close as we are. I don't want to ruin anything between us.'

'But if you could,' I asked, 'if you could wave a magic wand, you'd be his girlfriend?'

Sara snorted. 'You make it sound so childish.'

My cheeks were burning. 'It's not childish. It's just a question. Is that what you want?'

She took a deep breath; her gaze had drifted off towards the door before she set her shoulders and swigged out of the vodka bottle. 'Yeah. It's what I want. It's what I want more than anything.'

The doorbell rang. Sara jumped up as if stung. 'They're here,' she hissed, tugging on my arm. 'Come on, let's get this party started, eh?'

Hardly a party, I thought. It was mainly just us lot again and a few others that I barely cared about, people that I had invited just to fill the gaps. Ultimately it was just Sara, me, Dec and Jay that I cared about. With me and Dec playing gooseberry to their flirting. It really was like school again.

My legs were heavy and useless and my mind felt sluggish, but I pulled myself off the sofa.

'And Lottie?' Sara hissed, as she opened the door. 'Don't say any of this to anyone, OK? It's just between us. I've told you before. I don't want to ruin anything.'

147

'OK.' I nodded.

Why would I say anything? I was pretty sure Jay still liked her, the pair of them were just useless at communicating their feelings. Or too bloody cowardly. And I was happy to capitalise on that. Anything to prevent me being alone.

'I think you're wise to be cautious,' I said softly. 'You're good friends. Why spoil it?'

Her face was serious. 'I knew you'd understand.'

The smile on my face felt fixed and rigid, almost plastic.

–

I moved from room to room, feeling like I was in a bit of a daze. At Sara's insistence I had drunk some water, and this helped to clear my head a little.

The patio doors were open letting in a much-needed cool breeze, and I stepped just outside, taking in some grateful gulps. I noticed that Dec and Sara were sitting on the chairs along the edge of the patio. The paddling pool was still inflated and full of water. Sara's idea. She wanted to replicate my mum's swimming pool – although it was a poor relation and the murky water inside was making me feel a bit sick.

'Are you OK, Lottie?'

I turned round to see Jay approaching. He was coming from the kitchen clutching two beers in his hand. He stood next to me and gestured towards the pool. 'Are you going to paddle?'

'No,' I smiled. 'Aren't you tempted?'

'Not really. I think I'd rather just watch,' he replied and then gestured with his bottle. 'Hang on, I just need to give this to Dec and I'll come back.'

Jay approached Sara and Dec, speaking to them both but leaning in a little more towards Sara, his hand resting briefly on her knee. If this was some kind of naff cartoon there would sparks flying between them. I closed my eyes briefly and leant against the wall. I wanted the world to stop spinning for a minute.

'Are you sure you're OK?'

He was back. I opened my eyes and took in the sight of his handsome face, those kind, gentle eyes, his soft, full mouth. I shivered a little.

'Yeah, I'm good. I just have a bit of a headache.' I paused. 'Is everything all right with you?'

For the first time I noticed that Jay didn't seem to have his usual sparkle. His face was drawn and his eyes looked tired, as though he hadn't slept properly.

'There's a few things going on at home,' he said finally, so quietly that I had to strain to hear. 'My dad hasn't been that well. He's got heart problems and has to go into hospital for a check-up. My mum isn't coping. She struggles a bit with her mental health and she's had – well, I guess you'd call it a bit of a crash. It's not easy when she's like this, it can be a bit scary.'

'Oh, Jay, I'm sorry, that sounds hard.'

'It's OK. I guess I'm used to it. I'm a bit anxious at the moment, she's started to say things that don't really make sense and fixate on the past. It could be a sign she's spiralling. I'm a bit worried about her, and about Dad's tests.' He sighed heavily. 'I'm sorry, this is meant to be a celebration and I'm bringing down the vibe.'

'Don't worry, I like talking to you. I just wish I could help.' I hesitated. 'Does Sara know?'

His gaze shifted towards Sara who was still laughing with Dec. 'No – we don't really talk about stuff like that.

I'm not even sure Sara will understand, there is so much shit between our families. When her mum was dating my dad, it was really messy; my mum was so badly hurt by it all… I'm not sure she'd get it.'

'It sounded so hard. I know Sara's brother attacked your dad.'

'Yeah.' Jay sighed. 'It was a long time ago. Me and Sara were just kids really, but the whole thing tore our families apart. Dad was beat up badly and then he buggered off for a bit and left us all to deal with the mess. Mum just fell apart. Her husband had cheated on her and then left her. I remember my mum screaming and saying such horrible things to Sara's mum, but at the time no one knew how badly she was struggling with her mental health, I think everyone just thought she was nasty and bitter. When Dad came back it wasn't the same, it still isn't. I can tell there is still resentment there…'

This was probably the most Jay had ever opened up to me. I felt a warm glow filter through me. All I wanted to do was pull him into my arms and make him better. If we'd been alone, maybe I would have.

'Sara should understand that your mum couldn't help the way she reacted,' I said.

'Sara was hurting too I guess, and as time passed, we just avoided the subject. We're just resigned to the fact that our mums hate each other. That my dad is a massive problem between our families. I can't see that ever changing.'

'I guess some things are meant to be,' I said quietly.

Jay looked at me a bit oddly for a second and then he nodded sadly. 'Yeah, you're probably right. Maybe they are.'

I glanced over at Sara, watched how she was laughing with Dec in such a carefree manner. Maybe it was the drink inside of me, or maybe it was just the years of resentment building up, but suddenly I felt the fire inside of me light up.

'Doesn't it annoy you? How Sara is with you?'

Jay frowned. 'What do you mean?'

I chuckled softly. 'You know what I mean – she blows hot and cold. I know she's my friend, but I don't like to see that.'

Jay bowed his head slightly. 'I'm not sure she means it though; it's just her way isn't it. She's defensive sometimes… I think she struggles…'

I could tell he was thinking it over though and processing what I was saying.

I shrugged. 'I don't know, I just don't think I could put up with that. I'd find it hard to know where I stood with her.'

'Does she ever say anything to you?' Jay asked quietly, his eyes suddenly looking hopeful.

I gulped a mouthful of my water. This was my opportunity to be honest, to tell Jay what Sara had confessed to me earlier, but something held me back. I'd meddled before, but should I continue? My dad's words rang through my head, something he'd said to me at work only a few weeks before: 'sometimes you have to be ruthless.' I could tell Sara wasn't good for Jay. They'd only end up hurting each other, what would be the point in that? They would both end up miserable.

I could make them both happy. I really believed this.

'No,' I replied. 'No, she doesn't talk about you at all really.'

Disappointment flickered in his eyes but then the smile returned – stoic and brave. Jay was used to this. 'Yeah,' he muttered. 'Yeah, that's fine.'

I was about to say more. My hand reached out to touch his arm. I wanted to tell him what a lovely guy he was and how glad I was that he'd come today. I wanted to thank him for looking out for me since I had started at their school – but all of a sudden there was a burst of energy from the other side of the patio. Sara had rushed forwards, grabbing Jay by the waist. She was clearly pretty drunk now.

'Jay!' she trilled. 'Why aren't you dancing? You love this song!'

Jay flashed a nervous glance at me and then tried to untangle himself from Sara's grip. 'I'm not sure I'm up for that tonight, Sar...' He pulled his phone out of his pocket and glanced at it. 'I need to check on Mum really, I need to—'

'Jay! Come on! It's a party!'

Sara started to drag Jay. He was resisting and the two of them seemed caught up in a stiff little dance by the side of the pool. Then Sara tugged on his arm, the one holding his phone. Everything seemed to happen so quickly and yet almost in slow motion. I saw the phone fly in the air. I saw Jay's face twist and whiten as it flew towards the water. And then the horrifying splash as it landed.

'What the hell!' Jay rushed to the edge. 'Sara, what did you do? I need that!'

'I'm sorry.' Sara looked sick now. 'I'll replace it, or I'll get it fixed. I'll do whatever—'

'It's too late,' Jay snapped. 'I need it now. Why do you have to mess everything up?'

And then he stormed back inside.

–

A little later, I watched as Sara approached Jay in the kitchen, pulling him into a hug before the two spoke for a few minutes. I went to get another drink and when I came back, they had gone.

'Where are Sara and Jay?' I asked Dec, who was sitting awkwardly by himself on the sofa.

'They went for a walk,' he said. 'I think Sara wanted some fresh air. She offered Jay her phone to use as well. I think they went to the beach.'

'Oh…' I nodded slowly.

Dec looked at me with a knowing smile. 'Those two will always have something between them. It's just how it is. It's always about Jay and Sara. No one can get between them.'

I didn't know whether he was speaking in admiration or jealousy. All I knew was that my own stomach had shrunken inside of me. And all I felt was raw envy – naked, ugly and real.

Five Years Before

Lottie

It was much later. I had started drinking again, not really caring what it was – vodka, wine, beer – what did it matter? I felt numb to it all. The music thumped and swirled around me, but I felt like I was in my own quiet bubble. I floated from room to room. My stomach was acid, my throat was raw, my head was so heavy I could barely keep it upright.

Jay and Sara had been gone for over an hour. Were they even coming back? But from here I could do nothing. They were together. They would probably be together forever now.

I wobbled on the spot. The room was spinning. Light danced in front of my eyes. Someone grabbed my arm.

'Lottie, come here. Let's get some air.' It was Dec. He took me outside. The pool was glinting in the moonlight. It almost looked pretty.

Dec led me to a chair and sat me down. 'You don't look good,' he said quietly. 'Shall I help you to bed?'

'No... I'm fine here. Leave me.'

'I can help you clean up, too,' he continued, looking around the garden. 'It probably isn't as bad as it looks. Once we get started, we can—'

'Dec,' I interrupt, fighting back a hiccough in my throat. 'It's OK. I'm not that bothered. I'll stay here. Maybe I'll choke on my sick. Maybe someone will notice me then.'

Dec shifted uneasily on his chair. 'You are noticed, Lottie. We all notice you.'

I thought of Sara and Jay and made a snorting noise. Yeah, right. I barely mattered to them. But I couldn't talk to Dec about this. He was too sweet, too innocent.

'My mum doesn't…' I said instead, desperate to deflect. 'I never even hear from her now.'

'I'm sure she does notice you, Lottie. Parents just get caught up in their own stuff, don't they? I know mine work a lot and only seem obsessed with how I'm doing at work and how much money I'm making, but I know they care really.'

'I don't think mine do, not really.' I sighed, realising that a wound was beginning to open. 'Even when I was little, I was just another thing that they could show off, then they ended up fighting over me. Dad left without too much of a fight and thinks that he can sow affection by throwing cash at me, and Mum doesn't know what to do with me now that I'm no longer a cute little kid that she can dress up and control.'

I wasn't expecting those words to tumble out, but they did, spilling out of me like a tap that has been turned on full. I was a little shocked. I shivered slightly in the night breeze. Dec noticed and moved closer; he awkwardly put his arm around me and hugged me.

'I'm sorry, Lottie. That sounds hard.'

'I'm sorry I poured it all out to you. I just hate it sometimes. All I've ever wanted to do is find somewhere where I fit in, find someone who gets me.'

'I understand that, I do.'

Dec moved slowly towards me. I wasn't expecting him to try and kiss me but as his lips neared mine, I realised his intent and quickly turned away, giggling softly.

'No – Dec, I'm sorry, but I don't want that.'

Dec looked hurt, he pushed his glasses back and moved slightly away from me. 'I'm sorry, Lottie, I've been drinking. I wasn't thinking.'

'It's OK. Don't worry. I just can't…'

'You fancy him, don't you?' His voice was barely a whisper.

'No. No, I don't.'

I pulled myself up, trying not to laugh. My head was slightly clearer now, and my stomach was no longer rolling inside of me. The fresh air was clearly helping. 'I think I might go for a walk,' I told him. 'It'll make me feel better.'

'Do you want me to come with you?'

'No, stay here.' I smiled stiffly. 'Try and encourage these people to leave. I won't be long.'

Dec nodded. 'OK, but be careful.'

I told him I would be. The truth was I wasn't planning to go far. I moved towards the back gate, already tasting the sea on my lips.

'Lottie,' Dec called suddenly. I turned back. He was standing facing me, looking serious, his face creased in concern. 'You'll never stop them being together. Eventually it will happen.'

I nodded in reply but said nothing back. There seemed little point.

Dec thought he knew us all so well, but really Dec knew nothing at all.

I wandered down to the beach, knowing they would still be there as it wasn't far from the flat. The breeze was cool by now and it whipped at my face and body. I folded my arms across myself as I picked my way down the worn track that led to the waterfront. I don't really know what I was planning to do. Confront them both perhaps? Tell them they were wasting their time with each other, that all they would do is hurt and upset each other. They were better as friends, surely anyone could see that?

We should all just stay as friends – forever.

I crossed the road opposite the beach. It was empty of course. At this time of night, even drunken revellers had moved away. I stood for a moment just taking in the sight of the crashing waves, breathing in the salty air. The best part of living here had been this place – it was so refreshing, so pure. It helped to clear my mind when it felt at its most cluttered. In a stupid way, standing here in the darkness, I almost felt like anything was possible – like I was at the end of the world, waiting for my life to start.

I heard the noise. A slight giggle, a movement on the shingle.

Walking onto the beach itself, the sharp stones dug in where the soles of my shoes were too thin and flimsy. It was all I could do not to yell out in pain. Instead, I bit my lip, pressing forward – trying to work out where the sound was coming from.

I saw them straight away. They were against the groynes, or at least Sara was. She was pressed up against the wood and Jay was on top of her.

They were kissing hungrily.

Transfixed, I stilled for a moment, weird thoughts flashing through my mind, like: Wasn't Sara feeling the sharp rocks in her legs and bum as Jay pressed on top of her? Didn't they care that they were out in public? For a stupid moment, I thought they were just messing around, but then I heard Sara's groan. I watched as Jay thrust against her in both a primal and tender move.

Something exploded inside of me. It felt both terrifying and crushingly sad.

I quickly moved away, scared to make noise but also dimly aware that the two of them were so wrapped up in each other they would never have noticed me anyway. I was invisible again.

Back in the flat I pushed past Dec as he tried to talk to me, running into my bedroom.

Alone, all I wanted to do was scream. My body was hot and stiff, my stomach swirled with sickness and emotion. Every time I closed my eyes, I pictured the two of them shagging in the sand. That was it now. They would be a couple. They would fall in love.

And I would be alone again.

I thought of Dec, downstairs, still trying to clean up, still trying to make things better. I knew he was a good friend and possibly he fancied me, but he wasn't enough. And even if I could persuade myself to like him, he would be leaving to go to America in a few months.

He would still end up leaving me.

This room was still so new, so fresh – I'd barely bothered to decorate it. It was cold, unloved and plain.

We had much in common.

I walked over to my latest Jar of Joy, sitting smug on my windowsill. So many times I'd reached inside, drawing out memories to make me feel better. The one I had drawn out this morning still lay folded beside it. I knew the words off by heart.

Remember when you moved here, your first day of sixth form.

Remember how you felt when you first met
Sara. How she scared and intrigued you.
Remember when you first became friends.

I picked up the message and tore it up into tiny, tiny pieces and then dropped them around my feet as if they were flecks of ash from a fire.

I wished I'd never met them.

Day Ten

Sara

Today is my last day on shift before I have a week of annual leave, and I am determined not to be late. I booked this time originally thinking that I might take a last-minute break somewhere nice, but with all the stuff going on with Lottie I never managed to organise anything. To be honest, it's probably a good thing. A week to sort out my head, clear up my flat and make some decisions about my future is what I need.

I am already regretting my decision to meet up with Jay tonight.

The radio blasts out Nineties feel-good tunes mixed in with a few well-known ballads, and this immediately lifts my mood. As I dry and style my hair, I picture me and Lottie getting ready together. We always used to play music and sing along. Lottie adored all of the naff love songs and would learn each line off by heart, while I preferred rock and alternative stuff, something with an edge, but I started to soften to Lottie's music the more I spent time with her. It was always so heartfelt and emotional and often quite sad. Sometimes I'd look at Lottie's serious face while she was listening and wonder what she was thinking. If I ever asked her if she was OK, she would always tell me she was fine or laugh off any worries.

The Lottie I knew had been bright, breezy and fun-loving, which sometimes used to annoy me a bit, like she was almost a bit too free and easy. It was her relaxed attitude to things that had almost broken us, after all. Even thinking about how things had worked out and how she had ended up with Jay makes me feel a cool rage again.

Lottie was meant to be one of my best friends, but did I ever really know her at all?

I read the next Jar of Joy message before I leave for work. It's become a bit of a routine now, like brushing my teeth, and I'm finding that I'm not resisting it as much.

This message is short and sweet, but it immediately brings back a flood of memories:

> *Go to Monroe's.*
> *Pick something nice. Wear it the next time you go out.*
> *Remember how good we always felt when we went there, dressing up?*

I nod to myself. 'Ok, Lots, this is something I can do.'

I can sense Lottie next to me, her smile an infectious light. '*I knew you'd like this one, Sara. Dressing up is the best fun after all.*'

Monroe's the clothes shop is just a few streets away from the care home, and I admit it'll be nice to go in and treat myself to something new after work. I haven't done anything like that in ages. The thought immediately makes me smile.

It's just a shame that the next time I'm going out is tonight with Jay. It's only a drink at The Crown, but I still want to look nice. I squint at the jar and smile wryly.

'Jesus, babe. It's almost like you knew.'

I swear I hear her giggle drifting in the air around me.

–

'You're meeting your ex tonight?' Jess tugs at the covers of the bed we are making together and gives me an odd look. 'Is this a wise decision?'

'It's just a drink. Nothing more. We have lots to catch up on.'

'But this is the same ex that ended up with Lottie, the friend that died?'

'Yeah.' I sigh. 'It was messy. He broke my heart when we were younger. Then we had this one amazing night together at Lottie's party and I really thought it had changed things between us, but...'

'He fucked it up?'

'Yeah. He fucked it up. And then I went travelling and Jay and Lottie ended up being a couple. I guess they suited each other.'

'And you forgave them?' Jess blows out a deep breath as she strokes the covers flat. 'I'm not sure I could do that.'

'I didn't, well, not for ages, but shortly after I came back, they broke up. Jay moved away and not long after that Lottie got ill. She'd bumped into me outside my flat and I couldn't push her away when she told me about the cancer. I had to try and move on from the past.' I was trying to busy myself by bundling up the old washing so that Jess didn't notice I was getting upset. 'I found it harder to forgive Jay, though. We had known each other for so long. I'd trusted him, and I believed Lottie when she said she didn't mean for any of it to happen. She was so lonely at the time. I don't think she was thinking straight. I really don't think she set out to hurt me.'

'Ah, I see. Still pretty shitty of them.'

'Yeah, yeah, it was…'

As I take the washing down to the laundry room, my memories begin to stir again. I've been holding so much back because it was too painful or stressful to relive, but at this point it's difficult to stop the memories spilling over into my reality.

I remember the morning I was with Lottie, just a few weeks after that night on the beach. I had gone away for a bit to see my nan to give me and Jay some space; it had all been getting so intense after that night we had together. Jay's dad was in hospital, so I knew his head was all over the place. We had made plans for the future, they were exciting and a bit scary – Jay had asked me to decide what I'd wanted to do, to be sure.

And I had made my choice. I knew what I wanted. I had just needed to know if Jay felt the same way.

Being with Nan had helped. She wasn't a bit like Mum. She didn't believe in holding grudges or blaming others for other people's bad behaviour. She took my hands in hers and told me to follow my heart.

'This life is too short to be hesitant,' she had said. 'If love lands in your lap, keep hold of it. It's a precious thing. Don't let other people steal it from you. Sometimes, others can be jealous of true love when they haven't experienced it themselves.'

I knew she had been talking about Mum here and that made me sad. I didn't know much about my dad, only that he hadn't treated my mum that well in the time he had been alive, and then she had met Jay's dad when I was a baby, someone who she fell quickly in love with – but who broke her heart in two all over again.

It was no wonder she had been scared for me, but Nan was right, I couldn't live my life caged in a barrier of fears. Nan died shortly after I'd visited her after a short illness, but I never forgot the special time I'd had with her.

It was because of her I'd been finally ready to embrace my new life with Jay. I went back to mine and Lottie's flat first. I wanted to tell Lottie my plans and I hoped that she would be excited for me. However, as soon I saw her, I knew something was wrong.

I load the washing machine now, trying desperately to fight the sudden tidal wave of tears that hit me. I grip the machine and take a shaky breath. This was years ago. Why does it still affect me so much now? I'm surprised how clearly I can still see Lottie's face – how pale her skin was, how scared her eyes looked, how her hair was messed up, how her gaze shifted to the left as she couldn't quite look at me. How, when I moved nearer, I could smell a familiar scent on her, and my stomach bottomed out and my legs began to shake. Lottie caught my gaze again and I could see the sorrow and guilt oozing out of her like an open wound.

And then I heard Jay's voice behind her. Coming from her bedroom door.

The realisation dawned on me – hard and fast, like blows to my stomach.

'Have you two…' I couldn't even finish the sentence.

People talk about the world spinning but I'd never believed it could happen before, until mine did. I pictured Jay sprawled out in her expensive sheets – smug and satisfied. I'd only been gone a few weeks. I'd asked him to wait for me and he couldn't even do that. My head was fuzzy and unfocused. Lottie was quietly sobbing and all I wanted to do was pick her up and shake her.

'How could you?' I'd hissed. 'How could you do this? I thought you were my friend.'

'I am… Sara, I am. This was a mistake. We were both drunk. We didn't mean—'

'No.' I'd stepped away, disgust rising like bile in my throat. 'You're no friend of mine. You are nothing.'

I slam the washing machine close and then lean against it, noticing how my heart is hammering fast against the metal. A part of me died that day. A part of my trust, my hope, my love.

I don't know if I can ever get it back.

–

The rest of my shift drags and even my conversations with Derek do little to lift my mood. He is brighter today, and as he talks about his wife and their trips to Europe in their early marriage and how much they were in love, I'm glad that he's feeling better.

'We had it tough at the beginning,' he says, as I wheel him into the day room, which this afternoon is flooded with light. 'But I think in the end it made us stronger, if that makes sense.'

'It does,' I nod. 'And that was all because your wife was German?'

'My parents were Polish and had fled the war early. We lost so many to the war and I understand why they held the views they did, but that didn't make it right. Me and Alice were a different generation and Alice's family had faced their own pain and suffering. What good did it do to keep looking back at the mistakes before and clinging onto them? Life is for living. For moving forward and grasping opportunities when they come to you.'

I smile at this, as it reminds me so much of the words my nan said to me years ago about Jay. I miss her so much. I know she would want to help me right now. She always knew the right things to say.

'You ran away together though, didn't you? You didn't listen to your families. That was brave.'

Derek chuckled. 'Brave or stupid, one of the two. We were young and in love, so it seemed a simple decision at the time. Can you move me by the window, Sara? Where the jigsaw puzzles are? I fancy challenging my brain today.'

I do as I'm told and wheel Derek next to Esme, who is already busy slotting together the outer frame. She beams as we approach.

'Oh good, some help! I'm useless with this.'

'I've always been a dab hand when it comes to a puzzle, now let's see if you have all the edges sorted out.'

I stand back and watch the pair of them for a moment. They are so easy in each other's company. All around us is the gentle chatter of conversation; Sharon has put on the radio in the background and the room feels relaxed and calm. I want to curl up in a nearby chair and have a quick nap.

'You look dreamy,' Esme says, breaking my thoughts.

'She has a holiday coming up,' Derek fake grumbles, shaking his head. 'She is daring to leave us and do nice things outside of here.'

'What, like clean my flat?' I joke.

'No,' he says. 'You can get on with that Jar of Joy of yours. I want to hear about all the other things your crazy friend has made you do.'

'I will.' I smile.

Esme is still staring at me. 'You look unsure? Is this Jar of Joy not a good thing?'

'It's a lovely thing,' I tell her. 'But it's making me remember things that I think perhaps I'd rather forget. I'm not sure it is bringing me much joy at the moment...'

Derek taps my arm. 'Perhaps you can't see the joy yet, but it's there somewhere, waiting for you. Sometimes we have to confront the past before we can truly move on.'

–

Breathing deep, I stand outside Monroe's for a moment or two before I walk in. The shop has surprisingly survived difficult times when a lot of bigger retail outlets around here have closed down or moved on. People living here are quite loyal to the shop, though; it has been in the same family since the Seventies and at one time had been featured in glossy magazines as one of the best boutiques to shop in. I imagine back when it opened it would have looked fresh and modern with its double-fronted windows, high ceilings and brightly painted walls. Now, it looks a little tired and forgotten. The Monroe's name which was etched in black over the glass has begun to wear off a little, and now looks like it has been applied with a mascara wand. The outside used to be white when Lottie and I shopped here as teens, but at some point it was repainted pink. I'm not sure it looks any better, but that's probably only because of my own preferences.

It was Lottie who first dragged me here. I was never really that bothered about fashion or shops, I never really had the money to worry about it anyway. Most of my stuff was bought from the cool markets in Brighton, or were presents from my mum when she'd worked extra shifts. I lived in baggy jeans, oversized T-shirts and holey jumpers. The grunge scene might have passed, but I still fully embraced it. Lottie, on the other hand, wore decent gear. Her jeans were designer, her tops were minimal but beautifully cut and most of her clothes were unique and expensive. Lottie loved Monroe's because a) it was a tribute to her favourite actress and b) it was a proper, original boutique that made her feel at home. I wasn't at all comfortable being dragged in here. I remember how I'd peered through the window and felt my entire body lock up with resistance. I was sure the staff here would judge me. They wouldn't want a council estate kid like me touching their lovely clothes, yet still, I allowed Lottie to tug me in.

I push the door and walk in now; the bell still jingles softly which makes me smile. I scan the space, and it's much as I remember. Not much has changed over the years; the rails still dominate the sides of the shop, filled with expensive-looking vintage clothes. Towards the back I can see a new second-hand section that never used to be there, next to a pretty array of shoes and handbags. The seating is still pink, soft and plush and scattered in front of the two small changing rooms. Right at the back is the cash desk and above that is the huge Marilyn Monroe print that Lottie loved so much and always made me feel so welcomed somehow. There is something about that bright, welcoming smile that tells me everything is going to be OK.

Apart from one other woman, who is looking at the shoes, I'm alone in the shop. I breathe in the floral, sweet smell and memories rush at me all at once.

I see me and Lottie back here all those years ago, picking outfits for her party, our fingers moving through the rails as we inspected each dress. My heart had plunged when I saw the price tags, but Lottie told me not to stress out. She tried on dress after dress, each one looking beautiful on her tiny, petite body, before she settled on a slinky top that brought out the colour of her eyes and made her blonde hair shimmer.

'You look amazing,' I told her, and she'd grinned.

And then Lottie told me to pick out a dress. 'This is something I want to do for you,' she said. 'I want you to feel beautiful too.'

Something I had never truly felt before.

Five Years Before

Lottie

It was late morning, almost afternoon, by the time I woke the next day, sore and miserable and still clothed in my dress from the night before. My mouth was dry and tasted rancid and, after staggering to the bathroom, I went downstairs to get a drink, dreading what I might find. But the flat looked in a reasonable state. On the kitchen counter was a note from Dec – telling me he'd done all he could, and he hoped I was OK.

Guilt rose inside me; he was such a nice guy, I should have treated him better.

I poured myself a water and guzzled it down, trying to fix the throbbing in my head. I thought again of Jay and Sara on the beach and felt sick. I wish I hadn't gone down there; sometimes it's better not to see these things.

I was about to go off for a well-needed shower when I heard a movement behind me.

It was Sara. She looked awful.

'Lottie,' she said quietly. 'I need your help.'

We sat down in the kitchen. I tried to ignore my pounding headache and impending sense of doom. This was just like being a kid again when Mum would tell me about another one of her hobbies or outings, something new and exciting that she would cast me aside for. I was never the centre of anyone's life.

'I'm sorry we left the party yesterday,' Sara said.

I noticed how she said 'we' but tried not to fixate on it, instead busying myself pouring us both a fresh orange juice. I figured we could both use the vitamins. Sara wasn't exactly glowing either, in fact she looked like shit – her skin was dull, and her eyes lacked their usual sparkle. She didn't look like someone who had just shagged the guy she fancied on the beach.

'I felt so rough and as you know me and Jay ended up going for a walk...' Her voice trailed off as she accepted my drink. She took a sip and flinched slightly. 'Things have got kind of complicated.'

'Oh yeah?' I tried to act dumb.

'Yeah.' Her cheeks began to colour a little. 'We were talking and messing around a bit and then before I knew it, well, we kind of ended up having sex.'

She wasn't talking like this was the happiest event in her life. I sipped my own drink, trying not to recoil at the sourness. My stomach rolled a little, like a giant marble sat unstable inside of me.

'That's good, isn't it?' I probed. 'It's what you wanted?'

'Yeah, I guess. I mean – yes, it's what I wanted, but we were both drunk. I'm not sure if this is what Jay would want, not really. And it complicates things. We always agreed to be just friends and now things are... messy.'

She crinkled her nose at this and pushed aside her drink. 'I need to talk to him, Lottie, like really talk to him, but after we... well, finished, we started to walk back here. It was a bit awkward, you know – I don't know if either of us knew what to say. And then Dec ran out of the flat. He said Jay's mum had been trying to get hold of him – but of course I'd dropped his bloody phone in the paddling pool. In desperation she had called Dec. His dad was in hospital, he's really sick apparently. So Jay just – he just took off…'

'Oh shit, poor Jay…' I breathed out.

Sara nodded. 'Obviously I can't go and see him now, it wouldn't be right. His family need him, and they wouldn't want me there, I'd be the last person they'd want around. I could wait, I know – but I just want to tell him, you know? I want him to know that I am interested in taking things further, if he does. I understand if he just wants to be friends, but I need to know one way or another. This going back and forth is driving me mad.'

'He might not be in the right headspace now,' I reasoned.

'I know. I get that…' She rubbed at her head. 'Maybe it's selfish of me, but I'm going up to my nan's for a couple of weeks so I'm not going to be around. She needs some help after her hip operation. To be honest, I need the space. I just wish there was a way I could tell him how I really feel. If he had his phone, I could just message him or something, but that's not an option and I don't want to talk to Dec about it. He'd just mess it up.'

'I see…' I considered this for a moment or two. 'Well, maybe you need to take the more old-fashioned approach?'

'What do you mean?'

'Well, Mum still has the love letters stored in her bedroom that Dad used to send her. They are a bit grim to be honest, I read a few once and regretted it immediately. Those two were a right dirty pair.' I shuddered at the memory. 'But if you can't text or talk to Jay – surely a letter would make sense? You could tell him how you feel, lay it on the line. Ask him to contact you or something if he's really interested in being more serious?'

Sara seemed to brighten. 'That does seem a cute idea, but I couldn't risk delivering it to his place. If his mum saw me with it, she'd probably tear it to pieces.'

I forced a smile. 'Well, that's where I can come in. I've always fancied myself as a bit of a cupid.'

I found Sara a pretty notepad from my room, gave her a pen and left her in the kitchen writing while I had a hot shower. I was amazed at how much better I was feeling. The headache had bled away, and my stomach had settled. I sung softly under my breath, rubbing cream into my body and inhaling the sweet scent.

I was doing a good thing here. In the long run, I was helping both Sara and Jay. Everybody could see that they would be a mess of a couple, and I would only end up picking up the pieces later on.

It was so much better to intervene early on, to help them both move on. I was being the good person here.

Sara handed me the folded note. There was no envelope, just two simple pieces of paper.

She smiled faintly. 'I did what you suggested. I told him how I felt and asked him to call me while I was away if he was interested in something more. If he's not, I've given him the easy way out. He doesn't contact me, and we just remain friends.'

'At least you'll know, one way or another,' I told her. 'Don't worry, I'll make sure he gets it. What time are you going to your nan's?'

'Soon,' she replied. 'I don't want to stick around. Nan is struggling at the moment and I want to spend some precious time with her, you know?'

'I know,' I said, even though I didn't really. Dad's parents died long before I was born and Mum's lived in a villa in Spain. They called whenever they remembered and sent me money for my birthday, but it wasn't the same. I never really had a family of my own.

Holding Sara's letter tightly in my hand, I could almost feel the hope burning through it. Sara gave me one last tight smile before leaving to get her stuff ready.

'I know I'm probably wasting my time,' she said. 'Jay will probably just want to stay friends and that's fine, I just don't want him to make a fool of me. That's fair enough, isn't it? I just don't want him to treat me like a mug.'

'I'm sure he won't, Sara.'

'Thanks, Lottie,' she said softly. 'I know I wasn't always good to you, especially when you first joined our school, but I want you to know how much you mean to me.'

She gave me a tight little hug. I could still smell Jay's scent on her clothes. I pulled back and forced a grin.

'It's not a problem,' I said sweetly. 'It's what I'm here for.'

I watched and waited as she closed the bedroom door behind her and then drew a breath.

–

It didn't take me long to forge the letter. After all, I was well skilled in it after years of forging Mum's writing to get out of PE or miss a day of school when I was younger. Sara's loopy, almost childish handwriting was easy to copy. I tried not to cringe as I read her words, telling Jay how much he meant to her and how she had now realised that she wanted to be his girlfriend. How sad she was to be going away, but how she hoped it would give them the chance to realise what they both wanted and maybe, just maybe, they could give their relationship a chance.

"'If you don't want to be with me I understand, I do,'" I read aloud, hearing the cruelness of my tone but not able to stop it. "'I just need to know where I stand. I'll be at my nan's. I've put my number on the bottom of this letter in case you can't remember it. If you want to give things a go, call me – but if you don't, leave it. Your silence will tell me all I need to know.'"

It was sweet, it really was, and I knew it would have the desired effect on Jay. He would fall for the words, he would call Sara and they would delude themselves in their happy ever after for a little longer, meanwhile ignoring the obvious flaws. Would Jay just continue to let Sara treat him like rubbish? Would the pair of them shut everyone out? They would be a damaged couple. Everyone knew it – even they did, deep down – I was sure of it.

As I began to write, I pushed back the guilt. I was doing the right thing here. I was a daughter of divorce; I'd seen the end result of toxic love. An intervention was needed.

I'm going away for a bit because I'm confused and a little upset by everything. We shouldn't have done what we did last night. Sex was a step too far and I really regret it now. We were both drunk and emotional and it's not what I wanted. We know how our parents would react and I'm not sure that's the kind of stress I need. We should just be friends, Jay, but I'm not even sure we can be that now. Call me if you want to talk it through, but I understand if it's a bit heavy for you. If not, let's just carry on as before when I get back. I don't want to make a big fuss of this. I'd rather just forget it ever happened.

There. It was done. I folded the pages just as Sara had and put Sara's copy into my diary. I don't know why I didn't just throw it away, but something told me that was a step too far. Her words didn't deserve to be destroyed, just hidden, and one day, hopefully, she would thank me for this. I pictured us as older women; Sara would be married to someone else, have children of her own and Jay would be a distant memory. Maybe Jay would be with someone else – someone who could love and look after him.

Maybe one day, Jay could be with me.

The idea had only just spilled into my mind, a taunting and intriguing thought. After all, if I was with Jay I would be totally in control. I could stop this nonsense between them forever. And I would never, ever be left out again.

Maybe I was the solution?

–

Even though it was a baking hot afternoon and quite a trek, I decided to walk to Jay's. I needed the air. I just hoped that Jay wouldn't suspect anything and that my writing would be convincing enough.

I'd only been to Jay's flat once before; he was still living with his mum, a couple of blocks away from Sara's mum's place, and usually didn't have friends over because his mum got stressed out about it. His flat was on the third floor. I knocked on the painted white door and stood back nervously, wondering if his mum might answer. Sara had always made her out to be quite a cow and I wasn't sure she would be that pleased to see me either.

Thankfully it was Jay who answered. He looked flustered and a little confused to see me. I noticed that his hair was damp, like he had just stepped out of the shower. I felt myself flush a little. He really was quite cute.

'Lottie? What are you doing here?'

I handed him the letter, telling him that Sara had gone to see her nan and had asked me to bring it to him, because she couldn't 'face him herself'. I tried to ignore the pained expression in his eyes. He didn't open it in front of me.

'She doesn't want to be with me, does she?' he said flatly, fingering the pages. 'I should have guessed. I keep doing this to myself.'

'I'm sorry, Jay,' I said softly. 'I told her she needed to tell you. It's only fair.'

'It's a shame she couldn't tell me face to face. A letter?' He scoffed. 'What are we? Five?'

'To be fair, your phone is broken, and she was scared of bumping into your mum. She wanted you to know before she went away.'

'That's big of her.'

'I'm sorry,' I said again.

He swiped his hand across his face, a wry grin settled. 'It's all right. I mean, I thought after last night... but I guess I got the signs wrong again. I keep doing that.'

'She's been blowing hot and cold, Jay. It isn't fair on you.'

Jay shrugged. 'It's OK. At least I know now.' He shoved the letter in his pocket. 'I would invite you in, Lottie, but I'm getting ready to see my dad...'

'How is he?'

'Better. He'll need a stent in his heart, but apparently after that he should be much better.' Jay nodded, almost as if he was convincing himself. 'It's probably best that Sara said this, you know – I have lots on my plate at the moment. I don't need more complications, more stress.'

'Yeah, I get that.' I paused. 'But Jay, I'm here for you – you know? If you need a friend, or whatever.'

'Thanks, Lottie.' His smile was warmer now. 'I appreciate that.'

I watched as his hand subconsciously touched his pocket again and then he nodded and closed the door.

–

Sara rang me constantly while she was away, asking me how Jay was. She was upset that he hadn't contacted her but assumed that he had made his decision.

'I think he's got too much going on,' I soothed. 'What with his dad's operation and thinking about his job. He's still in line for that promotion apparently. Maybe it's not the right time for him to be in anything heavy.'

'Maybe,' Sara whispered.

'You're still friends, aren't you?' I said. The silence on the other end of the phone told me all I needed to know. As I suspected, Sara couldn't see Jay as a friend now. They had stepped too far over the line and now he had hurt her. She might like to pretend that they could carry on as usual, but I could see right through that.

'Maybe I need a longer break away from him. Away from everything?' she said finally. 'Dec joked that I should go travelling. That it would be a good way to clear my head. Maybe I should look into it.'

'Travelling…?' I repeated. 'That seems a bit drastic. You don't need to run away, Sara. I'll always be here for you.'

My thoughts were hurtling around inside of me. This wasn't what I wanted. I had always been frightened of what might happen if Jay and Sara ever became a couple, but I had never considered what might happen if Sara was no longer around. How could I manage without her?

'But it wouldn't be running away. It would be getting some space…' She paused. 'Anyway, it's probably a crazy idea. I'd miss you guys too much.'

I smiled. 'And I would miss you, just like I'm missing you right now.'

And I was.

But Sara was at her nan's longer than I had expected and as a result Jay and I spent more time together. The weeks soon sped away. I went to the hospital a few times with him to visit his dad. I even met his mum a few times and she was lovely, not at all the scary monster Sara had made out. I was a shoulder for Jay to cry on. He talked about Sara a lot, he was confused and hurt – but mostly he was frustrated.

'I can't keep wasting my time on her,' he told me sadly. 'It's messing with my head.'

I just made sure I was a reassuring presence. The good friend. The hand holder. I played my role well. I knew that Jay was coming to rely on me.

'What's going on with you two?' Dec asked one evening when they were both round mine. Jay had slipped out to the loo, and it was just me and Dec in the living room. His eyes were boring into mine. 'You've been stuck to each other like glue these past few weeks. Is there something I should know?'

'Nothing at all,' I smiled. 'I just care about Jay, that's all.'

Dec's gaze wouldn't leave mine. 'I don't know what game you're playing here, Lottie, but I know somebody is going to get badly hurt. It could end up being you.'

I held his gaze. 'That's not going to happen. Dec.'

I was confident I was in control.

—

Later that evening, I sat on the floor holding an old Jar of Joy. This one was from when I first joined Jay and Sara's school.

Sometimes I needed to remember a time that was good in my old house, or a happy memory of my parents – but this was not that time. Right now, I needed to engage with something more recent.

I reached inside and pulled out a folded piece of paper, my fingers fluttering at the edges, almost wary of opening it. But it was like I knew exactly what it would say, even though I couldn't be sure, I couldn't know what message was written on there.

Tears pricked my eyes.

> *Jay sat next to me at lunch today. He was so kind, asking how I was and if he could help with anything.*
> *He really cares about me.*
> *I think he could make me really happy.*
> *Remember his smile and the way he makes you feel.*
> *I'm certain he's the one.*

My breathing was a little unsteady and tears were now streaming down my face. I'd forgotten how Jay had made me feel in those early months. How kind he had been, how sweet.

It just made everything so much harder.

Day Ten

Sara

I leave Monroe's clutching a designer top that I found on the second-hand rail. It's quite a simple, delicate black T-shirt but the cut is lovely and the material deliciously soft. I haven't treated myself for a while, so I didn't feel too guilty buying it. As I walk back towards my flat, I wonder if I have time to wash and dry it so that I can wear it for my drink with Jay. After all, I want to look nice, even if it's nothing serious. I want Jay to think that I'm in a good place, that I'm doing fine without him – all of those empowering, feminist things they tell you to believe, but are hard to do in practice when you are faced with the man that broke your heart.

'Besides,' I mutter to a bored-looking Goose, as I sweep into the flat, 'this is not a date. It's just a catch-up, that's all. It's a chance to put some things to rest once and for all.'

I put my new top in the washing machine on a fast spin and then make myself a strong coffee. While I stand in the kitchen looking down at the street below me, all I can see are couples. Some are walking along hand in hand, others are drawn closer together, almost as if they are one, and there's a deep ache inside of me. It's not that I'm in need of a boyfriend; after the situation with Jay, I packed my bags and fled the country, travelling across Greece and Italy and then spending time working in Spain. There were plenty of flings and drunken encounters along the way and lots of amazing, uncomplicated sex. I'd never felt I missed having a boyfriend. Life had been too busy and exciting for that.

And then I'd come home and picked things up with Tyler almost straight away. I had worked with him before I left and he'd always flirted with me, and at the time he was perfect for what I was looking for – an uncomplicated and very satisfying shag. I guess I convinced myself it was all I needed. It was like I was continuing my foreign adventures back here.

However, now, as I stare down at the street, at the happy, laughing couples that seem to be taunting me with me their presence, I realise something startling.

I'm lonely.

I no longer have Lottie. I no longer have Jay. Everyone else I keep at a safe distance.

Which means that I'm achingly and painfully alone.

And I don't like it.

I remember the day Jay came to see me after I'd come back from Nan's. It had been the same day that I had gone to back to mine and Lottie's flat and discovered he was in her bed. I had fled back to my mum's immediately, unable to face him.

My bags were still in mum's hall, and when I went to answer the door, I remember casting them a dark look, wondering if it was worth unpacking them at all. One thing I knew for certain was that I didn't want to be here any longer.

I wasn't surprised to see Jay at the door, in fact I'd expected it. I had loads of missed calls that I'd already ignored from him. I didn't want to see him but at the same time, I knew I had to get it out of the way, like lancing a particularly annoying boil.

Jay at least had the decency to look exhausted. His hair was uncombed and his features looked messy somehow, the shadows had spoiled his usual good looks.

'I've been trying to call you all morning,' he said quietly.

'I know. You've clearly got your phone back working then,' I'd replied coolly.

'Yeah. I got a new one today.' His voice had dipped a little. 'Yours was one of the first numbers I put in.'

'That's good of you.'

'Can I come in?' he'd asked.

'No.'

He'd sighed and leant up against the wall outside my flat. 'Sara, I need to explain—'

'What? How you slept with my best friend the minute my back was turned?'

'It wasn't like that.' He was pleading a bit now. It made my anger flare even more. I couldn't bring myself to look at him. 'Sara – we were really drunk. I've been all over the place. I didn't know what you wanted.'

I was so stunned, I'd gasped a little. 'You got my letter, didn't you? The one I wrote before I left?'

'Yeah, I got that. It made everything pretty clear. You needed time.'

'Yeah, I just needed time to get my head around everything, that's all. I just wanted to put a little bit of distance between us. Jay, I was only gone for two weeks, not two years.'

'But I thought...' He'd shook his head. 'I thought you weren't interested.'

'How could you think that? I just wanted time, that was all. Did you even read the letter properly?'

'Well, I was upset. I didn't expect you to run off like that.' Jay's cheeks were red now. 'You knew my dad was in hospital, I had other stuff to worry about. Work has been challenging, I was hoping for a promotion and then all of this happened...'

'Exactly. You didn't need me to think about. I thought I was doing the right thing. I didn't want your mum to get even more stressed out if she heard about us—' My voice had broken on the word us. 'But then you decided that there was no us. You would rather shag someone else than wait for me.'

'It wasn't like that.'

'What was it like then?' I shook my head. 'Actually, don't tell me, Jay. I don't want to know. I'm not sure I'd believe any bullshit that would come out of your mouth right now.'

'Sara, please don't be like this. We need to sort this out. I don't want you to be hating me for one stupid mistake.'

But all I could feel was hatred, rising up like hot molten lava in my veins. It was mixed with disappointment, which was a far more difficult feeling to ignore. It felt as though my heart was being dragged slowly out of my body.

'I'm leaving.'

My words had surprised him. He looked at me, blinking slowly like he was having to really compute what I had just said.

'What do you mean you're leaving? We need to talk about this. We need to—'

'No.' My voice was loud, interrupting him. 'That won't be happening now. I can't drag myself through this again.

It's like I'm back there at eighteen crying over a stupid kiss.'

Jay had rubbed his eyes. 'But Sara, that was different. You—'

'No.' I was blunt. 'I'm done talking now.'

I didn't bother to tell him how I'd spent the day online, looking at options, how I'd decided that the money my nan had given me would be best used for travelling, for getting away from this place – him – for a while. I knew that I couldn't be with him now. I needed space. I wanted to take myself away from him, Lottie and their shitty little lies.

'You don't have to do this,' Jay had whispered. 'It's so drastic. If we just talked this through…'

'I'm done with talking through,' I'd repeated, my words ice cold now. 'I'm done with thinking and trying to work out if we can be together. It's clear we can't be, Jay, not in any capacity. Our families are right – we will just end up hurting each other.'

'And you're not willing to even talk about this?' he'd whispered.

'No,' I said coldly. And then, just so I could put an end to this conversation, I added the killer blow. 'I regret it all anyway. I never should have slept with you. It was a mistake, all of it. I wasn't thinking straight.'

I saw his face change, something harden within him. 'Yeah – maybe it's for the best. I don't think you're the type who'll ever be ready to settle down. You're too scared, Sara. Too scared of getting hurt, of showing your vulnerable side. It's so much easier to build an ice wall around you, isn't it? The only problem with ice walls is they eventually melt and then you're left miserable, cold and alone.'

I tried not to flinch, but that had stung. It really had.

'Bye, Jay. Go back to your lovely architect job. Go back to Lottie. Leave me alone.'

And I'd closed the door on him.

-

I tip my head back now, turning away from the couples down on the street. What on earth am I doing meeting up with him now? Isn't this the biggest mistake ever?

And yet, still I go.

The pub, The Crown, is an old teenage favourite of ours. A few years ago, the landlord was particularly slack on ID and a load of us used to get served underage. That landlord has long gone (probably fired) but I have nice memories of coming here as a young girl and feeling like a proper grown-up nursing my one vodka and lemonade all evening.

Jay is waiting outside for me. He walks towards me, smiling shyly. He looks good. It's clear he's worked out in the years since I last saw him. His muscles fill his tight white T-shirt in a shapely, not over-the-top, way. He has a tan, which makes his blue eyes stand out more.

Why does he have to look so cute? Surely it would be easier to hate him if he looked like a scruffy, smelly mess.

'Hey.' He stops in front of me, arms falling awkwardly at his side as if he's unsure whether to hug me, or even touch me.

'Hey,' I say back.

We stand like that for a few seconds and it's so weird. It's not us. We've always been so easy with each other, but I guess so much has changed since we were both eighteen. I'd only seen him a handful of times since I got back –

one of them being Lottie's funeral, and just thinking of that stings.

'Shall we go in?' He gestures towards the door and then walks behind me, holding it open so I can go in. As I pass him, I breathe in his familiar smell. It hasn't changed at all. It makes me want to bury my head in his chest and breathe him in further. 'You still drink vodka?' he asks.

I nod with a wry smile. 'Yeah, some things never change.'

'Grab a seat and I'll bring the drinks over.'

The pub is quiet. I scan the room trying to decide where I should sit us, settling on a small table by the unlit fire, away from the pool table and jukebox, but not hidden in a snug, cosy corner.

I sit down and try to steady my breathing. I don't know why I'm making such a big deal of this. It's just a drink, nothing more, and hopefully I can finally put things to rest with Jay.

He brings the drinks over and sits opposite me. I can tell he's nervous. His hands keep touching his pint glass, running his well-bitten fingernails over the condensation on the outside. He can't keep eye contact either. He keeps looking down, towards the table.

'I'm glad you came,' he says finally. 'I worried that you might not show up.'

'I wouldn't stand you up. That's not something I would do.'

'No, I hoped not.' He coughs. 'I wanted to talk to you at the funeral, but I realise now that wasn't the best time or place. I'm sorry I tried. You were upset. We both were.'

I shifted uneasily on the chair. 'It was the worst day ever, Jay. I don't even know how I got through it.'

'I'm glad you were friends with Lottie again, though. I wasn't sure, after...' His eyes finally catch mine and it hurts to look in them. To see all of the regret, pain and sorrow reflected back. I find that I am quickly looking away again and take a swig of my drink, any excuse not to feel that flare of pain.

'I met up with her properly after she got her diagnosis. It changes things, doesn't it? I realised life was too short to be angry with her about what happened with you.'

Jay nods. 'I was so upset to hear about her getting sick, Sara, truly. I didn't know. She must have got the symptoms not long after we split up – but she never told me, I swear. If I'd known, I would have come back to see her. I would've tried to help. I don't want you to think I deserted her.'

'I know you didn't. Lottie told me.'

I think back to the awkward meet up with Lottie in the park. I'd bumped into her initially just outside mine and Lottie had insisted that we needed to talk properly, there had been something in her eyes that told me it was serious. I had been avoiding the pair of them after finding out they were a couple when I came back from travelling, but now guilt bled into me as I realised how childish I had been. Just being with Lottie again made me realise how much I missed her. We had walked and talked for ages. Lottie had told me a bit about the cancer and how scared she had been. I remember how I'd taken her hand in mine and squeezed it, no longer bothered about all of the anger from before. It seemed so irrelevant and unimportant. Lottie had looked so small and vulnerable, her eyes full of fear.

She told me that Jay and her had split up just a few months after I'd got back from Spain. Jay had secured a job in Newcastle and wanted to move there, while Lottie loved her life in Brighton too much and wasn't prepared to go with him.

'The cracks were showing anyway,' she'd told me quietly. 'I don't think we were really that strong. It was just a relationship that kept going for whatever reason. I knew he didn't love me. I'm not even sure how I felt about him.'

She said she started feeling sick a few months after that. Her periods weren't right, she had bloating and sickness, and when she finally had her first smear at the doctors that was when they discovered the abnormal cells.

'Apparently its quite unusual for someone so young,' she'd said. 'Trust me to be different.' Her sharp laugh felt hollow as I pulled her into a hug. 'What if this turns out to be a bad thing, Sara?' she had whispered in my chest. 'I've still got so much to do. I don't want to live my life with regrets.'

'You won't, Lottie, you won't,' I had soothed. 'Everything is going to fine, I promise.' A promise given so liberally and yet at the time I had believed it with all my heart.

'And we are friends again now, aren't we?' she whispered.

'Yes, of course. I'm here for you – whatever you need.'

My friend was forgiven, we were strong again. Everything was going to be OK.

How wrong could I have been?

'I wish things could've been different,' Jay says softly, now. 'I messed so much up.'

'I guess we all have regrets.' I shrug. 'What did we really know?'

'Fuck all.'

We both snigger. Jay's already drunk his pint. He gestures to me for another drink, and I nod. While he walks to the bar, my eyes scan his body – still so slim and athletic, and with that slight bounce to his step that we used to tease him about. I smile.

He comes back and this time draws his chair nearer to me. The pub is a little busier now, so I guess I don't mind. At least I can hear him better.

'I was thinking about how we used to be as kids,' he says, leaning towards me. 'We shared everything didn't we? Our secrets, our fears – the lot.'

'I guess we had a lot in common,' I reply. 'Do you think we were rebelling a bit, too? We knew we shouldn't be together, so it made us want it more.'

'No, I don't think that at all,' he says firmly. 'It drove me nuts how our parents were, but it didn't change how I felt about you. There was always something—' He stops and shakes his head, takes another mouthful of his pint.

'What?' I urge, curious now.

'I dunno – I just felt like there was something special between us, a bond. It was like I always knew you.'

I don't answer, but I do know what he means. I think this is why what he did hurt so much more. I want to press him on that a bit more. Part of me wants to scream in his face: 'If we had such a bond, why did you break it so easily?' but I manage to resist. I don't want to drag it all up again, not now. It feels wrong now that Lottie is no longer here. Like a betrayal.

'I've never stopped thinking about you,' he says quietly. 'It's like you're always in my head.'

'And that's a good thing?'

He smiles. 'I think so.'

I remember what Lottie said to me. 'Did you ever love her? Lottie?'

His expression suddenly changes. All the joy seems to drain away, and his eyes suddenly become sad.

'I wanted to,' he says finally. 'I really wanted to, Sara, but I couldn't.' He doesn't speak for a moment or two, but then he adds the final words. 'She wasn't you.'

The music is getting louder in here and I find myself wanting to change the subject. I don't want the focus to be on me and I'm tired of feeling angry about him and Lottie. The vodka also helps relax me.

I ask Jay about his job as an architect, I ask him about his mum (he rolls his eyes, 'same old, same old'), about his dad (who left his mum not long after he started university and has a new girlfriend apparently, who is very young and *very* annoying) and about Dec (still talks to him, wishes he lived closer).

'In only a few years so much has changed, but lots hasn't, if you know what I mean,' he says with a sigh. 'I thought moving away would help, but it doesn't take you away from your family, does it? They're still as fucked up as they will always be. And then I come back, expecting things to be the same and—'

'Everything has shifted,' I finish for him. 'Except me. I'm still here.'

'Yeah – and dating someone else.'

I raise an eyebrow. 'Yeah, kind of. I'm surprised you know.'

'My mum told me,' he says. I can see he's trying to act casually but there's something about his tone that is more serious. 'She said she's seen the two of you around and then Dec confirmed it. Is it that Tyler guy – the one you used to work with when you were waitressing?'

'Yeah, it's the same guy. It's been going OK.' I refuse to think of Tyler's unanswered texts still sitting in my phone. Jay looks away briefly, and I try to ignore how that makes me feel.

'Dec said you seemed quite busy with him.' Jay smiles. 'You always said he was a playboy.'

I sip my drink. Interesting. I never mentioned Tyler to Dec much, I only wanted to prove that I'd moved on. Dec loved to tell me that I was scared of commitment, or some such bullshit.

'Ah, Dec.' I nod. 'I see I'm still the subject of great interest around here. The small-town mentality never goes does it? Even when our friends move to the other side of the world.'

'We just care about you, that's all,' Jay says carefully. 'Mum says she knows Tyler. He works at her mate's place. He's still a bit of a lad apparently.'

'A lad?' I laugh. 'Have you heard yourself, you sound like an old woman.'

'You know what I mean. He's not the type that wants to settle down. He's a player.'

This is quite ironic seeing as I'm due to be talking to Tyler about our relationship and his sudden need for more commitment. Who is the player here? Have I outplayed him?

'I think we've all got Tyler wrong,' I tell him. 'He's actually really sweet.'

'Oh, OK.' Jay nods sadly. 'Well, that's fine then, as long as you're happy. I didn't want to see you getting hurt, that's all.'

My fingers stroke my glass. I'm tempted to ask Jay what business it is of his any more, but I sense the shift in mood.

Jay looks a bit shaky and it's making me uncomfortable. I didn't want this night to be too intense.

'Fuck this,' I say finally, pushing my chair back. 'This is too full on. The pool table is free, shall we have a game?'

He gulps down the rest of his pint and then swipes at his mouth. 'Yeah, why not. You know I'll beat you though.'

'You know nothing,' I grin. 'Lots of thing have changed around here, Jay, like you said, and one of them is that I've got so much better at pool.'

–

We drink more. A lot more. The pool games which started with the best of intentions begin to become a competitive mess. I find myself giggling chaotically as Jay tries to help me get a position on the felt, one of my legs is hitched up, my body is halfway across the table.

I take aim towards my yellow ball, hitting it wildly with the cue and burst into more fits of laughter when it spins into completely the wrong direction. Jay has to help me down. I cling to his shirt, feeling a little dizzy and silly. Next to us a couple of men are waiting to play, I wave my cue in the air enthusiastically.

'Did I beat you?'

Jay looks at the number of yellow balls still left on the table and grins. 'Shall we just call it a draw?'

'You are admitting defeat this early?'

'I just don't think the pool table can take any more abuse.'

I am still pressed up against Jay's body. I've forgotten how good that feels, how he just seems to fit me so perfectly. My arm automatically snakes around his waist, my head longs to rest on his shoulder. I breathe in the scent of him and shudder.

'I should get you home,' Jay murmurs into my ear.

I nod. 'Yeah, let's go.'

We hand our cues to the waiting men and then step outside the pub. It's surprisingly chilly and I shiver automatically. Jay pauses.

'Are you OK? If I had a jacket, I'd offer it to you.'

'I think it's just the change from the heat in the pub.' I blink, feeling my mind begin to clear a little in the cool air. 'Can you hold me again?'

'If you're sure?'

I'm not sure of anything, but I like the way it feels when Jay pulls his arm around me. We walk slowly together, and I can feel his warmth bleed into me, filling me up. My skin is buzzing. It's like his touch is electric.

'I've missed this,' he says quietly.

'What?'

'Just us. Being together.'

For so long there has been a deep ache inside of me and I've ignored it, or tried to fight it, but now I feel like it's being soothed. How can it be wrong to be with someone who makes me feel so good? Maybe I've been wrong this whole time for being angry at a one-off event that happened when we were both so young. Jay always maintained it had been a mistake. He had been stressed about his dad and in the company of the gorgeous, lonely Lottie. Maybe he had just been drunk and reckless, and maybe I too had been reckless, running away instead of facing things head on. Had I pushed him into the arms of my best friend?

But he still did it, didn't he? He still chose Lottie over me. I can't forget that.

We stop outside of my flat and I hesitate. I think of my cold, empty bed and how much I would love to have Jay next to me, his hot naked body pressed up against mine. I know how good it will be. I actually shiver and he pulls me closer to him.

His hand gently strokes my cheek, he eases a strand of hair out of my face.

'It's been a lovely evening, Sara. Seeing you again, it's just been—'

My lips are on his before he can say anything more, hot and hungry. He tastes just as I remember. His mouth parts a little and I feel the tease of his tongue working against mine. Pressing closer to him, heat builds, desire growing, my hands pinching and clawing at his shirt.

This feels so good. And yet...

I pull away. We both stare at each other for a moment. The shivers are still snaking down my spine.

'I'm sorry,' he says. 'I shouldn't have let that happen.'

'It's OK,' I say. 'Don't worry.'

I smile weakly and then walk towards my flat. I can feel his eyes burn into my back. But all I feel is a mixture of desire and fear and I'm not sure which one is winning.

Five Years Before

Lottie

It came to the point where I didn't want Sara to come back from her nan's. There – it's the truth, I've said it. With Sara away, Jay and I were getting closer. He'd come to mine a lot, mainly to talk about his dad, who was recovering well after surgery. However, Jay still had worries and it wasn't something he felt comfortable discussing in front of his mum, who was still struggling with her mental health.

'I can't even talk to Sara about him,' he told me one night when he was round mine. 'She still blames him for everything that went wrong in her family. I can't blame her, I suppose, but I don't want to upset her either.'

'Let's celebrate your promotion,' I said, handing him a glass. 'Try to forget about your worries for a night. Your dad is going to be fine now, you know that.'

He nodded and smiled shyly. He had such a cute smile. 'I'm so glad you've been here, Lottie. It's been so hard. I'm not even sure my parents will stay together after this. They were so fragile before. Now my dad is talking about moving to Newcastle to be nearer to his family and my mum won't go. I feel like everything is changing...'

'I know, I get that. It's hard.'

I moved closer to him on the sofa. We carried on drinking, one glass after the next. Jay continued to talk a bit about his family, about his complex feelings towards his dad, how he hated the fact that his parents constantly split up and got back together again, but how he thought it might be final this time. I told Jay stuff, things I hadn't told anyone before – about how lonely I'd been growing up, the bullying I'd experienced, how I knew, really, that my parents didn't want me. How, even as an adult, I felt out of place.

'Neglect happens even in affluent households,' I said quietly. 'People seem to think that if you have money, you are immune to it.'

Jay wrapped his arms around me. 'I'm so sorry you went through that. You don't deserve it.'

I don't really know how it happened, but I guess the wine helped. I think I made the first move, kissing him gently on the lips, but he responded. My entire body softened and fizzed, I pulled him towards me, pressing myself against him, feeling his heat against mine. It was exhilarating, I was alive. His hands were suddenly on me, feeling over my top, stroking and caressing. I felt a burning need pulsing between my legs. I wanted him so badly.

He pulled away. 'Lottie, I don't know about this…'

'It's OK,' I soothed. 'I understand. I just want one night, that's all. One night to forget about everything else.'

'But Sara…' I saw the pain flash in his eyes. 'You know how I feel about her? This wouldn't be right.'

'But Sara doesn't want to be with you, does she?' I said the words kindly, but I knew they were slicing into him like a blade. He flinched and I touched his arm.

'I'm not looking for anything heavy, Jay. I just want one night, that's all. Nobody else needs to know.'

'I don't know…'

'You feel lonely too, don't you? Rejection is shit.' I stroked him slowly, feeling the soft hairs on his skin. 'Why do we have to be alone tonight?'

'Lottie, I like you, I do, but not—'

I kissed him again. 'I don't care,' I muttered. 'It doesn't matter.' I pulled away, stared deep into his eyes. 'Shall we go to my bedroom?'

Jay looked sleepy but content. He nodded. 'Yeah, sure.'

I took his hand and led him with fake confidence to my room, trying to ignore the shaking in my legs and the thumping of my heart.

Later, lying in the tangled sheets, I stared up at the ceiling waiting for my breathing to calm. Jay was already curled up away from me, sleeping softly. Minutes after we finished, he'd asked if it had been OK, staring at me with worried eyes and I'd told him that yes, yes, it had. I didn't tell him that I'd noticed that he could barely look at me the entire time we were together. That he'd barely kissed me. That this moment I had dreamt of had been cold, clinical and over in minutes.

Nor did I tell him that I'd heard him whisper Sara's name at the point of climax.

I kept these things to myself as I stared at the dark ceiling and wished that I could be the person he was looking for.

It was becoming more and more clear that I could never be.

–

Jay carried on sleeping the next morning. I, on the other hand, couldn't settle, so I got up and had a shower, then went to the kitchen and tried to clean up a bit. There was a feeling of sadness hanging in the air. I realised, as I loaded the dishwasher, that there was no love or warmth between me and Jay. I constantly felt cold and ignored, even with Jay curled up under my duvet. He'd kissed me and stroked my body, he'd fucked me in my bed and I still felt invisible. I couldn't stop the tears as they began to flow.

When I heard the key in the front door, I froze at first; Sara wasn't due back until the afternoon. I thought of Jay sleeping in my bedroom and my heart hammered hard inside of me.

Sara walked through the door and I felt myself crumble. It was all I could do to keep myself together.

'Hey!' She smiled up at me. She looked so pretty that morning. Her hair was glossy and shiny and loose on her shoulders; her face was naturally made up. She looked younger somehow, but not in a negative way – just well-rested and glowing. 'I'm back. I was hoping we could talk?'

I clung to the counter, my insides twisting and turning. A part of me hadn't expected Sara back from her nan's. I thought of Jay naked in my bed and nausea rose in my throat.

'Sara, I—'

'Are you OK? You look like you've been crying? Is it your mum again?' Sara asked, concern etched on her face. 'I know said I might have to stay on with Nan longer, but I couldn't take it. I was hoping to talk to you about Jay. He didn't call me, and I wondered if he said anything to you. I wondered if—'

'He hasn't said anything.' My answer was too fast. I shook my head quickly. 'I'm sorry, Sara, I've not really seen him.'

'Oh.' Her expression fell. 'That's OK, I just thought, maybe… I dunno.' She laughed awkwardly. 'I thought maybe there was a reason he didn't contact me.'

'I don't know either,' I mumbled.

The lies were tumbling down around me. I could see the pain on Sara's face, and it was awful. I never thought the guilt would affect me this much. I couldn't meet her gaze, I felt like my entire body was on fire. What had I been thinking? Sara would ask Jay about the letter, and he'd tell her what it said. They would soon find out what I did, and everything would collapse around me.

I don't know why I thought it would work.

'I'm sorry,' I whispered. 'Sara, I'm not feeling too good and I—'

'Oh God, is that why you look so pale?' She reached across and touched my arm. 'You should go back to bed. I can talk about Jay later, there's no rush.'

'Who is it, Lottie?'

Something changed in her expression. She paled slightly, like she could smell him on me. She retracted her arm and stared at me.

'Who is it?' he asked again.

I heard his voice behind me, and my whole body stiffened. I stepped towards the doorway, trying to prevent Sara from seeing into my room, but her eyes had already widened. She took a step forward.

'Is that Jay?'

'I—'

I was going to deny it, but then what was the point? I was tired and beaten. Slowly I moved to one side, tears blinding my eyes. Jay stood behind me, dressed in just his pants and a rumpled T-shirt. His hair was a mess, and his eyes were still sleepy.

Sara looked at him, and then at me and then back at Jay again. Her eyes had been wide with pain. She demanded to know what had happened. Jay was a stammering mess, he tried to protest but I told her the truth. I wasn't going to be anyone's dirty secret. Then she hissed those words at me – how could I do this. How was I even a friend. My protests were weak.

"You are no friend," she said coldly. "You are nothing,"

I watched as she fled our flat. I knew her heart was breaking, and part of mine was too. I hadn't meant to hurt her. All I'd wanted was a bit of love – that was it. A few minutes of selfish love.

I didn't want to lose Sara.

–

Jay tried to talk to Sara later that day. He rushed to Sara's mum's flat where she had fled, to try and explain himself. I waited at home expecting everything to be revealed. I thought they would work it all out, unravel my lies – but instead they turned on each other. The letter just caused more misunderstandings, Sara told Jay that she thought it had explained everything and Jay told her that the letter had been the reason he thought she wanted time away from him. Any hope of a reconciliation ended that day.

Jay didn't come back to my flat, at least not at first and he wasn't replying to my texts.

Sara called me later.

'You're welcome to each other,' she said coldly. 'I hope you'll be very happy.'

'It wasn't like that, Sara.'

'You knew how I felt about him, Lottie.'

'I didn't mean for it to happen,' I lied. 'It was a mistake. We were both lonely and upset.'

'Spare me your pity party,' she spat. 'I've been fucked over by two people I considered friends. I'm done.'

'What now?' I whispered.

'I'm taking Dec's advice. I'm getting the hell out of here. I don't want to spend another minute in this town. I need some space.'

'Don't go. Please don't go.'

She didn't answer. I felt myself crack open. I didn't want this to happen. She was leaving me.

'How long will you be gone?' I croaked.

'I don't know, Lottie. Why do you care?'

Of course I cared. I was the reason that Sara was going, and I was going to miss her so much. I had pushed away one of the few decent people in my life.

'I'm going to miss you so much,' I whispered.

She laughed coldly. 'Do you know what, Lottie, I actually feel sorry for you. You are so desperate for love and attention, but you have no clue how to get it. Jay will never love you; you know that right? You haven't gained anything.'

She put down the phone.

The next day she called again. She was leaving that day. Her mood had changed a little. She was still cold towards me, but there was a hint of forgiveness there. She didn't know I'd forged the letter. All she knew was that Jay had betrayed her, it almost didn't matter that it was with me. Jay had hurt her the most.

Once again, I was left wondering if I really mattered to anyone. Why was I always the secondary character in other people's lives?

Day Eleven

Sara

I wake up after a poor sleep and manage to force a quick breakfast down. Goose is begging for attention as I read through my messages (one from Jay, two from Jess and one from Tyler). The message from Jay is sweet, apologetic and saying that he is worried he moved things too quickly, he hopes I'm OK and asks if he can see me again soon. I don't answer yet, but I plan to later.

Tyler's message is confirming a date a little later in a park just down the road. My heart sinks a little when I reply, knowing what I'm going to say when I meet up with him; even though I know it's the right decision, I still feel a bit sad.

Jess's message is a little more concerning.

> Hey – I probably shouldn't do this, I didn't want to worry you while you're off, but Derek has taken a turn for the worse. I thought you'd want to know. I'll keep you posted.

I try calling her back, but her phone is switched off, so I message telling her to update me as soon as possible. I consider ringing Sharon, but I know she won't tell me much – although she can be tough at times, Sharon is a great believer in people using their holidays properly. She won't want me thinking about work and worrying myself.

The thought of Derek being poorly makes my heart hurt. I struggle to focus as I get ready. I know it's part of the job, but it doesn't make it any easier. There is something about Derek that has got under my skin and the thought of him suffering upsets me.

And I can't lose someone else so soon after Lottie. I just can't.

Goose must sense my upset, because she comes over to me and I spend some time fussing over her, remembering how much Lottie loved this cat and her unusual blue eyes. It was because of Lottie that I got her in the first place; I had never particularly been a cat person.

Goose's purrs soothe me as I stroke her, almost lulling me into a meditative state. The Jar of Joy catches my eyes but I'm reluctant to go over to it, knowing that I only have a few messages left to read – just a few tiny connections left to Lottie and then they'll be gone, there will be nothing more she can say to me.

Goose mews softly beside me prompting me into action. Rustling inside the jar, my fingers touch the message that is sellotaped to the bottom – the last instruction. What on earth has Lottie got planned for me there? A stubborn part of me almost wants to tear it off and read it before I should, but I can feel the weight of Lottie's demands resting heavily on me.

'*Follow the rules, Sara,*' I hear her whisper in my ear. '*It's not that hard. It will be worth it, I promise.*'

I do as I'm told and pull out another message instead. Goose clambers on to my lap, as if she's curious to see the results too, and with her in mind I read the words out carefully. This one is the longest so far.

> *I got so much joy from these jars, from keeping my memories – but also by keeping a diary where I could explore my thoughts and feelings in more depth.*
>
> *I want this diary to be in the safest of hands and I also want you to read it – when you feel ready to do so. My mum will know where it is, so please ask her to give it to you.*
>
> *I hope she is kind to you. She is a good person really.*
>
> *My happiest times were when I could share my feelings with you, Sara. I want you to know more about me.*
>
> *xx*

I frown. This message doesn't sit comfortably with me for a number of reasons. One, it means I will have to face Erica again, which quite frankly is never an enticing prospect, and two, I really don't feel comfortable reading Lottie's diary, this is something private, something that shouldn't be shared.

However, there might be a reason she wants me to see it. Maybe it will help in some way? And it would be another connection to her, something deeper perhaps.

'It's better than bloody Erica having it,' I mutter finally. 'I wouldn't trust that woman with anything confidential.'

Goose mews again as if in agreement and I smile; there is something about this cat that is so wise and aware. I rub her neck, knowing how lucky I am to have her.

'OK, I'll collect the diary,' I say grumpily. 'But first I have someone else to meet up with.' And this meeting I wasn't looking forward to at all.

–

Tyler and I buy coffees from the little kiosk in the park and walk over to one of the benches facing the lake. He looks good, clearly fresh out of the shower as his hair is still a little damp, and his face has a hint of stubble that I like. His eyes are liquid warm and engaging. We sit close together, but a little awkward. Neither of us had asked for any heavy commitments, our routine was often just to meet up, sometimes get drunk and more often have lots of hot sex. It worked for so long, until suddenly it didn't.

When we first officially got together, I'd only been back in the country a few weeks and was tanned, tired and a bit all over the place, living with Mum while I searched for a flat and a job of my own. That time had been weird. I'd heard from Mum that Lottie and Jay were still together and by then Dec had moved to America with his new job, so I wasn't keen to go out.

It was after a row with Mum (the usual 'what are you planning to do with your life') when I ended up in a grotty bar in town, being chatted up by some drunk creeps from the local rugby team. Tyler saw me and rescued me – the man that used to flirt with me when I was doing some part-time waitressing work at Gino's suddenly became my saviour. We spent the night flirting and laughing and then ended up having hot, frantic sex in his flat.

'I'm not looking for anything heavy,' he told me casually. 'But if you fancy hooking up again?'

I kissed his cheek lightly. 'Sounds perfect.'

And it was – it really was. I never had to get into anything deep with Tyler. There was no commitment, no 'meet the family' chats, no financial debates or stresses about the future. Everything was in the moment, which was made it fun, sexy and exciting. And in the end, unsustainable.

I look at Tyler's pretty face now and I know I could never love a man like him. I think I always knew that. That was why he was safe to be around; there was no risk of being hurt, no fear of where things might lead.

'Are you all right?' he asks now.

I nod. 'I used to come here with Lottie a lot, especially towards the end,' I tell him finally. 'She liked to sit by the lake, said the air made her feel better. Sometimes we'd go to the beach near her house if she was too weak to walk here, but weirdly her favourite place was here. She said it was more tranquil, less wild. I've always preferred the beach, but I guess we were different in so many ways.'

'That's the most you've ever said about Lottie,' Tyler said softly.

I turn to him and see that he looks kind of sad. I know that I never talked to him about Lottie, not really. I always liked to keep that side of my life separate.

'It had been so hard, so traumatic seeing her go through that,' I say, stumbling over my words. 'When I was with you, I could kind of forget – which sounds horrible when I say it out loud, but I don't mean it like that. It was just good to think about other things that didn't involve my break-up, or my sick friend, or sadness, or the worry of what was to come…'

'I get that.' He scuffs his feet on the floor. 'I was a distraction.'

I touch his knee and stroke it gently. 'It was a good distraction; it was what I needed.'

'But not any more?'

My mind automatically turns to Jay, of the way I felt to be held by him last night – like all the pieces of a jumbled-up me were finally slotting back together. It wasn't fair to stay with Tyler, no matter how much fun he was.

'It was only ever a casual thing with us, wasn't it? Maybe we let it go on too long...' I pause, not sure how to continue. Tyler is looking down at the ground. This is much harder than I thought it would be. 'Tyler, I never meant to hurt you.'

'I know.' His voice is quiet. 'It's my fault, I knew you didn't want anything serious, and I that's why I told you I didn't at the beginning. I didn't want to scare you off. I convinced myself that I was fine with it being a casual thing, but I guess I got too close to you. We should have ended this a long time ago.'

'Yeah, I think you're right.'

We sit in silence for a bit. Tyler sips his coffee and the gap between us seems to become ever bigger. I shuffle, feeling antsy and bad about things.

'We had fun though, right...?' I say finally.

A tiny smile settles on his cute face. 'Yeah, yeah – we certainly did. I'll miss that.'

I snake my hand over to his and slot my fingers through his. He squeezes it reassuringly. 'I'm sorry I didn't talk to you about Lottie, I've never been much good at opening up about stuff. I think my whole family is the same, we just store things up until we explode. It's not healthy.' I shake my head slowly. 'Honestly, Tyler, at the time you were really good for me. It was what I needed, but I'm sorry that I didn't end up being what you were looking for.'

'What about your ex?' he asks casually. 'Are you seeing him? He's back, isn't he?'

Heat rises to my face. Tyler's expression is soft, and I know he has no expectations – in all the time we were together we were never exclusive – but I still don't want to hurt him.

'Yes,' I reply quietly. 'We did meet up last night, to talk and stuff and it was nice, but I really don't know what it all means. I've got to start focusing on the future, and perhaps that means being single for a bit. I'm not sure what I want at the moment.'

Tyler squeezes my hand. 'I get that. I just want you to be happy, Sara. All the time I've known you, it feels like you've never quite been satisfied, it's almost as if something is missing.'

I stiffen, not quite sure how to take that. 'I'm happy, Tyler. I'm making the best of things.'

'I know you are, but I still get this feeling you're wanting more.' He releases my hand and turns fully to face me. 'I don't like to see you holding yourself back, I want to see you do whatever it takes to make you feel *good*. Whether that's your art, or travelling again, or just spending time finding out who you really are. I think you've spent so long protecting yourself from others, you've forgotten the joy of letting stuff in.'

'You're a nice guy, Tyler,' I whisper. I almost wonder why I'm breaking up with him.

'I'm not so bad.' He smiles. 'But you're even better. You need to start believing though.'

A short while later, Tyler and I hug goodbye – his embrace is warm and secure, and I realise I don't want to lose him totally.

'Can we stay in touch?' I ask awkwardly. 'Maybe just as friends?'

'Sure, I'd like that.'

Watching him walk away, I can't help wondering if I've made a huge mistake. But it wasn't right with him. He wasn't Jay.

The morning is already shaping up to be a sticky, humid one so I walk at a slow pace to Erica's, allowing my mind and thoughts to settle. It's already pretty busy out, with crowds bustling outside the shops and moving fast down the street. I can smell candyfloss and fried onions in the air and somewhere, a few streets away, a shop is playing loud reggae music which seems to intensify the feeling of summer.

Really, I should make my way to the beach, spread out a towel on the hard pebbles, lay back and allow myself to drift away while the sun heats up my skin. It's the perfect day to do it. Instead, I'm getting hot and sweaty as I weave out of the main town and head up towards the residential roads of Hove. In my pocket is Lottie's message, almost glowing red with urgency. I have no idea why she wants me to have her diary. I didn't even know she had one.

I had one for a short time when I was fifteen: bright bubblegum pink and covered in stickers. That was the age when things had started to change between me and Jay; we had moved away from being innocent friends at school who weren't allowed to play together, to something more awkward and difficult to understand. I remember how confused I felt if Jay spoke to another girl, or how I started to notice the flutters in my stomach every time he was close to me.

Mum found that diary. Horror had curdled inside me when I came home and saw it out on the living room table. Mum made out that she only read it because she had my best interests at heart, but that didn't wash with me. Those were my private thoughts she had invaded. Mum shouted at me, told me again that I needed to stay away from Jay and that if I had anything to do with 'that family' she would never forgive me. The diary was discarded in the bin, along with all of my hopes and desires.

Now, I pretty much hate diaries, they're too damaging in the wrong hands. They cause too much pain.

–

'Hello again...' Erica eyes me up and down with a hint of suspicion. 'I wasn't expecting to see you so soon.'

She ushers me in and I follow her into the large house that I'd always been so jealous of when we were teenagers. Now, I look around the place with tired eyes and can finally see what Lottie did – the cold floors, the blank walls, the expensive but stiff-looking furniture. Everything is so functional and formal; I can't feel any love or warmth at all, despite the heat of the day.

Erica guides me into the kitchen and offers me an assortment of coffees and fruit teas. I settle for a cold water. I'm too hot and flustered to drink anything else. I sit myself awkwardly on one of the high kitchen stools, while Erica leans up against the units. She's dressed casually in loose-fitting white linen trousers and a white shirt, and she looks a little better than the last time I saw her. Her hair is neatly brushed away from her face, and unlike last time, I can tell she has applied some make-up; her skin has some colour to it and her eyes are dark. However, I can still see smudges of grey shadow beneath her eyes and her cheeks look drawn in, like she has lost a lot of weight.

'How are you?' I ask carefully.

'I've been better,' she says stiffly. 'It's not easy, sorting everything you know? We knew this day was coming and Charlotte had prepared well for it, but even so, there is still so much to do.' Her shoulders slump a little. 'It's not anything any mother expects to do, is it? Bury her own child.'

Erica had always struck me as a stuck-up, offhand woman who had no time for her own daughter – and yet, I could see the pain clearly etched on her face. What must it be like to lose your only child? I suspect that Erica has many regrets, how could she not?

'I'm sorry,' I say finally, sipping my water. 'I can't even begin to imagine.'

'It must be hard for you, too. You and Charlotte were so close, especially at the end.' Erica pauses, a tiny frown visible on her face. 'It was a shame you had that fall out. I know she missed you when you went abroad. Charlotte always struggled making friends even when she was little. I think you were the first proper one she had.'

'Really?' I hadn't known this. Come to think of it, I didn't really know much about Lottie's life before we met, only that she had been to a school before that she hated. I remember how annoying I'd found her initially, thinking she was too posh and conceited for me. Looking back, I can't believe how judgemental I'd been.

Erica smiles a little and comes to sit on the chair near me. I can smell her strong perfume, mixed in with something else more bitter. Is it vodka? She wobbles a little as she settles herself. 'Charlotte always was a bit of a difficult child I suppose. She would make friends, but then become quite possessive of them, she didn't like them being with anyone else. As she got a bit older, I saw other changes in her. Maybe it was insecurity, I don't know. Me splitting up with her dad couldn't have helped – but she seemed to love her friends fiercely, to want everything they had. It was that envy that often got in the way of her making any true relationships.'

Jay, I thought. Was Lottie jealous of me and Jay? I'd never seen any evidence of that. If anything, she had been supportive and encouraging. But it had been Lottie that Jay ended up with, hadn't it? I quickly shook the thought away. It was easy to blame Lottie for everything when she wasn't here to defend herself and I knew how spiteful Erica could be towards her. Jay had made his choices back then; it wasn't up to anyone else. I wasn't prepared to blame the woman for a man's betrayal. Jay had chosen to sleep with her.

'I've been using her Jar of Joy,' I say, trying to move the direction of conversation. 'It's actually helped a bit to relive some of the happy times we spent together.'

'She loved her jars; I still have hers in her wardrobe. I don't even know what to do with them,' Erica sighs. 'I should throw them away I suppose, but that feels wrong somehow.'

'You could read them?' I offer. After all, maybe that's what Lottie wants – she seems to want to share her messages.

Erica stiffens. 'Read them. Why on earth would I want to do that?'

'I don't know…' I feel uneasy now, a bit silly. 'Maybe it will help to see what made Lottie really feel happy in the past. Maybe it will help you?'

'You have no idea what will make me happy, Sara,' she snaps. 'None at all.'

Silence falls. I sip my water again and try to force back the words I long to say to her. Why is she so scared of digging up Lottie's life a bit? Is she worried she will see something that she won't like?

'Actually, it's because of Lottie's Jar of Joy that I'm here,' I say eventually. Digging into my pocket, I draw out the last message. Erica takes the paper with shaky hands and takes her time to read the words.

'I don't understand, she wants you to have her diary? Surely that's private?'

'It's what she said.' I shrug. 'I'm not even sure I'll read it, Erica. Maybe it's not that sort of diary. Maybe it's just a journal or something?'

Or maybe Lottie has something she wants to tell me?

Erica shrugs and hands the message back to me. 'I'll go and get it now.' Her eyes glint at me. 'But I warn you, Sara, sometimes no good can be had from rooting around in the past. I know my daughter had the best of intentions, but for all of our benefits, I think we need to focus on the future now.'

Day Eleven

Sara

While Erica searches for the diary, I message Jess, asking how Derek is and, luckily, she replies straight away.

> He's perked up a bit. The doctor has been and given him some stronger drugs and he's sleeping a lot now. He's asking after you, which is sweet.

My heart thumps as I reply. I don't care if it's my week off or not, I'm going to visit Derek tomorrow. I need to reassure myself that he's OK. Besides, it always brightens my day seeing him.

Jay's message is still waiting for a reply too. My finger hovers over it, words forming in my mind of all the things I want to say to him. Is it fear that's stopping me from opening up completely? From admitting that I would love to give us another go – or is it something else, something more concerning?

I open up the message, biting the inside of my cheek, and start to tap out a response. Maybe it's time for me to let Jay back into my life. After all, Erica is right, we do need to start focusing more on the future.

Hi Jay, I tap, my fingers feeling fat and unyielding. *Maybe we can meet up again soon, if*

'Who's that you're messaging? Oh.'

Erica has come up behind me and I didn't realise. She places Lottie's diary carefully on the counter in front of me and I hear the slight tut under her breath as she walks back around the front to face me.

'It's just Jay,' I say, wondering why I feel the need to explain. 'He's down here for a few weeks. We met up.'

'That's nice,' Erica says, sounding anything but pleased about it. 'I'm sure he had a lot to say. To be honest, I was surprised he showed up at the funeral. I didn't like to make a fuss, but...' She smiles weakly but doesn't continue, her eyes still fixed on my phone. I push it to one side, the message unfinished. It can wait until later.

'He had to be at the funeral,' I say. 'They were together all the time I was abroad; they were close...'

How did it still sting me to say that? No matter that I'd been miles away in the sun, I knew those two had become a couple in my absence. It was almost as if they had been waiting for me to go away so they could properly get together. Friends don't hurt each other like that.

'It's interesting, isn't it,' Erica says quite calmly, 'how you can view things better after the event? I was never that close to Lottie, you know that. I can't sit here and pretend that I was the perfect mother, it was never something that came naturally to me. However, one thing I was sure of was how much she loved that boy. She really lit up when he was in the room, seemed to almost change as a person.'

'She did?'

I'd never actually been there when Jay and Lottie were together, thankfully, and as they had split up only a month or so after I returned, I was never subjected to their relationship. In a strange way, I'd never considered how being with Jay might have made Lottie happier – I just thought they had continued as they always had, just with the added benefit of sex. She must have really loved him.

'Jay broke her heart,' Erica continues, as if reading my mind. 'But what is worse is how he did it. First, by making that decision to take the job up north and then—' She stops, shakes her head. 'Maybe it isn't my place to say.'

Suddenly desperate to hear the rest, I reach my hand out over the counter. 'No, please, Erica. Tell me.'

'Well...' Erica releases a big sigh. 'Just before he left, Lottie told me he had cheated on her with someone else. Slept with another woman. She was devastated. She told me he didn't even care and told her that it was a sign that their relationship was dead and buried. He left soon after, took that job up north, and for all I know he continued to see the other woman. He left her broken.'

'That's awful,' I breathe.

'That's the kind of man he is, he lies and he cheats and he runs from problems.' Her voice is sharp. 'And he will do the same to you.'

I stare down at the table. An unsaid word drifts between us.

Again.

Erica pushes the diary towards me. 'Here. You came for this, didn't you.'

I pick in up carefully, as if it's precious. It has a soft, blue, velvet-like cover, some sections faded with time and wear. It's huge and weighty, a ten-year diary which, I realise when I peer at the dates, started the year Lottie joined our sixth form. Ten years from Lottie being seventeen right up until twenty-seven.

'I don't think she got a replacement when she finished this one,' Erica says quietly. 'When she was diagnosed, she didn't bother to diarise that.'

'I feel weird having this,' I admit. 'I'm not sure I can read it, it doesn't feel right, despite what Lottie says – but I can keep it safe.'

Erica shrugs. 'There must have been a reason why she gave it to you. Lottie always did things for a reason.'

My fingers trace the outside of the cover. I feel so conflicted. I know all of her thoughts and feelings will be in here, all her time with Jay, and I'm not sure I'm ready for that.

I slip the diary into my bag, ready to deal with it later. For now, my task is done. 'Do you think Lottie was happy with Jay, Erica?'

'For a time – yes, I do. She seemed pretty besotted. They were the only ones left, weren't they. You'd gone away and Declan was in America; I suppose it was natural that they came together.'

I nod. 'I guess so.'

'And maybe it would have worked out, if he'd been a better person. I take it you didn't know he cheated on her. Lottie never told you?'

I shook my head. 'No – I didn't know that, I assumed they had just drifted apart.'

Erica snorts. 'Well, I'm guessing Charlotte didn't feel comfortable talking to you about Jay. She knew you were... well, close to him. Like I said before, that boy can't be trusted. I'm sure it will all be in her diary. You'll probably discover more revelations there.'

A sick feeling washes over me. I am pretty sure Erica is right and this is partly why I don't want to go there.

'I better go,' I mumble instead. 'Thank you for your time, Erica.'

'Anytime,' she replies, sounding anything but welcoming.

I leave the house with a heavy cloud over me and a pinching sensation in my chest that won't go away.

Jay hurt Lottie: he cheated on her, and he ran away when she needed him most. Did I really want to let this man back into my life?

As I start the long walk back to my flat, I already know the answer. It's as if Lottie has provided me with it at just the right time.

I can't let someone like Jay hurt me again. I won't.

Needing some comfort, I put my headphones in and choose a playlist of songs that I loved back when I first went travelling. Just listening to the music again brings me back to that day when I stood in my bedroom, pulling my clothes into my bags, my mum watching, her face etched with concern.

'Are you sure this is the right thing to do, Sara? It seems so sudden. You shouldn't be making decisions on an emotional reaction.'

I knew she was probably right, but as I zipped up the bags, a rush of certainty took over. I wasn't happy in my life at that moment; I needed to get away, just for a little while. I was sure I would come back after a few months and find a new job. I had no clue that I would fall in love with the easy-going lifestyle of Spain.

Looking back now, I questioned if that was the real reason. Or was it the fact that, as the months passed, it became harder and harder to return to the life I had left behind – especially when Dec had called me to tell me

Jay and Lottie were now together. Why on earth would I want to go back to that?

'We will miss you, your brother and I,' Mum had told me.

I'd pulled a face at her – like my brother would care. He'd probably be glad to see the back of me.

Mum had touched my arm gently. 'I don't like the idea of you running away from things. You have so much here and people who love you.'

'I just need some space and time now,' I'd said calmly. 'I feel so confused about everything, I don't even know what I want any more. I think this will help me – I really do. You know I've talked about travelling before. Nan has given me money and it seems a good chance to use it.'

Mum had pulled me into a hug. She was never a particularly emotional person, so this had surprised me. As I'd melted a little in her arms, doubts had started to flicker – was I doing the right thing? I quickly pushed them away.

On the way to the station, my phone had rung twice. The first call was from Lottie telling me she would miss me and hoped that I would back soon. I hadn't wanted to speak to her, but my anger was directed more at Jay so I decided to hear what she had to say.

'You don't need Jay,' she'd insisted. 'I think his head is all over the place at the moment. You still have me.'

'But he read my letter, Lottie. He read it and didn't contact me. It's clear he doesn't want to be with me. I can't stand being around him now.'

Lottie drew a breath. 'Like I said, I think his feelings are all over the place at the moment. I told him not to mess you around and maybe that influenced him a bit, I don't know. I'm sorry if it did.'

'No – it's good that you were honest with him.'

My body had been so heavy as I walked. I wished me and Jay could've been more honest with each other, all the time we'd been mucking around, acting as friends but never quite sure what our true feelings actually were. It was no wonder it ended up such a mess.

'I think Jay just likes having fun,' Lottie had said quietly. 'He wasn't exactly missing you while you were away.'

My heart cracked open a little more.

'I'm sorry,' she had said again quietly.

'No, it's OK.'

At least I had made the right decision to go. I was putting myself first. I wasn't letting my feelings for Jay hold me back. It was time I freed us both.

'Thanks, Lottie,' I told her then.

I felt her relief bleed through the phone. 'I'm going to miss you so much. I can't wait to see you when you get back.'

I didn't answer.

'You do forgive me, Sara, don't you?' she had pleaded softly. 'I was drunk and not thinking straight. I didn't want it to happen. You're my best friend.'

Lottie had sounded so pitiful that I couldn't stay that angry with her. I knew how much she longed for love and affection. It wasn't her fault that Jay didn't want me.

'I just need some time. That's all.'

After I'd hung up, a second call came through. It had been Jay.

I declined the call. And I did the same thing when he tried again five minutes later.

He then sent me a message while I was on the train.

> Please call me, we need to talk before you go.

But my mind was made up. I didn't want distractions any more. Jay had made his choice and I was sick of going around in circles.

> It's too late Jay, I've already left. We can talk when I'm back. Please just leave it now.

It was the hardest text I'd ever sent, but it had been necessary and at the time it had felt right.

In the days that had followed, as I explored new streets in the blazing heat, looking for any bar job I could get hold of, thoughts about Jay started to melt away. I felt like I could breathe again.

I knew that I could probably find it in my heart to forgive Lottie, but Jay – Jay I wasn't so sure. That man had smashed me into a million pieces. How was I going to come back from that?

And now, as I tread in a similar blazing heat back to my flat, sweat trickling down my back, I send another cold and succinct message to the same man.

> Last night was a mistake. It's too soon after Lottie dying and it doesn't seem right. Please don't contact me again.

I feel sick as it sends, but despite the rush of my heart and the slight queasiness in my gut, I know I'm being true to myself. All Jay and I do is keep hurting each other. And the last thing I need is more pain.

Once I reach home, I fumble for the key, desperate to get in my secure and quiet space. My music is still playing, but now it's an old Eighties song, a Kate Bush track that is both sad and mournful. The lyrics tug at my heart; it was a song that Jay had loved as much as I did.

I lay down on my sofa and for the first time in ages I cry. I cry for Lottie, for Derek, and most of all, I cry for myself – I just let the tears flow out from me until I am totally exhausted.

I have never felt so alone in my life.

Three Years Before

Lottie

Jay and I kind of stayed together, but it was never real, never substantial. I knew this. We were just the ones left over when Sara left and Dec too, for a job in London. Jay was depressed for a time and spent a lot of time alone in his flat.

He thought about phoning Sara occasionally but soon talked himself out of it. After all, she had left him. She clearly didn't care. He needed her and she went. He convinced himself it wasn't meant to be and yes, maybe I had a hand in that.

We were on/off with each other for the next two and a half years. When Jay had been drinking, he would come to mine, and we would talk and often sleep together. I was his pity shag and my self-esteem was so low I just accepted it. Jay never wanted me, I knew that. He told me that he didn't want to string me along. He told me he could never love me. Many times, he tried to break off our weird relationship, but I begged him not to. I told him that everyone left me in the end. He was the only one still here. Out of guilt we clung to each other.

By the end, we were a mess, barely even friends. Jay resented spending time with me and I hated the fact that he could never see me as anything more than he did.

Dec came to visit us. He was completely pissed off with the entire situation and tried to talk some sense into me. Instead, we ended up getting drunk together and having disappointing sex in a back alley by the pub. I knew Dec would tell Jay. I think he was hoping it would make Jay end the whole charade. I was hoping it might make Jay jealous and it would make him see sense.

Jay didn't seem to care either way. Actually, he thought it was kind of funny. The three of us were so fucked up – it was like we had completely lost our way since Sara had gone.

We didn't realise Sara was back from her travels until we saw her in town. We were in the park, ironically having another disagreement. Jay was telling me that he was leaving for good. He had a job in Newcastle, and he wanted to move there to be closer to his dad, to escape the mess of his life. When I started to cry, Jay pulled me into a hug.

'I'm sorry, Lottie. You never should have been caught up in this crap.'

When we drew away Sara was just standing there, like a ghost from the past. She had a rigid grin on her face, but I could see the pain flashing in her eyes.

'Hey.' She smiled. 'I'm glad to see it worked out for you both.'

I think Jay was about to tell her the truth, that we weren't a couple, that we never had been, really – but Sara interrupted in her usual blunt way. She started telling us too brightly about her fun times in Spain, how she had a new job in the care home and how her new boyfriend Ty was 'amazing' and made her so happy. I tried to ignore how much Jay stiffened next to me as she spoke.

When she walked away, Jay turned to me. I saw tears sparkle in his eyes.

'This is why I have to go, Lottie. I can't be with you; I can't be here any more. I will always be in love with Sara, so it's best for everyone if I go.'

And then he left me standing in the park, my whole world crashing down around me, and I knew then – above everything else – that I deserved this. I had caused this. All the pain and lies had been for nothing.

I was still desperately alone.

Day Twelve

Sara

I call Jess almost as soon as I wake up. My mouth tastes of sludge from the one-too-many glasses of wine I drank before bed, and I don't even dare to look in the mirror because I already know I look a state.

'You sound like shit,' Jess says straightaway.

I rinse out a cup that is sat by the sink and force myself to down some orange juice. The vitamins have to help, right?

'I feel like shit,' I admit. 'The last day or so have been tough.'

'So, come on, tell me about it – I'm all ears. You've caught me on break. This saves me having to hear Sharon's boring holiday plans.'

'Can she hear you?' I whisper, cringing on Jess's part.

'No, of course not, but you know she'll be in here any minute and if she spots me on my own, she will attack. I'm defenceless. Within minutes I'll know every single bloody detail about their next Norwegian cruise.'

I smile. I need Jess's energy today. I wish I could suck some of it into me. 'Well, for starters, I finished with Tyler.'

'You finished with Tyler?' Jess breathes out. 'That man is gorgeous. It couldn't have been easy.'

'It was easier than you think.' I lick my dry lips. 'I don't really think I should be with anyone at the moment.'

'There are certain benefits to being single that's for sure. I can get you on one of my apps.' Jess pauses. 'Or are you talking about being proper single, like no sex or anything?'

'Proper single.' I start to pace the flat, trying to ignore the dull headache at the back of my eyes. 'I think it's the only way.'

'Wow – you're serious. What else happened? Is this to do with the Jar thingy?'

'The Jar of Joy. And kind of.' I stop pacing and rub my temple, trying to place my thoughts into place. 'I ended up meeting Jay again. We went for dinner, and it was nice, but confusing and we ended up getting closer than I planned...'

Jess sucks in a deep breath. 'Really? OK, so what happened? Did you shag? Are you seeing him again?'

'No. I told him not to contact me again.'

'That's pretty final.'

'I know, I know...' Pressure builds in my head. 'But the thing is – Lottie's instruction was for me to pick up her diary from her mum's.'

'Her diary? Oh my God. Have you read it?'

I glance at the heavy book which is still where I left it on the coffee table, sat right next to the empty-looking Jar of Joy.

'No, not yet. Lottie wanted me to when I'm ready, but it doesn't feel right. Anyway, when I got to her house her mum told me all sorts of things, mainly about Jay, which has basically made me hate men and want to stay single forever.'

'Oh! That *is* a lot. And that's why you told him to leave you alone?'

'Yeah, I feel like I need a breather.' Taking in the small space of my flat around me, I can see that I've already let the mess and clutter get on top of me. It's no wonder I feel so low when I have this chaos all around me. I begin to pick up some of my clothes off the sofa and the discarded books off from the floor. 'I think I need to sort my life out.'

'Well, I can join you in that one. When you come back to work, we can make some plans.'

'Sounds good,' I say, as I notice an old, stained cup under the sofa. God, I really am gross. 'How is Derek?'

'Better. Much better. His medications seem to be kicking in so he's much brighter.'

I straighten up, still clutching the dirty old cup, a trail of musty clothes hanging over my arm. 'Oh, Jess, that's the best news. Tell him I'll pop over later.'

'Sara! You're meant to be on holiday.'

'I am on holiday, that doesn't mean I can't visit a dear friend.' I turn back to the table and smile. 'Besides I have something to show Derek. I think he might be able to help me.'

–

The next few hours are spent deep cleaning. I play my music loud and fling the windows open, not caring what the neighbours think. I've been living like a ghost recently anyway. Cleaning takes my mind off things. It's easier to ignore the message from Jay that is sitting unread on my phone, and it means I don't have to start thinking about what I'm going to do about Lottie's diary. I'm all for fulfilling her wishes but this is a step too far.

'Maybe we can store it away somewhere,' I say softly, imagining she's there next to me. 'That way it will always be safe.'

I can feel Lottie next to me, shaking her head and smiling sagely. '*I know you want to read it, Sara. You want to know what really happened that summer, don't you? You know everything will be in there.*'

Except do I want to know? Aren't some things best left in the past?

For now, I put the diary on my small bookshelf out of harm's way and decide to worry about it later. I have a hot date to get ready for.

–

'You look good.'

'I know you're lying.'

'I'm really not. You have colour in your cheeks and Jess tells me you've managed breakfast this morning.' I sit myself next to Derek, tidying his cover as I do so; I like it to be nice and tight across his bed because I know he feels cosy.

'Yes, a few mouthfuls. I eat like a bird now, I'm turning into skin and bone, not that it matters.' His mottled hands dance briefly on the top of the sheet. 'It's not as if I'm going to be going dancing anytime soon, is it?'

'I don't know – maybe I can tempt you out with me.' I wink at him.

He smiles sadly. 'You shouldn't have bothered coming in today, Sara. I know it's your week off. You should be doing fun things with people your own age, not worrying about an old codger like me.'

'Perhaps I like being around codgers,' I tell him lightly. 'Besides, I needed to check on you. I can't have you getting poorly on me again.'

Derek tuts softly but the sad expression hasn't left him. I try to ignore the heavy feeling in my stomach, it seems to get worse every time I look into his large, soulful eyes.

'So, what have you been up to?' he asks in a sudden chirpier voice. 'You can tell me all about it over a cup of tea.'

I grin. 'That's a deal.'

I don't waste much time at the tea trolley, nodding briefly to Ade who is wheeling another resident outside. It's another lovely sunny day and the home is much brighter, with the doors wide open and the smell of summer spilling in. I can hear the sound of a lawn-mower in the distance and the gentle sound of chatter. It's soothing.

Back in Derek's room, I hand him his tea (super strong, just as he likes) and then walk over to the window and tug back the curtains, throwing the window open.

'You need some summer air in here,' I say. 'It's too stale in this room. It's enough to make anyone feel rubbish.'

I put pillows behind Derek so that he is more comfortable and move his bed into a more upright position. When I sit back down, we take a few moments just to enjoy the silence – although silent would be the wrong word. Derek's smile grows as the sounds from outside filter into the room; the strongest is that of a bird, singing sweetly from just by the sill.

'That'll be a blackbird,' he says nodding. 'You can't mistake those notes – beautiful and sorrowful at the same time.'

'I can take you out next time I come. You'll be able to hear them better.'

Derek sips his tea thoughtfully for a minute and then speaks. 'Tell me what you got up to.'

So I do. I haven't got the pressure of being at work and having to rush my time, so I go into detail about my date with Jay, about my visit to Erica's and about all the memories Lottie's stupid Jar of Joy has brought up.

I reach into my bag and pull it out, placing it carefully on the table next to Derek.

'There are only a few messages left. I feel so conflicted. Part of me wants to get it done and dusted because remembering all of this stuff is so hard… but then again, I know that once I stop, that'll be it. I'll have nothing left of Lottie.'

'You have her diary though.'

'I'm really not sure I can read that, Derek.'

Derek sighs softly. 'She left it to you for a reason. You know, people use diaries for all sorts of reasons. For some, it's a private, hidden thing but for others its more of an outlet, a way of documenting true events. Some people hope that their diaries will be read one day.'

I consider this. Maybe it's true, Lottie could well have wanted this all along.

'Maybe it's more that you're scared of what you might find out,' Derek continues. 'You tell me the messages have been difficult enough. It sounds as though you have shut a lot of life away, Sara.'

I bow my head. I don't want Derek to see I'm getting upset. 'I just think it's easier to move forward than to keep focusing on the mistakes of the past. Why would I want to get hurt again?'

'Did you ever properly talk to Lottie about what happened between her and Jay? How they got together, or even what led them to split up?'

I shake my head. 'When I got back from working abroad, they were still together, but they split soon after and Jay moved up north. I didn't see Lottie for ages after that. The first time we just bumped into each other in town. It was awkward, but I agreed to meet up with her again. Then she told me she had cancer.' I pause, I can feel the emotion building up inside of me. 'What was the point of asking questions then? Lottie had enough of her own crap to deal with. Jay had left her, she didn't get on with her mum and her dad was bloody unreliable – so I stepped up. It's what friends do.'

Derek eyes me over his cup. 'And you are a very good friend, Sara.'

'Thank you.'

'But I think now this is Lottie's way of helping you – this Jar of Joy. The diary. She wants to give you the answers that you couldn't ask at the time. She wants to help you move on. This is her gift to you – not the jar itself, but the freedom it will provide.'

I churn this over. It makes sense in a way, but the thought is still scary. Am I really going to have to start thinking about the past more? I'd spent so long carefully constructing my safe little wall around myself. Was I really prepared to knock that all down?

'Are you really happy working here?' Derek asks carefully.

I hesitate before speaking. 'What makes you ask that?'

'Just a funny feeling really,' he replies, shuffling a little into position. 'I mean, don't get me wrong, you're great at your job, dedicated, kind and hardworking. It's just…'

'What?' I urge.

'Well, I can see you working somewhere else, that's all,' he says. 'I watch you sometimes, when you are drawing with the other residents. I can see the talent spilling from your fingers, the small smile that takes over your expression. My wife was an artist, you know? I recognise the happiness that she had, it just poured out from her. When you work, I can see you are just going through the motions, but you are young and talented with your whole life in front of you. I wouldn't like to see you waste it.'

'I was going to do something with art after my degree…' I shake my head. 'It's too late now though.'

'It's never too late. There are always solutions, Sara, but sometimes you just have to search a bit harder for them. The best things are worth fighting for though – that's what I believe.'

He closes his eyes and sighs softly. I stand up, briefly touching his warm hand.

'I'm sorry, Derek, I'm tiring you. I'll go now. I can come back tomorrow.'

'You're not going anywhere.' His eyes remain closed. 'I want to know what the next message says first.'

'Really? I can tell you all about it when I next come.'

'Sara' – his voice is stern – 'I have little entertainment as it is now. Please do me the honour of including me in your exciting moments.'

I laugh. 'OK, OK, hang on…' I dig my hand into the jar, hit by another wave of sadness at its emptiness now. It's silly, but I feel like it's a sign that Lottie's joy is disappearing.

Carefully, I unfold the message. It's on pink paper this time, her favourite colour.

> *Go to the cat rescue where we went that day on a whim and found Goose. Isn't she the best cat ever?*

234

Find an animal I would love and donate in my honour.

I read the words out loud, trying to ignore the slight tremor in my voice. That had been a strange old day, but one of the best. It was the day Lottie had found something for me that I hadn't realised I'd ever wanted – a pet!

'Goose?' Derek frowns. 'Bit of a daft name for a cat.'

'It is, I suppose. But she's white and has a long neck for a cat. She's kind of awkward looking. The first time I saw her, she reminded me of a goose. Lottie wasn't too sure though.'

'No? What did she want to call her?'

'Fifi,' I say, grinning. 'I thought that was too soppy. Too girly, but Lottie loved it.'

'You won in the end though.'

'Yes, I guess I did.'

'You should go today. It sounds like you'll have a nice afternoon surrounded by animals. If you see an old frail one, think of me. Maybe you can call the poor sod Derek.'

We both laugh.

Derek reaches towards me and squeezes my hand.

'Look after yourself, young Sara. And remember to put yourself first sometimes. You need to stop worrying about your friend, about your ex-boyfriend, about me. Instead, focus on what you want and need. Learn to follow your heart.'

And with that, he closes his eyes again and I know this time the conversation is really over.

–

I grab some lunch from the corner shop near work and then pick up the bus that will take me into the next village where Rowlands Cat Rescue is. As I sit on the threadbare seat, nibbling on my sandwich, I think back to the last time we went there. It wasn't long after Lottie had been diagnosed and she had bundled us both in her car, insisting that we went to see the cats in an attempt to cheer her up.

'You know how much I love them,' she'd told me eagerly. 'I often pop by just to donate and spend some time fussing over them. It takes my mind off my own troubles for a while.'

I had never really been a cat lover, but I'd been won over by Lottie's enthusiasm. It was just so lovely to see her smile. As soon as we had stepped into the centre, Lottie had spotted the little white cat sitting alone in a cage.

'Oh, Sara,' she had gushed. 'Look how cute this one is. How could anyone abandon her?'

'A little goose…' I'd replied, my gaze fixed on her.

'Goose! Are you crazy? She is far more a Fifi! Look how pretty she is. What sort of name is Goose anyway!'

I don't even know how it happened so quickly. Lottie could've never taken her on, Erica was always so scared of dust and germs, especially now that Lottie was poorly. I really didn't want a cat in my flat at the time, but seeing how much Lottie loved Goose I couldn't resist. I knew Lottie could visit her at mine and I had to admit, there had been something about that tiny little cat that had made my heart melt. Lottie eventually accepted her name, she even admitted it suited her.

Now I couldn't imagine life without Goose, her gentle purrs and warm little body made me so happy.

I hadn't loved cats at first, but Lottie had shown me how to let them into my heart.

The bus pulls up a few roads away from the rescue centre and I hop out. As I walk the rest of the way, I have mixed feelings about coming back. I know how much Lottie loved it here. Just seeing the low, timber building makes me feel a rush of affection. I gently pat the statue of a wise-looking tomcat that stands by the doorway as I walk in, something Lottie said she used to do for luck.

Inside the scent of fur, food, and wood chips hits me. I nod at the smiling woman at reception, pick up a few leaflets and then make my way down the corridor of cats, dozens of cages containing tiny animals – some old, some young, some poorly – all sitting and waiting to be found by the right owner.

'It always breaks my heart,' Lottie had said, her fingers touching the wire on the cages. 'I want to take them all. I see the loneliness in their eyes. I know what that feels like. It's horrible.'

I pause in front of a tired-looking black cat. I'd never questioned Lottie about that comment. I always thought we had done all we could to help her fit in, but Lottie had joined us so late in sixth form. I knew she had struggled with friendships before and I guess, in all honesty, I knew she had always been on the fringes of our group, too.

Had I done enough to help her?

A tiny mew distracts me from my thoughts. Staring at me through the bars is a small, skinny cat with longish blonde fur and the brightest blue eyes I have ever seen on a cat. I read the description on the printed card by her door.

> This cat is believed to be one or two years old. We currently call her Marilyn because of her blonde good looks. She was abandoned as a young cat and needs someone to show her love. She can live with other cats.

I stare into the eyes of this sweet little creature and feel my heart pound. Lottie wanted me to find a cat that she would love and donate in her honour. There is no doubt that she would love this cat. It is her in animal form – a tiny, sweet-looking thing.

'But you're no Marilyn,' I whisper to her. 'You're a Fifi.'

A few minutes later, I'm not filling out a donation form. I'm filling out a request to adopt.

Fifi is coming home with me.

Two Years Before

Lottie

I didn't plan to wait outside Sara's flat, but Dec had told me where she lived, and something drew me there. I think mainly it was the shock. I needed someone to talk to.

Jay had left to move to Newcastle a few months before. He was kind and dignified and still wanted us to be friends, I was hurt and cold – refusing to accept that we could ever be that again.

Days after, I'd visited my doctor. I went there wanting tablets to help me sleep, but I happened to mention the bleeding and cramps I'd been experiencing. I'd not had a smear appointment before but had no reason to think anything was wrong. Even the doctor seemed calm, telling me they would just test me in case. It was good to check these things.

Weeks turned into months, and now I was going to hospital appointments on my own. I had no boyfriend to confide in, no friends, and I certainly didn't want my patronising mother sat beside me. When the consultant led me into her nicely furnished room and asked if anyone could be with me, I told her no.

She told me I had cancer whilst I was sitting on my own, clutching my designer handbag tightly on my lap and staring blankly into space. The darkness inside of me seemed to open up a little bit more.

'You need people around you,' she'd soothed. 'This can be a difficult time.'

I blinked back at her. The only person I wanted was Sara.

So here I was.

—

I followed her at first, too scared to call out her name, too afraid of what she might say when she saw me.

She walked towards the park and I was her shadow, noticing how tanned she'd remained since she'd returned from Spain. How her movement was relaxed and casual, how her long dark hair seemed more glossy than usual.

At the park she stopped at a bench to adjust her trainers and that was when I walked up to her. She immediately stiffened; her eyes narrowed a little bit as I approached.

'Sara, hey! I was just walking past and I spotted you,' I gushed.

'OK…' She shifted on the spot, looking like she was keen to get away. 'How are you?'

'Erm, not so good…' Where did I start? How could I tell her?

'Oh.' She pushed her hair away from her face. 'Are you and Jay good, still?'

I noticed how her voice stalled a little on Jay's name. The ache inside of me felt hollower. I had done this. I had caused all of this. I'd thought it would help me keep people closer to me, and instead I had made them all run away.

'We're not together any more. He's in Newcastle.'

'Oh.' Her eyes widened. 'I didn't realise. Newcastle? That's a long way...'

'He got a leadership role up there. He's doing well. It's close to where his dad lives now.'

'Right.' Sara nodded slowly. 'Look, Lottie – I'm sorry you're hurt and that, but I don't think...' She coughed, glanced away from me again. 'I don't think I can do this. Too much has happened, you know. It's too hard.'

'I have cancer.'

The words just fell from my lips. It was like Sara was frozen for a moment, then she took a deep breath and studied me for a few seconds.

'What?'

'It's pretty serious. I have to have chemo. Radiation. They hope they've caught it in time, but it's aggressive...'

'Shit, Lottie. I'm so sorry.' She grabbed my hands. The warmth bled into mine and I shivered.

'I need you, Sara. I need a friend,' I whispered. 'I'm so sorry for everything that happened but I can't be on my own right now, I can't.'

'I know. I know.' She pulled me into a hug, squeezed me hard. 'It's OK. I'm here. I'm here for you.'

It was all I needed to know.

Day Thirteen

Sara

Two cats greet me as I blink open my eyes in the morning. This is a pleasant surprise. Fifi is a gentle and curious cat who has slipped into our home easily. I'm also surprised how generous Goose has been towards her; I knew she was a laid-back creature, but she has practically ignored this home invader and carried on as normal. It's made my decision feel less crazy and more rational.

'*You love cats really*,' I hear Lottie say. '*They make you happy. You need to let more things into your life*.'

I shake this off and keep myself busy, feeding my housemates and preparing myself for the day ahead. I have no plans as such, but I have a feeling that Lottie's jar will direct me somewhere interesting today. There are only three messages left and this includes the one that is sellotaped to the bottom. I'm not sure what Lottie can say in these limited words to make me feel better. At the moment, I can't say the jar has done much for me except leave me a little sad about the events of the past.

'How does this help,' I mutter, as I step over the puddle of cat that is Fifi sprawled out on the floor. 'I don't know how reminiscing and remembering the good or even sad times is a positive thing. It's like wallowing in the juices of the past.'

I pick up Lottie's diary and skim through it, recognising the large loopy style of her handwriting.

This diary starts with her time in sixth form, when she first met us all. It had been Jay who had persuaded me to give her a chance. Jay always did tend to see the best in everyone.

I am tempted, for a moment or two, to sit down with the diary and start to read like Lottie requested. I'm curious as to what she wants me to see, but I'm not sure I'm ready for it. What if I don't come off well here? What if I read something I don't want to?

I'm still dithering when my phone rings. I put the diary back down and pull my phone out of my pocket. It's Jay. Again. I sigh, wishing he'd just get the hint and leave me in peace for a bit. I chuck the phone back on the sofa and turn my attention back to the Jar of Joy. Jay calling was a sign, I'm sure of it. I'm not ready to read Lottie's words, not yet anyway.

Instead, I open the jar and extract one of the last folded pieces of paper.

> *Go to London, like we did after I first got diagnosed and you wanted to treat me. Do you remember what we did? I want you to relive the day.*
>
> *I also want you to visit your brother Kyle. I know he lives there now. You need to talk to him.*

Kyle. Fuck. I puff out a breath.

Out of all the things I expected Lottie to ask me to do, this was not one of them.

—

I didn't want to go, I admit it, but as always, I felt honour-bound to follow Lottie's instructions. It's almost like I could feel her watching over me and I didn't want to upset her. Deep down, I knew I hadn't been the best friend to her, not really, and if I could do one small thing like this to appease her memory, it seemed right.

But Kyle – that really was pushing it.

On the train, travelling up to London, I brought up his number on my mobile. I couldn't just turn up unannounced, but it was hard bringing myself to actually make the call.

It's fair to say that I've never been close to Kyle. There are seven years between us and the age gap made a difference. Kyle was always my big, angry, slightly scary older brother. Some of my earliest memories are of him kicking off, shouting, smashing the place up – making my mum cry. He was excluded from school, he would fight with his mates and most of the time he would fight with himself, punching walls or hitting his own body in an attempt to calm his own inner rage.

Mum never said it was linked to Dad's death, but I could put two and two together. I was too young to remember Dad – only three when he died, while Kyle was ten and already big for his age. Kyle said he remembered Dad a lot, and I know he missed him.

Kyle got worse after Dad's death; he was a big ball of rage of resentment and the only person who could make any sense of him was Mum. She home-schooled him, trying to educate him between her cleaning shifts. She took him to different doctors and therapists. She stayed calm all of the time while he shouted abuse or kicked another hole in the wall.

There was no room for me in this set up. I couldn't get close to Mum – if I tried, Kyle would turn nasty. It was easier to stay away. I played outside a lot, even from a young age, and met up with the other estate kids. By the age of five I became good friends with Jay. His dad used to look after him while his mum worked and sometimes I would be invited around for tea.

I liked it at Jay's house. It was calm and peaceful. I liked Jay's dad – he was sweet and funny. I didn't often meet his mum. Jay said she worked long hours as a teacher.

I think Jay and his dad knew that I was avoiding being at home, but they never questioned me about it. My mum would pick me up and sometimes she would stay for a cup of tea. She and Jay's dad would sit together in the kitchen laughing. It was the first time I heard her do that for ages.

The year passed quickly. Kyle was thirteen. I was six. My best friend was Jay.

And my mum made the huge mistake of falling in love with his dad.

Kyle picks up on the third ring.

'Hey.' His voice is gruff as always, but there is a softness there that I wasn't expecting. 'Is everything OK?'

'Hey,' I say back, the word dry in my mouth.

I never call Kyle. Never. On the occasions that he visits Mum, I'm rarely there. When he was released from prison, he moved into a flat in London and I didn't bother to see him.

Sometimes I feel guilty about that. Mum keeps on at me, telling me about the rehabilitation Kyle has gone through. How he has had intense therapy and is now on medication to help with his mental health. According to Mum, his girlfriend Jenny is nice – she helps to keep him on track. I understand why Mum is desperate for us to be

245

back in touch again – our family is so small and fragile now – but there is always something holding me back.

It was Kyle's temper that nearly destroyed me and Jay and it got in the way of our chances of being together. It was Kyle's reckless act that drove a huge wedge between our two families.

And what nobody knows is that I saw it all.

Mum and Jay's dad had been outside the flat, talking. Well, arguing is probably the best word for it. They had been seeing each other for over a year. They tried to keep it hidden from us all, but we all knew, no one was stupid. Mum spent more and more time at Jay's and I guess Kyle started to feel a bit rejected. As a result, he stayed out more. He started hanging around with older kids on the estate that my mum hated – the ones that were rumoured to carry knives and drugs. I may have only been small, but I knew the risks that were involved. The rows at home were explosive and it only led to Mum falling into Jay's dad's arms even more.

Jay hated it. He wouldn't talk about much to me, but he didn't like what his dad was doing to his mum.

'This is what he's like,' he told me once. 'He always has other women. He acts like it's no big deal, but I heard Mum crying last night. She hates him doing this to her.'

'Does she know about my mum?' I asked.

Jay shrugged. 'She knows Dad messes around. They always argue about it.'

I couldn't understand why Jay's mum put up with it. Every time I met her she had come across as strong and even a bit scary. She rarely smiled and wasn't as friendly and welcoming as Jay's dad. I could see why lots of people liked him.

That night, outside the flat, I was watching out of my window. I was meant to be in bed, but the raised voices had drawn me to look like a moth attracted to a flame. I wasn't used to seeing Jay's dad looking angry or my mum crying. The scene unsettled me.

Mum was begging him. She was pulling on his arm, telling him not to end it. Jay's dad didn't seem the same person at all. He was cold and stiff. He pushed Mum away. I couldn't hear all his words, but what I did carved through me. Words like 'pathetic' and 'needy' and 'deluded'. My brave strong mother seemed to crumble in front of him. I touched the glass as if I could reach her. She went to grab him again, tugging on his arm, telling him that he couldn't stay with his wife, he didn't love her.

That's when he delivered the killer blow. He laughed as he did it.

'I'm not going back to her, you daft bitch. I've met someone new. Someone better. You were just a stopgap. That was all. A good shag.'

My mum slapped him.

Jay's dad stood there, stunned, I think, and then he slapped her back. Hard. Mum fell to the floor. I cried out.

Kyle was there in an instant. He'd heard the shouting and run out to find our mum on the ground clutching her face. When he looked towards Jay's dad's face, I saw something in his eyes I'd never seen before. He actually roared, like a tiger, and launched himself forward.

I stood frozen, watching the scene unfold. Watching as my brother kicked, hauled and punched a grown man to the ground. I saw my mum screaming, trying to drag him off and I heard Jay's dad crying out as the blows landed one after another.

And then I watched as Kyle righted himself, rubbing his bloody fists against his chest. His eyes seemed to catch mine and they still glinted with ice and rage.

I'd never been so terrified in my life.

I crawled back into my bed, crying soft tears. I didn't tell mum what I saw. I didn't tell the police when they called, I didn't tell anyone. I just tucked myself away in the safe place in my mind. But the truth was, I was terrified of my own brother. And I still was. I'd seen what he could do, I knew what he was capable of, and I never wanted to be near that again.

And yet here I am, on the phone to him.

'I'm coming up to London. I thought maybe… I could pop by,' I say now, trying to sound casual.

There's a pause. 'OK. That'll be nice, but, Sara – why now?'

'I just thought…' I shake my head, staring out at the flashes of countryside passing by the window. 'It's been so long. Maybe we finally need to talk. We are family after all.'

'Yes.' His voice is soft. 'Yes, we are that.'

He gives me his address and some instructions. I tell him I'll be there around four. My head feels dizzy with indecision, my skin prickles with worry.

'Sara,' he says, before I end the call.

'What?'

'I'm really glad you called. It will be good to see you.'

-

I walk around central London in a bit of daze, but I'm determined to honour Lottie's instructions. I start off browsing our favourite bookshops on Booksellers Row

248

in Cecil Court, which is a seventeenth-century lane lined with second-hand and antique bookshops. Me and Lottie used to joke that we would love to own one of them and spend our days behind the dusty shelves, gossiping and giggling.

When we were here before, Lottie ended up buying an old edition of her favourite *Grimm's Fairy Tales*.

'It reminds me of when I was really little and things still felt normal,' she told me. 'Dad used to read these stories to me before bed, putting on the voices and everything. It felt like a really special time.'

I browse the shelves a bit but nothing catches my eye, or perhaps I'm not in the right frame of mind. I head instead to the little pancake place a few streets away which was where Lottie dragged me, telling me we had to forget about calories and healthy living for the day. At the time, I was trying to keep fit by running and watching my sugar levels, but I couldn't resist being naughty with her.

The cafe is just as I remembered, small and cheery with bright painted signs and an immediate scent of sugar and maple syrup that hits you as soon as you walk in. It's pretty quiet, so I order a tea and a lemon and sugar crepe and take my seat by the window.

It's hard not to think of when I was here with Lottie. She had been in such a lovely, chatty mood despite it only being a few months after we had first got back in touch after her diagnosis. I had thought she was so brave, sitting there delicately eating her food and not seeming stressed about the news that had hit her.

'I will beat it,' she told me finally. 'I have so much I still want to do; I'm not going to let something like cancer stop me.'

I think I'd smiled then, unsure as to how to respond. I didn't want her to know how sorry I was and how guilty I felt that our friendship had restarted at such a bad time and only due to the circumstances.

'And if I don't beat it…' She shrugged, wiping the sugar off her lips. 'Well, it just means it's my time. It happens to us all eventually.'

'Don't say that, Lottie,' I'd begged.

'I will say, because I'm done with being scared.' Her eyes had shone as she spoke. 'I've spent my entire life being too scared to be who I wanted to be, or even try to be happy – well, no more. This life is mine and mine alone and for as long as I have it I'm going to bloody try and enjoy it.'

I stared back at her, admiring her strength and determination. Would I be the same in a similar situation? Possibly not.

Lottie slid her hand across the table to meet mine. 'It's making me appreciate that I have to be grateful for the things I have. I spent so long trying to do that, with my Jars of Joy and journals – trying to focus on the good things in my life, but I think I never quite succeeded. I was always distracted by envy, or fear.'

'Envy?' I blinked at her. 'Who were you envious of?'

Lottie sighed. 'It doesn't matter now. I don't want to even think about that now.'

'OK, fair enough.' I nodded, not wanting to stress her out by pushing the point.

'At least Mum is being sweet now. She is making a fuss of me and doing loads of research, insisting that we find the best consultants, investigate the newest treatments.' Lottie scoffed. 'It's like she's finally realised I exist. Even Dad visits more now and they don't argue any more –

instead it's all whispered conversations when they think I can't hear them.'

'That must be hard.'

'I'm getting used to it. It's always been difficult being the only child. I feel like all the pressure is on me to either impress or disappoint them.' Her gaze fixed on mine. 'Don't you miss your brother at all, Sara? Do you still not see him?'

I pulled my hand away from her grip, suddenly feeling uncomfortable. 'No, I don't. We lead completely different lives.'

'That's a shame.' Her voice was quiet, barely a whisper. 'I'd imagine having a sibling would be a special thing. They are an extension of you really, aren't they. I would love to have that connection.'

'There is no connection,' I said, bringing an end to the conversation.

Lottie had nodded like she understood but I knew she didn't. How could she? No one else knew what it had been like to live with Kyle. No one else knew what I had been through, seen.

Why on earth would I want that back in my life?

The waitress brings over my pancake, the sugar on it sparkling in the light. I take it, thanking her politely, and hope she didn't see the tears in my eyes.

I cried the first time I came here with Lottie and I'm crying again now, but I've realised one important thing: Lottie could easily have been talking about me when she said she was too scared to face things. After all, it was me who always ran away, me who pushed people away, me who hid from reality.

Maybe I have to learn to live my life properly too.

Day Thirteen

Sara

Kyle lives in a block of flats in Clapham. I have to jump back on the train to get there and use my phone to find the address. It is a grim-looking grey building, built alongside the back of the railway. There is a faint scent of piss as I climb the concrete stairs, but it's thankfully cool inside the building. The sound of music plays from one flat and laughter from another. I try and fight back the fear that is threatening to spill out of me.

The same mantra keeps playing out in my head: *He's my brother. My blood. Isn't it time I stopped avoiding him? I am doing the right thing.*

Thankfully, Kyle lives on the third floor; I don't think I have the energy to climb much higher. On the external walkway, as I pass the various front doors looking for forty-nine, there is an assortment of stuff outside people's front doors – overflowing plant pots, battered bikes, children's scooters – and it takes me a while to pick my way across. Kyle's grey door is unsurprisingly bland. I take a deep breath and then rap on the brass knocker.

After a few seconds, the door opens. A slim woman faces me. She is pretty and blonde with a sunny-looking smile. I recognise her from the photos Mum has showed me – Jenny. We have never actually met.

'Sara?' She grins and then rushes to me, pulling me into a hug. She smells of that expensive perfume I'd always wanted to treat myself to. 'I'm so glad you came. I've been wanting to meet you for so long.'

'Well, I…' I pull myself away, not sure what to say, and then notice that Kyle is standing right behind her. His hair is cropped short now and he has a trim beard that suits him. When he smiles at me, I barely recognise him. Kyle didn't smile much as a kid.

'Sara, come in,' he says warmly. 'I don't want Jen to suffocate you before we've even had a chance to talk.'

–

I sip at my tea, peering around the room in surprise. It's really nice in here. I'm guessing it's Jenny's taste. Everything is co-ordinated perfectly; the sofa and armchair are cream leather and filled with colourful cushions, the walls are neutrally painted but brightened with interesting art prints and the floor is cloaked by a huge and plush rug. Jenny spends a few minutes buzzing around me, asking polite questions about my job, my flat. I find I'm answering them in almost parrot fashion. Not meaning to be rude or anything, but unable to lighten the awkwardness that hangs onto me from just being here.

My eyes fall on a photo by the TV. It's one of the three of us – me, Kyle and Mum.

'That was taken just before I went to the young offender's unit.'

In the photo, Kyle looks so much older than his thirteen years. His eyes are sunken and there are dark shadows underneath, like smudges on his skin. I look up at him now. He seems different, brighter, more awake. The shadows have gone.

'I'm glad you came.' He sits next to me on the sofa. 'Every time we come to see Mum I ask after you. I wanted to visit, but Mum didn't think that would be a good idea.'

I shrug. 'I've never really been one for visitors.'

'But it's more than that, isn't it?'

'I should leave you to talk for me a bit,' Jenny says, smiling a bit too brightly. 'You have a lot to catch up on.' She rushes out of the room, closing the door firmly behind her.

Kyle sighs softly. 'So, come on, tell me. Why have you been hiding from me for so long? Ashamed of your criminal brother?'

My cheeks flush. 'No, no nothing like that.'

'Then what is it like?'

I shift awkwardly on the seat. I feel too hot, my skin is itchy and I suddenly have the urge to run of here. I close my eyes briefly and it's back, that memory of Kyle laying into Jay's dad – the screams. The blood.

'Sara' – his voice is softer now – 'what is it?'

'I – I was scared of you.'

He doesn't answer at first, and I watch as he twists his fingers in his lap; his head is bowed and his shoulders are hunched. He seems to have shrunk to half his size.

'It makes sense,' he says finally. 'I guess I was kind of scary. I had so much pent-up rage. So much frustration. I scared myself at times.'

'I saw what happened that night,' I continue quietly, aware that my voice is shaking. This is the first time I've actually said the words out loud. 'I was watching out of the window that night and I saw what you did to Jay's dad.'

'You saw?' He looks up, his eyes are wide. 'Shit, Sara, didn't you tell anyone?'

'No. I guess I was too scared to. I wanted to forget.'
I shake my head softly. 'I didn't even tell Jay. He was so
upset about it, why would I want to bring it all up? I was
terrified we would never be friends again.'

'Jay was always a good friend to you. He knew none
of this was your fault.'

'It still pulled our families apart though, didn't it? Jay's
mum never forgave ours. Their marriage fell apart. You
ended up—' My voice breaks.

For the first time, Jay reaches over and touches my arm.
'I ended up getting help, Sara. It was what I needed.'

'You hated everyone,' I whispered.

'No,' he replied firmly. 'No, I didn't. I loved you all
very much. I still do. I just didn't know how to show it.'

It's hard to talk about stuff that has filled up your life for
so many years. I could have completely opened up, broken
down that wall I built around myself and told Kyle exactly
what I thought and how I felt, but just the idea of that was
exhausting. And what good would it serve now? Sitting
here now, staring at the old photo of Kyle with his tired
eyes and drawn expression – I realised that the same man
wasn't sat next to me now. So much had changed with
time.

'I've had a lot of help,' Kyle says, as if reading my mind.
'I'm not saying I'm perfect, but, you know, I'm better than
I was. I have coping techniques and medication. I know
what my triggers are. I look after myself better.'

'That night was so scary, seeing you like that…'

'I know and I'm ashamed. I hated seeing Mum hurt,
but that was no excuse to do what I did,' he pauses. 'Mum
told me that you and Jay were very close after for a long
time.'

'Yeah, I guess we were. At school we were friends and then…' I think of that night on the beach. I hadn't let myself think of that night for ages but suddenly it all comes flooding back – the sharp stones against my legs and back, Jay pressing closer onto me, his breath warm on my face, his hand reaching down and—

'Sara, you're blushing,' Kyle laughs. 'You clearly still have feelings for this guy.'

'I'm not,' I protest a bit too loud. 'It's just complicated that's all. Mum doesn't like him, and he ended up with my best friend.'

'The girl who died? Mum told me about her.'

'Sounds like you and Mum do a lot of talking.'

Kyle sighs. 'She's my family, and so are you, Sara. We don't have a lot of it left. I've always been interested in your life even though I understood I needed to stay away.'

'I know.' I feel myself calm. 'I'm sorry. I didn't come here to argue.'

'So, what did you come here to do then?'

I tell him about the Jar of Joy and the instructions left by Lottie. I'm glad he doesn't pour scorn on it or laugh at me. Instead, he just listens, nodding patiently.

'I came here because I'm sick of running away from everything, Kyle,' I say firmly. 'I want to start facing up to my life.'

'Well, Sara – that's one thing I understand better than anyone.'

We talk for hours. Jenny comes into the room and joins us. I like her, she's bright and funny and perfect for Kyle – they are so relaxed in each other's company. Weirdly, I find that I'm sharing all sorts of things – the reason why I gave up on art and moved abroad, how I felt coming back and hearing that Jay and Lottie were together and how things changed again when Lottie told me she had cancer.

My body starts to relax as I talk, it's like I'm letting go of so much bottled-up frustration and worry. Kyle and Jenny don't judge or interrupt, they just listen and when I come onto the subject of Jay, they really get it.

'It must be confusing for you,' Jenny says gently. 'You've spent so long telling yourself you can't be with him, no wonder there's a block there.'

'The problem is, you've been listening to other people and not yourself.' Kyle eyes me with a stern expression. 'You can't hold yourself back because of some family feud that was over years ago, I don't even think mum cares about it any more. And you can't stop yourself being happy because of Lottie, those two were together ages ago, and it sounds like it wasn't that successful anyway.'

'It wasn't,' I admit. 'But that doesn't make it any easier. Jay still hurt me when he got with Lottie, I gave him that choice all those years ago. We had got so close, and I opened myself up to him. I told him what I wanted, and he wasn't interested.'

'You told him all of this?'

'Yeah, I wrote it in a letter. I couldn't speak to him at the time because he was looking after his mum and dad and I had to rush off to care for Nan – but everything was in that letter, my heart and soul and he didn't respond. It was like he didn't care. Within weeks he was with Lottie.'

Jenny breathes out. 'Shit, that's tough.'

'Yeah it is,' Kyle agrees. 'But he was younger then and people change, don't they? Let's not all judge ourselves by our behaviour in the past.'

I bow my head, feeling a rush of guilt. Here I am, making peace with the brother I'd shunned for years, but

I struggled to do the same with the one person who had been closest to me for so long. Why did I find this so hard?

'Is it because you're scared that he will hurt you the most?' Kyle asks gently. 'Is that why you're too afraid to let him back in?'

Tears well in my eyes. Yes, that's it. Of course it is. I've spent so long building up defences, protecting myself from pain and rejection, why would I want to subject myself to more? Surely, it's better to keep the danger away from me and try to stop the temptation.

But why did that feel so wrong?

Jenny gives me a box full of tissues and I take a handful, mopping at my eyes, my nose, my face until I finally calm myself down.

'You've been through a lot,' she soothes. 'It's no wonder your head is all over the place.'

I smile gratefully. 'I blame Lottie's stupid jar, if it wasn't for her making me dig everything up from the past and remember everything I wouldn't be in this state.'

'Yeah, maybe,' Kyle says. 'But if it wasn't for Lottie, you wouldn't be here with me, would you?'

'And we are really glad you came,' Jenny adds, squeezing my hand.

There is so much kindness coming from them. Kyle isn't the same angry little boy he used to be, and why on earth did I expect him to be? We had all been through trauma and come through the other side. We were allowed to heal and grow.

'There's something else we'd like to tell you, before you go. We haven't even told Mum yet.' Kyle moves over to Jenny and wraps his arms around her. 'We are going to have a baby. You'll be an auntie soon, Sara. Our little family has just got a little bit bigger.'

One Year Before

Lottie

The treatment was getting so hard. Long days spent getting chemo pumped into me. Days after, feeling sick, exhausted and beaten. Sara was there every step of the way. When I moved back to my mum's, she helped me. My mum was trying to be better, and our relationship had improved. She even let my dad visit occasionally, although it was always strained.

But Sundays became mine and Sara's special time together. We would watch films, play board games and, if I was well enough, go for walks.

My favourite place was the lake. Always the lake. There were so many times when I tried to tell Sara the things that I had done. I knew I didn't have much time left. The doctors started talking about 'making me comfortable' and 'palliative care'. After so long fighting this thing, I knew I was facing months, maybe less.

Death was inevitable.

I had to make my peace. Even though it was much harder to write stuff down, or to even look at my Jars of Joy again, I had to believe that I could right my wrongs.

I loved Sara too much not to.

Day Fourteen

I can't believe I hadn't thought about adopting another cat before. For at least an hour this morning, I've been sitting and watching them play. Goose is like a kitten again, chasing the younger cat around – they are having so much fun. It strikes me that Goose might have been lonely, sitting in this flat all by herself. I should have got her a friend a long time ago.

'Everyone needs someone. It's no fun to be alone,' I whisper, watching as my two pets curl up together on the sofa. A feeling of dread snakes around my insides. I stare at Lottie's jar – only two messages remain and then they are all gone.

Soon I will have nothing left. I will be alone again.

I reach out and touch the glass. All of this has been so emotional, reminding me of my up-and-down relationship with Lottie. We probably weren't the closest friends that have ever existed, we had so many differences and we misjudged each other – but there was something that drew us together. We were both passionate, strong-willed and ultimately kind. We were both seeking the love and security that we never really got from our lives growing up – Lottie because her parents were so cold and distant, and me because my life was so chaotic and disorderly.

Ultimately, we were both looking for love – which we never actually found.

God, that's so shit when you think about it.

I make a quick call to the care home to check on Derek. I'm back next week, but I don't want any nasty surprises. Ade answers and, to my relief, he tells me that Derek is doing better than ever, the drugs really are kicking in now, and I end the call feeling much better than I did.

My phone buzzes in my hand. I glance at the screen and see it's another message from Jay. He clearly doesn't understand what 'leave me alone' means. I open it reluctantly and read the text slowly, it takes a while as the words seem to swim in front of me.

> Hey Sara.
>
> I'm sorry, I know I shouldn't keep trying to contact you like this. Your message was pretty clear. I just don't like leaving things like this. There are still things I'd like to say, if you'd give me the chance.
>
> I'm sorry about the kiss, it shouldn't have happened, but if I'm honest I don't regret it. The truth is, I've never been able to get you out of my head, Sara. I know that's my problem and not yours, but I just felt like it needed to be said.
>
> I will respect your wishes and I won't call again. I'm going back to Newcastle tomorrow anyway, I'm needed back at work.
>
> If I don't hear from you again, I'll understand – but I needed you to know how much you mean to me, how much you've always meant to me.
>
> I wish we could find a way to stop hurting each other.
>
> J x

The words were like bullets tearing into my skin. I click out of the message, blinking away the tears, and try to ground myself by staring at my cats again. I'm doing the right thing – I know it. Jay and I are bad for each other. We can't build on something that was based on teenage infatuation, family divide and ultimate betrayal – that isn't sustainable. I also can't forget what Erica had told me about Jay cheating on Lottie. Even if he didn't want to be with her any more, he could've treated her better. Instead, what had he done? Hurt her and left her heartbroken. That is something that I don't want to bring into my life.

Not again.

We aren't some kind of modern Romeo and Juliet. We are nothing like it.

My phone suddenly rings, making me jump. Surely, it's not Jay?

It's not, and weirdly I feel a mixture of relief and regret. I answer the call quickly.

'Mum? You OK?'

'Yes, yes, I'm fine. I'm just calling because I spoke to Kyle.' Mum's words are tumbling out so fast, I'm having trouble keeping up. 'He said you went to see him yesterday. Sara, that's so wonderful.'

'Well – I thought it was about time.'

'He was so happy, and so am I.' She pauses and I hear her sniff. 'He told you about the baby?'

'Yes.' I grin at the thought. 'I can't believe Kyle is going to be a daddy. He's actually a grown-up now.'

'Our family is finally starting to heal,' Mum replies quietly, and I can hear the crack in her words. 'I've waited for so long for this and at last I can see it. We are together again.'

'Yes, Mum, we are,' I say, and I realise that I'm as relieved as she is.

'I really feel like things are looking up, Sara. We are moving forward.' She pauses. 'And it's about time, we have spent too long being sad and bitter.'

I blink back the tears. 'Yes, Mum – we really have.'

–

The second-to-last message from the jar sits open on my lap; the instructions are clear, but Lottie's intentions aren't. I honestly don't know why she would want to remember that day.

> Go to the lake where we went the day I told you
> my cancer was terminal. Remember the words I
> told you – it's important, I promise.

In truth, I've avoided the lake ever since. How could I forget standing by the water edge, listening as Lottie told me her devastating news. I had been useless really, muttering platitudes that I knew meant nothing and would do no good – but what else can you do when someone tells you they are dying? Especially someone so young with her whole life in front of her. It was so desperately unfair. So wrong. So unjust.

But what else can I do, Lottie wants me back there. She wants me to remember and I've agreed to honour her last wish.

Reluctantly, I pull on my trainers, take a deep breath and step out of the front door.

'*It's OK,*' I hear Lottie breathe by my ear. '*You're almost there now.*'

But it doesn't matter if I'm close to the end or not, this isn't getting any easier.

–

It's only a thirty-minute walk away and I'm glad to have the time to clear my head. It's not as hot today and a cool breeze helps ease my journey. I try listening to music to begin with, but I find every song is making me feel either emotional or more stressed, so I decide to focus on the sounds around me instead.

We did this walk together the last time, when Lottie told me she had something to tell me and suggested we go down to the lake together. She had been in a good mood that day, full of smiles and jokes which lulled me into a false sense of security – I actually believed that she was going to tell me good news. Perhaps an all-clear. As we walked, I was thinking of all the things we could do together after she told me – a holiday perhaps, another trip to London, happy things that friends should do together.

'This is nice,' she had said, grinning. 'Just walking and being together. I missed you so much when you went abroad. I was so upset when you didn't come back after six months.'

'Yeah, I guess I just got caught up out there. It was a different life for a bit,' I said, not telling her that Dec had already warned me that Lottie and Jay were 'kind of dating' and how I might want to prepare for that if I came back. Turns out it took me two years to prepare and even then it still hurt like a bitch.

'I feel like we lost so much time,' she said gently. 'All that time you were away and then when you first came back, you didn't even contact me.'

'It was awkward…' I felt bad saying it. 'You know. You guys were still together.'

'Barely.' She half laughed. 'Do you know I didn't bump into you by accident in town that day we met up? I'd actually been waiting outside your flat. I wanted to knock, but I was too scared that you might not want to talk, so I ended up following you instead.'

'A bit creepy…'

'I know, I know, but when I got that diagnosis I felt so alone. Mum couldn't cope with it. Dad thought he could throw money at it. Jay wasn't there. I needed you.'

'I'm sorry,' I said, because what else was there to say? I did have regrets. I knew I had lost lots of time hiding away when I probably should have been facing up to my problems. I didn't think about the knock-on effect it would have on those around me.

As I reach the lake now I take the same circular route that I took with Lottie before. The wind whips at my hair as I walk close to the water, watching the ducks circle gracefully on the surface. I peer down into the shallows and can just about make out the golden scales of a carp skimming below. I'd forgotten how nice it is here, how peaceful. The lake itself is tucked away from the rest of the town, so apart from a few dog walkers and a young family feeding the swans on the other side, I am alone.

Lottie always loved it here. The sea was too wild for her. Too unpredictable. The lake was where she felt safe.

I take a seat on the same battered old bench where I'd sat with her before. I tip my head up towards the shielded sun and draw out a long breath. I remember her words when we sat here before. I think they have been lodged into me ever since, like invisible ink carved into my bones.

'I'm dying, Sara,' she said quite calmly. 'There's nothing I can do.'

I remember how I'd suddenly noticed how frail Lottie had looked sitting there; how had I missed that before? Her skin was grey and drawn, her cheeks sunken and her arms and legs looked too thin and reedy against the frame of the bench. Had I just ignored these signs because I was too scared to see them?

It was then when I became flustered. I argued. I insisted that there must be more things we could look into, surely not every avenue had been investigated. I took her tiny hand in mine and realised it was like gripping twigs. I was suddenly so scared of hurting her. I burst into tears.

'I'm so tired, Sara,' she said. 'But it's OK, really it's OK.'

'OK! How is any of this *OK*?'

She shrugged. 'I think I'm done with being angry. It's not helping. I've realised, probably a little too late, that bitterness only ends up eating you up. I wish I'd spent more time being grateful for the small things I had rather than wishing that everything was different.'

'But this is so unfair.'

'Yeah. It is.' She smiled weakly. 'But that's life, isn't it. We're all dealt a hand. We never quite know how the game will play out.'

We sat in silence for a bit then. I was still sobbing softly, trying to think of solutions, anything to make things better, and Lottie remained calm and poised, staring out towards the lake as if she had just told me the weather report for tomorrow.

We always were so different.

'It's when something like this happens that you start to evaluate your life better,' she said quietly, her gaze still fixed on the water. 'I think of some of the mistakes I've made in the past – some of the regrets I have – and I wish that I'd done things differently.'

'You can't be thinking stuff like that now, Lottie.'

'No, maybe not.' She paused for a moment. 'But maybe I can figure out a way to fix a few things – it'll give me some peace.'

'What do you mean?'

What was Lottie talking about? Was she upset about Jay? I knew she hadn't spoken to him in some time. Or was this about her fractured relationship with her parents – I knew it was something she often felt sad about. She turned back to face me and for the first time that day, her expression was so sad. My heart sank, waiting for more bad news – but when she finally spoke her words surprised me.

'You have been such a good friend to me, Sara. I know we haven't known each other that long and perhaps things could have been better at times, but you came at a time when I really needed you. I'd always dreamt of having a friend like you, someone I could aspire to be one day. I think in many ways you made me stronger. I only wish I could have been better to you.'

'Oh, Lottie – you have been a good friend.'

She shook her head sadly. 'I should have never dated Jay. It wasn't right. You need to know, I—'

I quickly interrupted her. I hated to see her beat herself up about this, especially with everything she was already going through.

'Forget about Jay, Lottie. We were never going to work, and I don't have ownership over him. I shouldn't have stayed away for so long like a wounded child. I should have been happy for you.'

'There wasn't much to be happy about in the end. We didn't exactly work out well either...' Her gaze drifted off again. 'But I do think maybe we should talk about it.'

'Not yet we shouldn't. We have plenty of time for that. Today is about you. Just you.' I pulled her into a hug, feeling her delicate body press against mine. I really did believe, even then, that we'd have so much time together – that we would have lots more talks and walks and opportunities to put right the wrongs of the past.

How could I have guessed that Lottie was just weeks away from leaving me?

I sit here now, blinking away the tears. Why does Lottie want this all coming back to me now? Was it the unfinished conversation? Or was it just the fact that we had sealed our love for each other, here on a battered old bench in the faded sunshine.

Somebody once told me that grief is an assault on your emotions and that you never quite know what will strike you next. This is exactly how I feel now, as pain, fear, anger, regret and sorrow seem to be swamping me at once. Will this ever get easier?

And now I'm still left with questions. Was there something more she wanted to tell me? Was she going to open up about Jay cheating on her, or was there more? Was there something else I needed to know?

I reach for my phone.

One person could provide me with the answer of course, but how could I trust them? How would I know that anything Jay told me would be the truth?

But there was someone else. Somebody who had been close to them both.

Somebody who might be able to give me some much-needed answers.

I find the number and press dial before I had second thoughts.

And then I take a shaky breath.

Day Fourteen

Sara

'Sara?' Dec sounds surprised to hear from me. Of course he would be. I never call him. He's always the one that has made the effort to stay in touch. I've always been rubbish at that.

'Dec...' My words catch. 'I need to talk to you about Jay, Lottie, me – everything. You were there with us the whole time. You saw it all. I need a fresh perspective.'

'Oh.' A pause and then he finally speaks. 'I did wonder when this might happen...'

'Why did Jay hurt us so much, Dec?'

The family across the lake have moved· away now, probably to the little cafe across the bridge where they'll buy ice creams and cold drinks. I am quite alone here now, apart from the birds and ducks and Dec's disembodied voice on the other end of the phone.

'Sara, I'm not sure I'm the best person to be talking to here. It doesn't seem right, I'm not even in the country any more. It's Jay you should be talking to. He was so upset when I spoke to him earlier, and you won't listen to him and—'

'I can't talk to Jay. I'm not sure I believe him at the moment.'

'Well, you should for once. Maybe all this would've never happened if you just trusted people.'

'What's going on, Dec?' I snap.

I hate it when he goes on one of his desperate rambles like this. I can never make head or tail of what he's trying to say. He used to be like this at school, turning bright red like a tomato and stuttering while he was trying to get his words out. It was endearing sometimes, except when you really wanted to find something out.

Dec sighs loudly. 'It's you that keeps hurting Jay, Sara, not the other way around. For once, you need to stop pushing him away.'

I shake my head. 'That's – that's not true.'

He sighs. 'Maybe it's not, maybe it's more complex than that, but I hate seeing my two dearest friends tear each other apart because they're not listening to each other. There's stuff you still don't know.'

I draw a breath. 'So, tell me. What is it? I know Lottie was trying to say something before but she couldn't—'

'I can't, Sara. It's not my place. You need to talk to Jay.'

'Why should I?' I demand, fury overtaking me. Maybe it's the emotion of being at this place again – of thinking of Lottie – or perhaps it's the frustration of years of not really knowing what was going on.

'Why should I listen to a man who has spent his time hurting and cheating those closest to him,' I continue, my heart pounding hard in my chest. 'First me and then Lottie, treating us both like we don't matter. Perhaps I could forgive him for messing me around, we were young and stupid after all, but Lottie? What did she do to deserve that?'

'Lottie?' Dec sounds confused. 'What are you going on about?'

'I know about Jay cheating on her. That's why they split up,' I say plainly. 'It probably broke her heart even more.'

There is a pause and then Dec sighs loudly. 'Sara, that's not what happened. It wasn't Jay that slept with someone else, it was Lottie.'

'How do you know that?' I demand.

Another pause. Longer this time.

'Because she slept with me.'

It takes a few seconds for his statement to resonate. 'You? She slept with you? How?'

'I'm sure I don't have to explain the details, Sara,' he scoffs. 'I was down visiting, and Lottie was a bit upset. Her and Jay weren't getting anywhere. It was clear he just wanted to be friends, but she wanted more. We all got drunk and suddenly Lottie was all over me. I later worked out that it was an attempt to make him jealous, not that I really cared at the time. I always had a soft spot for Lottie and I guess I hoped she might have liked me a bit too.' He laughs harshly. 'Who was I kidding, eh?'

'And did it work? Did it make Jay jealous?'

'Of course it didn't. Jay didn't care what Lottie did. He was still getting over you. He was always getting over you.'

Still getting over me? That didn't make any sense.

'Dec – Jay was the one who decided he didn't want to take things any further with me. I put my heart on the line for him. I wrote a letter telling him how I felt.'

'The letter?' Dec sounds confused. 'But it was the letter that finally broke Jay's heart.'

'What? What do you mean?'

'After he read it, he was devastated. It was a pretty low blow, Sara, writing him something so cold and uncaring. He said you clearly weren't interested in him and then you went off travelling. To be honest I thought you were better than that. I wanted to say something to you at the time, but Jay told me not to. He just wanted you to be happy.'

I take a deep breath, my head is swimming with this new information and nothing is making sense. 'No, Dec. No, that's not what happened!' I stand up, my heart is racing now. I start to pace the area around me. Why is Dec saying all of this stuff? It simply isn't true... 'Jay has told you it all wrong,' I say as calmly as I can. 'I never told him I wasn't interested. After that night we got together, I was excited – a bit nervous, yes, but I was excited to see what might happen between us. But he was caught up with his dad being ill and I couldn't text him because his stupid phone was broken, so I wrote him a letter. I told him exactly how I felt. It was meant to be romantic and sweet—'

'Really?' Dec's voice has turned to ice. 'I read it, Sara, after you left. I saw what you told him. It's no wonder he was upset. It was like you didn't care.'

'Hang on...' I shake my head, trying to make sense of this. 'You read my letter, the one where I told him I wanted to give our relationship a go? Where I told him that I wanted something more and that if he wanted the same thing, he should call me? I waited and waited, Dec, and that call never came. When I got back, I found Jay with Lottie and he was so distant, so I just assumed—' The words are choking up in my throat. 'Dec, what is it you're telling me?'

'I–I don't think Jay got your letter. Not the one you wrote anyway.' He pauses. 'Who gave him the letter, Sara?'

'Lottie,' I whisper. 'She did it as a favour. She told me...' I wobble a little on the spot. How could I have been so stupid? It's all making total sense now. 'When I was here – with her before – she told me she hadn't been a good friend. She told me there were things I needed to know, but I just dismissed her. This was it, wasn't it? She wanted to tell me what she'd done. She'd pushed me away from Jay.'

'I think so.' Dec sounds sad. 'She was very confused, Sara, and a bit lost. I think she just wanted what you had.'

'But I had nothing in the end.' I can hear my heartbeat thudding in my ears. My breath is shaky. I stop pacing. 'She even encouraged me to go travelling, she told me it would be good for me. But she just wanted me out of the picture. I thought she was my friend, Dec, and all the time…'

'I'm sorry, Sara, but you needed to know the truth,' he says gently. 'For what it's worth, I do think Lottie loved you, but she was very mixed up. She thought she could be happier if she could have a life more like yours. She thought the answer was with Jay.'

'So, in pursuit of her own happiness, she destroyed mine,' I say frostily.

Her latest message is still in my pocket. I pull it out and scrunch it up between my fingers and then toss it into the water.

All her bloody Jar of Joy has done has caused more pain. I want nothing more to do with it.

'I'm sorry to have thrown all this at you,' Dec says. 'I wish I was there to help you guys sort it all out. I couldn't leave you in the dark, though, thinking that Jay was this bad person. He has been beating himself up for too long. He deserves better.'

'Yes,' I reply quietly. 'He does.'

He deserves so much more.

I walk home in a trance, trying to process everything Dec told me. For some reason, things aren't settling properly in my head. I feel like a jigsaw where all the pieces have been shaken up – nothing makes sense any more.

Why did Lottie lie to me for so long? Why did she push me and Jay apart? What letter did she even give him, and how could she have done that to me knowing how much I liked him? I think of all the times I sat with her during her illness, holding her hand, nursing her through the bad times, and bitterness floods me.

Could she have really done this? Or had Dec – strong, reliable Dec – made a mistake somehow?

'What was I to you, Lottie?' I mutter aloud. 'I was never really your friend, was I? You just used me when there was no one better around.'

For once I can't hear her reply. All I hear is an icy silence echoing around me. It's like my friend was never there at all.

And what was the Jar of Joy – was it something to make her feel better about the pain she caused? Or was it a final laugh in my face?

Did I ever really know her at all?

As soon as I get back into the flat, I stride past my welcoming cats, pick up the stupid jar and smash it in the sink, well away from their delicate paws. I stare numbly at the shattered pieces that are left, the sprinkles of glitter and the naff stickers that Lottie had stuck on. Regret and bitterness spike in my veins.

'I never wanted you,' I hiss. 'I never wanted any of this.'

The last message still remains, stuck to the base of the glass. I walk away leaving it there. I don't want to read it. I don't think I ever will.

Later, after I'd forced myself to eat and allowed Fifi and Goose to curl up next to me and comfort me, I pick up Lottie's diary. Once again, I leaf through the pages, staring blankly at her curved, loopy writing, wondering if I can bring myself to read her words. Surely it would be more lies and delusions. Who knew what went through Lottie's head.

And then I spot it. Nestled in the middle of the diary is a folded piece of paper. I tug it out, my heart beating fast, but I know what it is before I even open it. I remember how I'd folded this pale sheet over and over, how my hands had shaken writing the words. I open it, my breath ragged and my eyes damp.

It's my letter to Jay. The final proof. She did take it. So then what on earth did she replace it with? Any tiny doubts I had quickly fade away.

Lottie had destroyed the one good thing I had in my life. The only man I had ever loved.

I need answers. My hands are still shaking. I flick through her diary searching until I find the right date, the day that she started at our school.

And then slowly, I begin to read, once again hearing her voice flood my mind.

> 'I just need a few more seconds, OK? Just a few more...'
>
> This was it. My first day at this sixth form college and I was absolutely terrified. What if it was a big mistake? What if I didn't fit in – again!

Six Months Before

Lottie

I was busy finally. Every spare minute was spent on this final Jar of Joy. It was my final gift. The only thing I could think of that might work.

I want her to remember the good times, like I always did.

As I worked, the light shined through my window making the glass on the jar glow. It was like a little piece of magic in my hands. I used one of my old jars from my childhood. The glitter and stickers were a little aged, so I did my best to brighten it up. I knew I didn't have much time.

Downstairs, I hear the doorbell go and then her voice as she spoke to my mum at the door.

'I'm here for Lottie.'

I smiled sadly. The truth was, she always was.

I'd realised it far too late.

Day Fifteen

Sara

I woke up late. I'd been up most of the night reading. The diary lay discarded by the side of my bed. Lottie's words flood me, like a cold wind sweeping through my brain. I pull the covers tight over my body as if it would protect me in some way.

All of Lottie's feelings have now been revealed.

Her desire to get with Jay.

Her weird jealousy of me.

The letter she had forged.

And the lies she had told to try and keep us both apart.

It was all there, right in front of me. Lottie wanted me to read it, so I guess she needed me to know what a horrible, fake person she had really been. I shake my head at the craziness of it all.

'You were never my friend,' I hiss, getting out of bed and kicking the book across the room. She was the worst type of enemy – a silent one, only interested in destroying and hurting others.

I am done.

I busy myself. I can't face breakfast, so I feed the cats and get myself half decent instead. I put the radio on to try and distract my brain. When a dance record comes on that reminds me of Lottie, I quickly change the station.

Eighties music floods the room instead and I instantly relax. I pick up the shattered glass and broken remains from Lottie's jar and throw it all away, rinsing the sink so that every trace of her stupid glitter is gone. I pocket her last message, meaning to throw it away later. I don't think I can ever face that one.

I try to ring Jay. I need to speak to him. I have so much to say, but his phone clicks straight through to voicemail.

'Hey,' I say, leaving a croaky message. 'We really need to talk. I've found some stuff out. Please call me. It's important.'

I wonder if he's already gone back to Newcastle. I debate jumping on a train and following him up there, but I don't even know his address, and it's not like I can knock at his mum's and ask for it, I'm still probably the last person she wants to see.

I pace the flat. I can't stay here. It's already getting hot, and my mind is racing. The only other person I want to confront is dead and can't answer my questions.

I scoop up my bag and head out of the door.

There is only one other person who can cheer me up when I'm feeling like this.

–

'Twice in one week? Aren't you meant to be on holiday and getting a break from here?'

Derek is back in the main resident's sitting room. He is looking so much better. He has colour in his cheeks now and his bright smile is back, I immediately feel my spirits lighten just seeing him.

'Well, I just can't keep away, can I?' I say, smiling. 'Besides, I wanted to update you on the Lottie saga.'

Derek leans forward. 'Take a seat and tell me more!'

I perch on the armchair next to him and tell him the whole sorry story. I watch as his eyes widen at the key points, then as he nods delicately as I draw to a close. Once I finish, he taps my hand lightly with his long, thin fingers.

'That is quite a lot, Sara.'

'I know.' I bow my head. 'I can't believe I didn't notice these things before. I've been so stupid. Why didn't I see what Lottie was up to? Instead, I just ran away like I always do. I never gave Jay a chance to sort things out with me.'

Derek sighs softly. 'Now is not the time for regrets. We could all spend hours looking back on our lives and wishing we'd done things differently. I think you should be seeing this in a different light.'

'How?' My voice cracks. 'How can I see this any differently? It's a mess, all of it. I thought Lottie was my friend, I thought she cared for me…'

'I think she did, but she sounded like a very confused young woman. I think Lottie saw your life as a reflection on her own – it showed her what she was missing. She sounded like a very lonely and mixed-up person.'

'But that doesn't make what she did right, does it?' I say, feeling indignant.

'Not at all.' Derek smiles and squeezes my hand. 'But it does mean that you can have a little bit of empathy towards her. You've admitted before that you and Jay were uncertain before, both of you were putting obstacles between yourselves. Who knows what might have happened if you had gotten together when you were younger, maybe you weren't ready?'

'But we didn't get the opportunity to try.'

'Maybe not – but you did get the opportunity to spread your wings, to travel, to see some of the world, and Jay got to focus on his career. Who knows what would've happened if you had both stayed together in the same town. I'm not saying what Lottie did was right, but she was young, jealous and foolish and maybe her actions haven't been that damaging because it sounds to me that you both still have feelings for each other.'

I nod slowly. 'I do still like him, Derek, but I've pushed him away again. I keep doing that to him. I'm worried that this time it might be for good.'

'You have to find out, one way or another. Your heart needs to know the answer.' Derek's voice is firmer now. 'Life passes too fast, Sara. If you are given a second chance you should grab it with both hands. Don't be an old man like me, sitting here with regrets.'

I squeeze his hand. 'Thank you.'

'Try not to be angry with Lottie,' he adds. 'I think she is seeking your forgiveness now. The diary, the Jar of Joy – they have all been ways to bring you back to the truth. Lottie wants you to be happy, I think she wanted to give you your joy back. She wanted to put things right.'

'There's one final message of hers,' I say, digging it out of my pocket. 'I was going to throw it away, but maybe—'

'Read it,' Derek urges. 'It might bring an end to all of this.'

Gently, I unravel the crumpled paper. My heart is in my mouth as I read the words.

'Oh my God,' I whisper. 'Why does she want me there?'

Derek looks confused. 'Are you OK, Sara?'

I nod, even though I know my face is on fire. 'Yeah, I'm fine. It's the last place I want to go right now, but I will.'

I just hope Derek was right and it will bring me some kind of closure.

–

Jess hugs me on the way out. 'Are you OK?' she asks, fussing around me. 'You look so pale – and I worry I've not been much of a friend, since, well, you know…'

I hug her back, suddenly realising how much I've needed this, a simple hug. I feel like I'm melting into her. 'I'm fine, Jess, honestly. My head has been all over the place, but it's not been all bad.'

I give her a quick run–down of events. She is clearly shocked over Lottie's actions, but Derek has given me a different perspective.

'I don't think Lottie was in a good place for a long time,' I say. 'But when I came back from travelling, she was different. Maybe the illness gave her perspective, but I think she had grown up too. That last year we spent together was special, I don't want to forget that. I think I was the friend she needed then, the one she'd always been looking for. And she was good for me too, we had so many special moments together. There were times when she tried to talk to me about stuff from the past, but I just shut her down, selfishly I wasn't ready for that. I guess that's why she did the jar. She needed me to know the truth.'

Jess smiles. 'I'm glad you can see the good in all of this.'

'I think I'm starting to. I'm back talking to my brother. Mum and me are a bit stronger than we were – hey, I even don't hate Erica as much as I did.' I half laugh. 'In a weird way Lottie has sorted out half of my problems.'

'Except you and Jay?'

'Maybe no one can help us,' I say quietly, my stomach clenching. 'Even I don't know the answer to that one yet.'

—

I head straight to where Lottie instructed me to. I'm still confused as to why she has chosen this place. It's so specific, so personal.

And so sad.

I crunch across the stones to the same groyne that I had sat against all those years ago. The sea is much calmer today and of course it is daylight now, not night. I sit myself down on the damp pebbles and stare across at the same beach outlook that I had before. It's busy today, there are families gathered, sitting on towels and blankets. Windbreakers snap in the breeze. A dog runs between the stones yapping excitedly. If I look up, past the beach, I can see the tiny winding path that leads right up to Lottie's back gate.

All those years ago me and Jay had been alone here. We had just kissed at first, hesitantly, unsure, all those years of teasing and bickering suddenly unleashing in a drunken and lustful need. Jay had pulled back, staring in my eyes with an uncertain gaze.

Was this what I wanted? Was I sure?

The throb between my legs and the heat that was rising throughout me told me all I needed to know. I pulled him towards me. Soon we were tugging and pawing at each other. Jay's hand slipped under my dress, he found my breast and squeezed it. I remember crying out, not in pain but in lust. I pushed aside my knickers, hitched up my dress. All I wanted was Jay inside of me; I needed him.

The crash of the waves that night and the sharpness of the rocks against my skin only made me want him more. I remember his weight as he pressed against me, the first thrust of him as he entered me, the ripple of pleasure that overcame me as he stroked and teased me.

That night had been so rough, so quick, and yet so perfect. Afterwards, we both lay with our arms wrapped around each other, tears in our eyes, sand and stone stinging our skin.

'Was that OK?' he'd whispered.

I'd kissed his chapped, salty lips and laughed.

It had been more than OK. It was wonderful, amazing, everything I had ever wanted and yet…

I had never told him that.

I had got up. Pulled up my knickers and laughed it off.

If only I had told him that night, instead of making out it was no big deal, none of this shit would have happened. Lottie was right in her diary: I was never clear with Jay. I sent him mixed signals. My own insecurities had caused this mess.

It was because of me that Jay and I had failed before we'd had a chance to begin.

Tears begin to flow, and I don't fight them off this time, I don't see the point. I'm not hiding any more. I can see the person that I am.

I need to break free from her.

'Sara?'

I look up.

Jay is standing in front of me. I have to blink several times, hardly able to believe it. I rub at my streaming eyes.

'Sara? What's wrong?'

'I thought...' I shake my head. 'I thought you'd gone?'

'I nearly did,' he says, 'but then I remembered I had one more message.'

Jay holds out a jar in front of him. I stare at it blankly for a moment or two. 'Hang on. You have one too?'

He nods. 'Yeah. Erica brought it over after Lottie's funeral. It's filled with memories, of places we used to go.'

I pause, thinking this all through. 'Was that why you were at the cafe like me? The flats?'

Jay smiles. 'Yeah, Lottie wanted me to revisit all our favourite places...'

'I thought you were checking up on me.'

'Well – it was good to see you, too.'

I shake my head. 'But this makes no sense. Why did she make us both one?'

Jay shrugs. 'I'm not sure. Maybe so I stuck around for a bit? So I got to remember the fun things we did together – to honest, most of the memories reminded me of you, not Lottie.'

'Funny that,' I say quietly.

'Also, I still have one last message – well not so much a message, it's a letter.' He pulls it gently out of the jar. 'And it's addressed to both of us.'

> *Dear Jay and Sara,*
>
> *I hope you are reading this as I planned, on your spot on the beach. I'm sorry it's come to this. I hoped that I might have had the opportunity to tell you the truth to your faces, but I always was a bit of a coward and was always better at writing stuff down than actually saying it out loud. I hope you can see that I meant no malice in my actions, I*

was misguided and naive and a bit of a bitch. For all of these things, I'm sorry. I really am.

Above everything else – I mistook your love for each other. I didn't quite realise how important you were to one other. By stepping between you, I did a terrible thing and for that I have so much regret.

I genuinely love both of you. Sara – I wanted to be your best friend, your only friend. And Jay, I wanted to be loved by someone and I was so scared of losing you both, of being alone.

Stupid, isn't it? It's only now that I realise that I could have had both of your friendships if I hadn't been so bloody selfish. I think when you are alone a lot, you forget to see the bigger picture. I spent too long focusing on the things I didn't have, rather than seeing the things that I did have right in front of me.

I forgot to see the joy.

That's why I made you both the jars. I bet you both thought they were pretty naff, but I hope you can understand my thought behind them. I wanted you to re-experience some of the important moments we shared together – even more vital, I wanted you to remember what it is that matters.

I may have been guilty of trying to break you two up, of telling lies and trying to be something I wasn't – but you two aren't innocent either. Sara, you have constantly hidden yourself from any conflict or stress. You are too afraid to embrace the life you really want. And Jay – you too were fearful of saying or doing the wrong thing. You have to take chances sometimes. I know you both fear rejection, but a life of loneliness is far worse. Believe me. I know.

And you are both rubbish at telling each other how you really feel!

I love you both so much and now all I want is for you to be happy. Stop letting others be the excuse for you to not give this a chance. Your family will have to accept your decision, and they will because they love you too. You are no longer Romeo and Juliet. For a while I was your poison, but now I'm gone. Now you are Jay and Sara. This is your life and yours alone and it's desperately short, so please embrace it.

I was wrong to be jealous of you. I want you to continue finding joy, not find reasons to hide away from it. I am much happier now, which is ironic because I'm dying – but I've finally accepted and learnt to love the person I am. I am also so grateful to have my friendship with you back, Sara – the time we spent together was precious and I have memories, laughter and joy that will stay with me forever (and hopefully beyond – whatever that may be).

I now want the same thing for both of you.

You are so lucky to have each other, don't let it go again.

Be brave.

And above all, let love win.

Lottie

XXX

Day Fifteen

Sara

Jay folds the letter back up and lets out a deep breath. 'Wow.'

I can't talk, not straight away. Around us is the chatter of happy families, the crash of the waves, the call of the seagulls – but suddenly it's like Jay and I have been sucked into a tiny vacuum, just the two of us. All I can hear is the soft sound of his breathing.

'Did you know any of this?' he asks.

'Most of it – I'd just started to find out,' I say, and then I tell him everything I know. I watch as his face crumples as the facts hit him. It breaks my heart to see the effect my words have on him. 'I'm so sorry,' I whisper even though it wasn't my fault, not really.

'I need to process this,' he mutters.

We sit down, our backs against the groyne. Jay is still clutching the letter in his hand. He shakes his head.

'I can't believe she did this – all this time she was coming between us.'

'To be honest, Jay, I think we put enough obstacles between ourselves.'

He stares at me blinking. 'But if I'd received your letter – the one you were meant to give me – everything would have turned out different.'

'Maybe.' I stretch out my legs, giving thought to this. 'But who knows? We were both different then. I was so scared of commitment, of being hurt. We were both young and daft. We were both still so worried about upsetting our parents. Maybe it wouldn't have worked out anyway. Lottie did a bad thing, but she might've been right – we weren't in a good place for each other.'

'And what about now?' Jay asks tentatively.

'Now?' I smile weakly. 'I dunno – I guess we're still young and daft.'

'Are you still scared of commitment?'

'No, I don't think so.' My eyes fix on his. 'Are you scared of upsetting your parents?'

Jay laughs. 'I think I've upset them a million times over. Do you know what, I don't think they'd even be bothered about us.'

I shrug. 'Maybe not. It seemed like such a big thing at the time, didn't it?'

'They have their own crap going on.' Jay pauses. 'I think all they ever wanted was for us two to be happy.'

'Lottie was right, wasn't she? We have to start looking for the joy in things, don't we?'

Jay reaches out and touches my face tenderly. A shiver feeds it way right down to the base of my spine, like an electric spark igniting me.

'Sara,' he says quietly. 'You know how I feel about you, don't you?'

I stare back into his eyes, those beautiful clear eyes that I used to dream about on the lonely nights when I was trying so hard to forget about him. Lottie was right, I had always been so scared of love, I tried to push it away. I thought it was the thing that end up harming, or even destroying, me. But I knew right now that it was the thing I needed more than ever.

More specifically, I needed Jay.

Jay leans towards me and when our lips meet I actually gasp. It's not like before, it's more hungry, more urgent. My hands claw his hair, our tongues meet. I want him so badly that the desire is making my body shake. I've waited too bloody long for this.

I pull away.

'Not here,' I say, my gaze burning into his.

And then I take his hand and lead him away.

—

Back at my flat we can't keep our hands off each other, it's like that first time again – desperate and keen – except this time there is a different energy in the room, an understanding that we are both taking this seriously. I lead Jay into my bedroom, and we continue kissing hungrily, tugging our clothes and groaning desperately – both knowing that we have waited too long for this.

I push Jay on the bed and clamber on top of him. His body is perfectly firm and a little more defined than I remember; my fingers trace the newly formed muscles.

'Been working out?' I tease.

Jay smiles. He is also exploring my body. He strokes my breasts, my stomach, my hips. 'You are still as perfect as I remember,' he says.

The sex is fast, hot and urgent. I thrust against Jay, loving the feel of him inside me and wanting more. We come together in a loud sticky mess. Jay laughs. I have tears in my eyes. We both cling to each other almost too scared to let go.

'I've waited for that moment for so long,' he says, his breathing ragged. 'I can't tell you how many times I've dreamt about being back here. With you.'

'And now you are,' I murmur back.

We have sex again, but this time it's slow and sensual. Then we take the time to explore each other's bodies, and with every touch, I shiver. Jay kisses my neck and then continues down to my chest, my stomach and beyond. I am burning with lust, with love and with overriding joy. When I stare up at the ceiling, I swear I see stars dancing above me.

It is so perfect; it almost scares me.

Jay comes back up. He strokes my face.

'Sara. Why are you crying? Didn't you like it?'

'I loved it.' I smile weakly at him. 'But I'm so scared something will happen.'

'What do you mean?'

'Things have got in the way before – our parents, Lottie, even us.' I sniff. 'What if goes wrong again? I'm so scared of being hurt, Jay. I know it's pathetic but it's true.'

'I'm not going to hurt you.'

'I know – I know you don't want to – but you can't know. You can't know what will happen in the future.'

Jay leans up on his elbow. 'No, that's true. I can't. But I know we have to stop being scared of what might be. Look how amazing tonight has been. I'd rather risk having more nights like these than walking away and never having it again.' He kisses me gently on my lips. 'We can be happy, Sara. We are allowed to be and together we can face whatever comes our way in the future.'

He pulls me towards him, and I curl up into his warm body, my head resting on his chest like a pillow. It's so late now, we are both aching and tired. I feel myself begin to relax and soften as my mind begins to drift. Lying here in his arms feels so right. It's like it's always been this way. Just me and Jay. Us against the world.

'Sara,' he whispers. 'It was always you. Always.'

I smile into his chest.

'It was always you, Jay. Even though I tried, I could never forget you.'

Day Sixteen

Sara

My last day of leave and we have so much to sort out. In the space of a day, so much had changed. Jay and I sit in my small kitchen, eating breakfast together and smiling shyly over the table. Everything has shifted now. I am content, warm and happy and even though a little bit of fear dances beneath my emotions, I am learning to embrace it. Fear doesn't have to be a bad thing. For the first time in so long, I feel alive.

Jay bends down to fuss the cats, who are desperately trying to get our attention.

'I never took you for a mad cat woman,' he teases.

'I never really took me for a cat person full stop, but Goose and now Fifi have filled a gap in my life.' I shrug. 'I couldn't be without them now.'

He smiles. 'It just shows what happens when you let love in.'

I pull a face. 'Urgh. Don't be so cheesy.'

He rights himself again. His face is more serious, his gorgeous eyes are fixed on mine. 'So what now, Sara?'

'What do you mean?'

'Well, you have your life down here. I'm in Newcastle. We have our family to think about. All the stuff that Lottie revealed. What are we going to do next?'

I sip my tea. 'I guess we need to talk.' I hold his gaze. 'But first, shall we go back to bed? We have a lot of catching up to do.'

Jay doesn't need asking twice.

–

We visit Jay's mum first. I'm dead anxious. I haven't seen her for years, but she barely reacts when Jay brings me into the flat. Her smile is warm and welcoming. We have tea with her and tell her our plans and she seems pleased for us.

'This is the happiest I've seen Jay look for ages,' she told me quietly, when I helped her take the cups out into the kitchen. 'I've been so worried about him. He's been through a lot; you know, stressing about his dad and then that business with Lottie – she totally drained him.'

'I always thought…' I said hesitantly, unsure of how to put into words the fear I had about her reaction, knowing that she had never liked my family. She simply rested her hand on mine.

'The past is the past, Sara. You can't worry about things that were done by other people. I misjudged you in the past when I shouldn't have. I'd like to think we've all moved on now.'

We hug at the door, and I feel some of my worry ebb away.

'You see,' Jay says. 'I told you it wouldn't be that bad.'

We cross the estate to my mum's flat. We know the two still aren't friends, but I'm hoping my mum will be just as understanding. She opens the door with a beaming smile, clearly pleased to see me, but a concerned look passes across her face when she sees Jay beside me.

We step inside and I tell her everything. I feel quite exhausted by the entire story. Mum's gaze flicks between mine and Jay's. Finally, she pulls me into her arms.

'Oh, Sara. What an ordeal.'

'Yes, for us both.'

'Indeed.' She nods, her teeth worrying her bottom lip. 'I feel so bad. If I hadn't had had my own dramas, maybe you and Jay would've been fine back then. I hate to think of how unhappy you both were.'

'It's OK,' Jay tells her. 'We're together now, that's all that matters.'

Mum nods. 'And what are you going to do now, Jay? Are you moving back here?'

We tell her what we've discussed. I notice how her expression clouds a little. She sniffs but continues nodding.

'I'll still visit lots, Mum, after I have a new nephew or niece to spoil, but I need a new start – I think I've needed one for a while.'

'And you're sure this is what you want to do?'

My voice is firm. 'I've never been more certain.'

Her smile is bright. 'Then you must do it.' She takes both our hands in hers. 'For what it's worth, I always thought you two should be together. There is something about you – it's almost magical. You don't want to let that go.'

I'm not as keen on visiting the next person, but Jay insists it's the right thing to do. We have loose ends to tie up. We have chapters to close.

I knock at the door awkwardly, my stomach feeling the same hollow ache it did the last time I was here.

'It's horrible being here, knowing Lottie will never be back,' I say quietly. 'Despite everything she did, I still miss her. I always will.'

Jay rubs my back. 'I know.'

Erica opens the door slowly. As she peers through the gap, I see she is the same broken woman from before. Her face is still unmade-up, her hair is not as groomed. It is like there is a part of her missing.

'Both of you?' Her voice is clipped. 'To what do I owe this pleasure?'

'We just wanted a quick word, if that's OK?' I say.

Erica seems to consider this for a moment, then shrugs and lets us in. Once again, I am walking through her sparse minimal space until I find myself in the large kitchen. Jay is beside me feeling just as stiff and awkward as I do.

'Why are you here?' she asks.

I pause before talking. I could hit her with everything – what we had found out from Lottie, the lies we had discovered Erica herself had been telling, all of the deceptions that had been created to try and keep me and Jay apart, but what would be the point? Looking at Erica now, all I can see is a lonely, tired woman. A woman who knows that she failed her own daughter. By throwing more accusations and blame at her, what was I going to achieve? She's already grieving; she's already in pain – I don't need to add to that.

Besides, as Jay hooks his hand into mine, I can tell by Erica's resigned face that she knows we are together now. We don't need to point-score.

Instead, I pass her the small bag I'm carrying in my other hand.

'This is for you,' I say gently.

Erica takes it, looking confused, and then pulls out Lottie's diary. She holds it awkwardly. 'I'm not sure Lottie wanted me to have this,' she says finally.

'No, maybe she didn't, but I can't keep it. It's not right,' I say carefully. 'I think maybe Lottie's diaries, her Jars of Joy – all those things should be kept together.'

Erica places the diary on the counter and bows her head. 'Yes, maybe – I'll put it somewhere safe. You're right, her things should be together. I'm just not sure—' Her voice catches and her hand leaps to her mouth. 'I'm sorry,' she whispers. 'I'm not very good at this.'

'It's all right, Erica.' I go over to her, help her sit down. Jay offers to make her a drink and she asks for a strong coffee. For a few minutes we busy ourselves looking after her. I make her eat a biscuit (she looks like she hasn't eaten for days) and then we both sit beside her on her wobbly bar stools.

'I read her Jar of Joy,' Erica says finally, her voice still shaking a little. 'That's not like a diary is it? There were old messages in it, from when she was little. It made me so sad, reading all the things that had made her happy. Silly things, little things – like us two watching films together, or baking cakes for her dad.' She scoffs gently and then sips her drink. 'I thought for so long that she was a happy girl. She had everything she wanted. A pool, horse-riding lessons, designer clothes, nice holidays – but not once did she write those things in her jar. She was happiest with us, with me and her dad, but we were always so busy…'

'Erica, don't blame yourself,' I say gently. Even though a bit of me does blame her. After all, if she had been a better mum, Lottie might not have grown up to be so vindictive and jealous.

'I changed after the divorce. I know that now. I was so selfish and bitter.' Erica shakes her head. 'I can't keep pretending. I messed up.'

'But Lottie had those happy memories of you, right?' Jay says. 'She held onto them. They made a difference to her. You have to remember that.'

Erica sniffs. She probably knows it was a small thing, but it was all she had right now.

'I was thinking…' I say carefully. 'About Lottie's ashes?'

Erica looks up sharply. 'What about them?'

'I was wondering if we could scatter them by the lake? Lottie always loved it there and it would be a nice place to remember her. We could maybe get a bench and dedicate it to her?'

Erica nods slowly. 'Yes… Yes, I like that idea, Sara. It would be good to do something like that.'

'We are never going to forget her,' I add softly. 'She taught me a lot. She has helped me in ways I wasn't expecting.'

Erica looks up and smiles for the first time. It lights up her face. 'She loved you, both of you. You were good friends to her and I'm guessing she possibly wasn't the easiest to be around at times, but Lottie had a good heart underneath it all. She was just searching for happiness, that's all.'

'I know,' I say back quietly.

I hope she was right in her letter, I hope she found a little bit of it.

It still hurts me to think that Lottie died without that.

–

Our last visit is probably the hardest one. I squeeze Jay's hand as I walk through the door. Luckily Sharon sees me straightaway, and although she's disappointed with my decision, she understands. She gives me a hug.

298

'You are great at your job,' she says. 'But I always had a feeling your heart was someplace else. There will always be a door open here if you need it.'

I insist on seeing Derek before we leave. Sharon gives us permission to take him for a walk around the grounds. He looks up as soon as we approach, a cheeky little grin crossing his face.

'Ah, Sara, please tell me this is the elusive Jay I've heard so much about?'

Jay attempts a polite bow. 'Pleased to meet you, sir.'

Derek bats him away. 'You daft bugger, none of that please. But you can push this bloody thing if you want to be helpful.'

'Actually,' Jay says gently, 'I've been offered the opportunity to have a coffee with Sara's friend, Jess.'

Jess is standing a few feet away, grinning. I knew she was desperate to grill Jay. I am cringing at the thought of what she might ask!

'Me and you are going for a short stroll together,' I say to Derek, taking hold of the wheelchair. 'I hope that's OK?'

'Of course it is,' Derek replies. 'Sounds like a perfect afternoon.'

It was Jay's idea that I should speak to Derek alone. He knew how much the man meant to me. As we walk across the grounds with the sun beating against my face, I could feel the tears begin to build in my eyes. How was I going to be able to leave him behind?

'This is the last time I'll see you, isn't it?' Derek says finally, sounding quite cheerful about the matter.

I stopped walking and put the brake on the chair. We were in a quiet, shaded spot quite far from the house.

'It's not the last time,' I say. 'But I've handed in my notice today. I've only got a week's notice and Sharon has said I can forgo that because of all the stuff that's been going on, but I'm not moving to Mars, Derek—'

'You're moving to Newcastle.'

'Yeah, yeah, I am. There is a vibrant art scene there. Jay has a spare room and—' I shake my head, trying to gather my thoughts. 'It sounds crazy, Derek. Everything is moving so fast and yet it's not. This is the most sense anything has ever made. I want to do my art. I want to move away. I want to be with Jay. He's even happy to put up with my mad cats. I know it's a risk, but I'm sick of being careful all of the time.'

'You're doing the right thing,' Derek says. 'I always said you were bloody wasted here.'

I laugh. 'I want to train as an art therapist. I want to work with older residents, help people with dementia and trauma – that sort of thing. I think I can be good at it.'

'I know you'll be good at it.' Derek tuts under his breath. 'You don't need to convince me, Sara. I've been waiting for you to find your happiness and finally you have.'

'But I'll miss you,' I say quietly.

'And I'll miss you. But I'm an old man with not much time left and you're a young girl with a life to lead. I will be happy knowing you're free.'

I can feel my tears building and try to fight them back. 'I'll visit.'

'You don't have to do that.'

'I want to.' I smile. 'Besides, I still have family here, Derek. Like I said, I'm not moving to Mars. You don't get rid of me that easily. I can come and tell you all my training dramas.'

Derek laughs softly. 'In that case, I'll look forward to it.'

We sit for a while, just enjoying the weakening late afternoon sun, and then I start to wheel Derek back, conscious that he needs his rest.

'I hope I'm not making a big mistake,' I say, as we approach the house. 'What if Jay hurts me again? What if I hate the course?'

'Life is full of "what-ifs" – the secret is to embrace them, don't run away from them. You will cope with whatever is thrown at you, Sara. You are strong and capable. You'll be fine.'

'You think so?'

'Of course.' Derek chuckles as we hit the main path. 'Your friend gave you the greatest gift. She helped you find your joy, and whatever mistakes she made in the past, she ensured she helped you get back what you needed.'

I glance up and see that Jay is waiting for me by the entrance. He smiles as I approach and my entire body lights up. He is perfect.

Derek is right, I have been given the greatest gift. One I have longed for for so long.

Suddenly I hear a breath of laughter and a familiar voice floods my ear.

'*Thank you,*' Lottie says softly. '*You were the greatest friend. Be happy now, because I finally am.*'

I turn my face to the sky and I smile.